Horrible Husbands

HORRIBLE HUSBANDS

JESSICA HUNTLEY

JOFFE
BOOKS

Joffe Books, London
www.joffebooks.com

First published in Great Britain in 2025

© Jessica Huntley 2025

Cover art by Nick Castle

ISBN: 978-1-83526-876-6

TRIGGER WARNING

Please be advised that this novel contains scenes of physical and domestic abuse which some readers may find upsetting.

Dedicated to my best friends, Alice and Katie, the real-life version of 'The Bitches', who I love with all my heart . . . but not enough to kill your husbands for you. You're on your own!

CHAPTER ONE

Lisa
Fourteen years ago

A scream claws and rips its way up her throat, suffocating her. There's nothing she can do to stop it. The sound explodes from her mouth as he grabs her hair in his clenched fist, covers her lips with his other dirty hand and pulls her behind a row of thick bushes.

The darkness envelops them whole.

One minute she was walking back from her friend's house after leaving a party earlier than planned, and the next she was being dragged behind a bush kicking and screaming.

She knows she shouldn't have been walking alone in the dark, but it wasn't that far; only through the park, the same park she knows like the back of her hand and has walked through a hundred times before. She hears horror stories all the time, on the news, about young girls being attacked by strange men, but never did she think it would happen to her.

No one can see her and that's what he's counting on. As she manages to scramble to her feet, he shoves her and she trips on the uneven ground, spiralling to the grass, and feels the sting of a thorn as it embeds into her left palm. Wearing high heels on grass is never a good idea, and now they feel like shackles, weighing her down and impeding her escape. Maybe if she hadn't worn them, she would have been able to get away and run for her life.

She attempts to crawl away again. Her short skirt rides up to her hips and she feels the cool breeze brush across her bare bottom.

'Such a slut,' he says. 'Wearing a thong with a short skirt. You're just asking for it.'

He grabs her left ankle and drags her back towards him. She kicks out, hoping to stab him with her high heels, but her feet catch nothing but air. She screams and claws with her fingers, but nothing she does stops him from laying his full weight on her quivering body. He growls as he smothers her mouth with his large hand, pressing down so hard she can't even breathe. He's wearing a black balaclava, the only thing visible are his black eyes.

'Shush now. This won't take long.'

But he's wrong. She's there, in hell, for eternity.

He snaps her thong away with one swift movement. She hears a zip being undone and then he's inside her. And it hurts. It's her first experience and it's nothing like she knows it should be. She shouldn't have tears in her eyes, and she shouldn't be terrified, and it shouldn't be a stranger on top of her, and it shouldn't have happened outside in a park. She's not ready. She wanted it to be special.

This is all wrong, but there's nothing she can do to stop it. Her body goes limp. Maybe if she lies still, he won't hurt her. Maybe if she doesn't fight back, he'll get bored.

But she's wrong about that too.

It spurs him on.

She whimpers like an injured animal.

'I told you you'd enjoy it, you slut.' He sniffs her cheek and mops up the tears with the material on his face. 'Hmm, your tears taste good, baby.' He licks his lips. He sounds young, maybe in his twenties, but she can't be sure.

Laughter erupts from somewhere nearby. She's saved! There are people walking through the park.

He clamps a hand over her mouth. 'If you make a sound, I'll rip your insides out.'

She makes another whimpering noise like a cat as the laughter slowly dies away and eventually disappears.

'Now,' he says in her ear, 'where was I?'

And he continues.

CHAPTER TWO

Holly
Now

There's something about the smell of sweat that makes my skin bristle with goose bumps and sends a tingle of adrenaline through my veins. I'm not talking about body odour, because that's completely disgusting and makes me gag just thinking about it. I'm talking about *sweat*. Musty, warm, slightly tangy maybe. In a way, it's similar to the smell of blood, which I also happen to like in a bit of a strange way. Plus, whenever I cut my finger, I enjoy sucking that tiny bead of blood and feeling the buzz of sweetness against my tongue. We all do it. I'm not a crazy weirdo.

But back to sweat.

Some people will argue that sweat doesn't smell until it mixes with bacteria on the skin and that's what causes an odour. Those people are wrong in my eyes. Sweat does smell. And I happen to like it, so it's all I can do not to lean over to where my male client is dripping below me and take a big whiff.

I'm not a sex worker.

I'm a personal trainer.

Sweat is part of my job description. If my clients don't leave my sessions a hot, sweaty mess then I feel like a failure and I haven't done my job properly. However, I'm not one of those personal trainers who push clients until they puke or almost pass out. There's a fine line between working hard and working to failure. That sort of extreme training is reserved for the elite sports professionals, not the mere mortals who come into my gym. However, clients don't come to me to have a casual chat during their sessions either, because if they can talk during their workout, then I'm doing something wrong and they're not working hard enough. If they want someone to open up to, moan about their lives, gossip about their neighbours or swap the latest beauty trends, then they don't come to me. Everyone knows that. If a client decides they want me to train them then they know exactly what they're signing up for: hard work, results . . . and *sweat*.

Like Kevin Bolton . . .

Kevin is a balding, middle-aged man who came to me wanting to lose three stone, begging me to train him so he could look good naked in front of his wife. That's what he said during our first meeting and assessment session. I told him, 'Look, Kevin, I'm sure your wife already thinks you look good otherwise she wouldn't still be married to you, would she?' His response was, 'Okay, let me rephrase that . . . I want to look good naked for me.' That was the correct answer.

I accepted the challenge. Because, at the end of the day, that's why I became a personal trainer. It's not about looking good for other people. It's about looking and feeling good for yourself. It doesn't matter what you look like, as long as you're happy and love yourself no matter what your size or shape.

Now, Kevin is six months down the line. He's lost two of the three stone and has already told me he feels and looks great, his sex life is better than it's ever been, and he can run around after his kids without getting out of breath or feeling like he's about to have a heart attack. He's stopped eating takeout food every single night, and now only eats it once a month. He has upped his water intake and started counting his daily steps. I'd call that a success story. That's why I love my job. Being able to help people not only change their lives but live longer is my goal in life. Yes, most people come to me to lose weight, but my end goal is to change their lives, no matter what form that may come in.

I stare down at Kevin, who's lying on the mat below me, dripping all over it after completing his core exercises at the end of his hour-long session. I always add in core training at the end because if you do it at the start then your core is already fatigued by the time the main bulk of the training starts and you'll be less likely to perform the exercises safely and correctly. Besides, the core gets trained during every single exercise, whether it be bicep curls or squats if you're doing them properly, so I sometimes question whether sit-ups are even necessary.

Almost every client I train starts by telling me they want a flatter stomach, and they need to do more sit-ups. Then they proceed to tell me they've done so many different core exercises, taken these so-called fat-burning pills that will melt away stomach fat and have even tried wearing waist trainers to cinch in their waists (women mainly, although I have had one trans woman who wore a waist trainer, and I told them to stop it immediately). The bottom line is that you can't target your stomach fat. You can't just tell your body to burn fat from your stomach today and a bit from your butt tomorrow. It doesn't work like that.

Abs are made in the kitchen. Because everyone has stomach muscles under their body fat. And that's exactly what I told Kevin at the start. He listened to me when I told him that he couldn't just come to me twice a week for two hours and expect to get results. He had to work hard during the other one hundred and sixty-six hours of the week too. And, God love him, he's worked his butt off and I'm proud of him.

Not all my clients listen to me, but Kevin does, and his results speak for themselves. In fact, he won the award at the gym for 'Best Transformation' last month.

'Okay, you're done. Great work, Kevin.' I hold out my right hand to him, which he grips firmly, and I pull him to his feet, fighting the urge to sniff him as he straightens out his sweaty grey T-shirt. I always question why people wear grey when they work out. It shows every sweat stain. That's why I stick to wearing black.

'Thanks, Holly. What a great session. Same time Thursday?'

'You bet.'

'What are you up to now? Another client?'

'I have two hours free, so I'll be doing my own workout, then taking an early lunch before a full afternoon of clients and a spin class tonight.'

'Wow, you don't stop, do you?'

I smile at him. 'I like keeping busy, but sometimes I do feel as if I live at the gym. Maybe I should just set up a blow-up bed in the back room.' We share a laugh as Kevin wipes his gym towel across his forehead.

'I'm sure your husband would miss you if you did that,' he says.

'Hmm, you're probably right,' I reply, keeping my internal thoughts to myself.

I doubt my husband would even notice I was gone.

'Thanks again, Holly. See you on Thursday.'

'Bye, Kevin. Good luck with your presentation tomorrow. You'll smash it.'

He grins like I've just paid him the biggest compliment in the world. Last week he told me before our session that he had a big presentation the next week and it was really stressing him out at work and causing a bit of tension at home. The fact I've remembered hits the mark. I always like to go the extra mile for my clients.

'Thanks!' He walks towards the male changing rooms with a spring in his step.

I head to the corner of the gym where there's a desk set up. The personal trainers here use it as a place to sit and complete paperwork after a training session while also keeping an

7

eye on the gym floor. No one is at the desk, so I slide into the seat and take a sip from my water bottle, which I left there this morning when I arrived at work at 6 a.m. I run my right hand through my black, pixie-style hair, rearranging a strand that's slipped out of place.

Sometimes I like to sit and watch people. I don't do it in an obvious way, but it is a fascination of mine to see all the different types of people who come into the gym.

There are the regulars, who walk in and exude confidence and who always use the same bench in the same area of the mat and stay for the exact same amount of time.

Then there's the older crowd, who usually come in together and take over half the cardio machines. They never use any other piece of equipment.

There are also the newbies, who look as if they've just walked into the wrong room and are constantly looking around for the nearest exit or for someone to come and save them. They're my favourites because they may start as shy and nervous, but after I've shown them the ropes, given them a tour and introduced myself, they grow in confidence and watching their journey is always inspiring.

I stand up and head to the changing rooms. It's time for my own workout.

* * *

I'm used to people staring at me. They think I don't notice the sly, side glances, but I do. When you have a disability as obvious as mine then, unfortunately, you get used to being stared at. I don't think people do it to be rude. They're just nosy and, in my case, fascinated that I'm able to be a personal trainer while having only one fully functioning hand.

I was born with moderate symbrachydactyly in my left hand, also known as an underdeveloped hand. It's where most or all the finger bones are missing (in my case my three fingers between my thumb and baby finger). It makes lifting weights a challenge. I can't lift a heavy dumbbell with my left hand or use a kettlebell properly, but I've made do by training with resistance bands, which can hook over my arm. I'm able to squat using a barbell if I use the squat rack and can usually demonstrate most exercises to my clients, although sometimes I resort to using videos on the internet if I'm unable to pick up a weight safely. The point is, I haven't let my disability hold me back and I think that's why I'm the most popular personal trainer at the gym. People see me as someone who has overcome barriers, and they can relate to that, or at least respect it.

There have been a few accidents over the years, but I've learned to adapt my needs to suit my job and modify exercises where needed. Plus, the gym I work at has been extremely helpful and willing to provide me with extra support should I require it. But I do get a lot of stares. Mostly from newcomers to the gym who find it odd to see a fit woman of thirty-two working as a personal trainer with only one complete hand.

I finish my set of ten squats using the barbell and rest it back on the squat rack. It's not as heavy as I usually lift, but seventy kilos is still more than my body weight and I don't lift any heavier without a spotter present in case I lose my grip.

Two muscle-bound men are standing just off to the side, huddled close together, shooting glances at me and whispering. I can see them in the mirror. And I don't think they're complimenting my toned butt or squatting technique because they're smirking and attempting to hide their laughter.

I turn around and approach them. 'Can I help you, gentlemen?'

They both have the decency to turn red. One of them (the one with the shaved head and black tattoos on his arms) takes a casual drink from his water bottle.

'Just admiring your technique,' he says, squeezing his lips together. The one behind him (who has bright blond hair) looks up at the ceiling, avoiding eye contact.

I smile sweetly. 'Thank you very much.'

'What's your one rep max?' Baldy asks me.

'One hundred and ten kilos,' I reply.

Blondie raises his eyebrows. 'That's impressive for a . . .' He stops and turns an even deeper shade of red.

'Now,' I say, folding my arms, enjoying making them squirm, 'either you're about to insult my gender by saying it's impressive for a woman or you're about to insult my disability by saying it's impressive for someone with one hand . . . so, what's it going to be?'

Blondie and Baldy glance at each other, hoping the other will speak first.

After five long seconds, Baldy shows me the palms of his hands. 'W-we didn't mean . . . I mean . . . I wasn't suggesting . . .'

I raise one eyebrow and look at Blondie. 'Relax, guys,' I say with a laugh. 'I'm just messing with you.'

They both blow out a sigh and laugh.

'But if I see you sniggering and joking behind my back again, or at anyone else here, then I'll ban you from my gym. You got it?' They clamp their mouths shut and nod as I turn on my heel and stroll back to the squat rack, my head held high.

* * *

Forty-five minutes later, I've finished my workout and am performing static stretches on the mats in front of the bank of televisions high up on the wall. They're on mute, but the subtitles are on, so I follow along on the screen while I hold my quad stretch.

The gist of the news story is that a woman was found dead last night only twenty minutes from where I live in Edinburgh. I work in the city centre, but my house is in Roslin, a small village about seven miles south of the capital. The woman who lost her life was found floating in the Water of Leith, the main river that flows through Edinburgh, at about ten o'clock last night and has been identified as Leanne Prince, a hairdresser from the nearby village of Juniper Green.

'Oh my God!'

I take my wireless earbuds out as the woman on the mat beside me shrieks and covers her mouth with both hands. She's halfway through a set of sit-ups at the time.

'Are you okay?' I ask.

Tears fill her eyes, and she starts to shake. 'I–I knew her. She's my hairdresser.'

I forget about finishing my stretches and immediately drape an arm around the poor woman's shoulders as I usher her onto a nearby bench. Another personal trainer comes over and asks if everything is okay, so I ask him to bring some water. By the time he returns, the woman has stopped crying but is now very pale.

'Here, drink this,' I say, offering her the plastic cup. 'You're in shock.'

'I–I just can't believe she's dead.'

'When was the last time you saw her?'

'Two days ago. No one knows how to do my hair like Leanne. I had my hair coloured—'

'It looks lovely.'

'—and she was telling me how excited she was for her niece and nephew to visit this weekend. Oh God . . .' The woman sniffs loudly.

I'm at a loss for what else to say, so I beckon Jane, another trainer, over and quietly explain the situation. Jane looks horrified and glances up at the television, but the news has now changed to something else. Apparently, there's going to be a freak heatwave in Scotland this weekend. It's been known to happen.

Jane is much better at dealing with emotional people. It's not that I don't empathise with the woman who's just lost her hairdresser, but this is severely eating into my lunchtime. Plus, and I say this with the utmost respect, I just don't really care that much.

'What should we do?' Jane asks me.

I glance at the woman who's now sobbing into a damp tissue. 'You're asking me?'

'Should we call someone?'

'Who?'

'Do you want us to call someone?' asks Jane, raising her voice ever so slightly so the woman knows she's talking to her.

The crying woman shakes her head. 'No, thank you. I'll be okay.' She stands. 'It's just . . . who's going to cut and colour my hair now?'

Jane and I swap glances. 'My hairdresser is fantastic,' I say in as cheery a voice as I can muster. 'She knows all the best gossip and even gives you a scalp massage at no extra charge.'

'Really?' says Jane. 'Who is it?'

'Kelsey from To Dye For.'

'Ooh, I've heard she's good!' says Jane.

I nod over-enthusiastically and then offer a hopeful smile to the woman, who nods.

'Thank you, I'll give her a call.' She takes a few steps towards the changing rooms.

'Are you sure we can't call anyone for you?' I ask.

'No, I'll be fine. Goodbye.'

Jane and I watch the woman leave the gym and then sigh at the same time.

'That poor woman,' says Jane.

'She'll be fine. Honestly, Kelsey is a whizz with hair—'

'No, I meant the woman who died.'

'Oh . . . right. Of course. Yeah . . .'

I head to the changing rooms and sit down on one of the benches, checking my phone. The WhatsApp icon is lit up, which can only mean one thing: the girls have been chatting.

Time to catch up with what's been going on with Lisa and Penny.

CHAPTER THREE

Lisa
Now

The woman in the mirror doesn't look like me. It's hard to even conjure up an image of what I used to look like before my life went down this uneven road. Before I became someone I no longer recognise and adopted a persona of a loving, happy wife who is delighted to have a doting husband, a full-time job and a roof over her head. Because that's about as far from the truth as it can get. I long for the days when I used to wake up in the morning full of hope and excitement for the day ahead, not knowing what the future would bring, but those days are so long ago now I sometimes wonder if they even existed at all. They play out like deleted scenes of a movie in my head. Instead, I'm now terrified of saying or doing the wrong thing and being punished for merely breathing. Every day is fraught with tension and fear, which exhausts me to the point of collapse.

I sometimes question why I bother covering the bruises on my face every day with make-up. It's not like anyone notices or cares. The dark shadows under my eyes tell the world I'm exhausted, yet I know they are from sleepless nights of being too terrified to fall asleep. The paleness of my complexion tells the world I'm weak and malnourished and my frail body shows that I don't look after myself because I don't care about the way I look. Whereas I know it's because I'm not allowed to put on weight, and I can't show off my body in case I give men the wrong impression.

But the bruises tell a different story. People tend to not comment on them because it would be considered insensitive to do so and they don't want to get involved with anything serious. My colleagues tell me my hair looks limp and lifeless and that I could do with a fake tan, but they don't ask about my black eye. They don't want to know the truth because the truth is too real for them to handle, too messy.

The only two people who would care if they knew are Holly and Penny, but I haven't seen the girls in almost three years. They wouldn't recognise the woman I am today. Whenever I do show my face in a video or picture I send them via WhatsApp, I pile on the make-up to hide the bruises.

Gosh, is that how long it's been? Three years. We all lead such busy lives and finding the time when we're all available is like trying to juggle fifteen different diaries at once. It never flows smoothly because one of us always has something that crops up. It doesn't help that we live in different countries. I live in Truro, England. Penny lives in St Davids, Wales, and Holly lives in Roslin, Scotland. We couldn't live further apart if we tried while still living in the UK. Penny did consider living in California for a short amount of time with her husband, Drake, but that idea was quickly extinguished when she found out she was pregnant and then had the twins. They did, however, move out of their London home and settle in St Davids, near where Penny's Aunt Silvia, her only surviving relative, lives.

Leaning a little closer to the grimy bathroom mirror in the staff area at the back of Boots where I work, I apply another layer of concealer under my eyes because the first layer is now cracking and causing the lines to appear deeper.

I'm a pharmacist, so at least I have decent access to medication and the latest beauty buys that guarantee to get rid of dark undereye bags. The labels don't say anything about covering dark bruises, but they're relatively the same thing. I'm still recovering from the broken ribs my husband gave me a couple of weeks ago. At first, they weren't that bad, but now it's hard to take a breath without thinking my ribcage is going to burst open.

I dab a small amount of concealer around my left eye, wincing as my finger grazes the sore, swollen spot. He caught me good and proper last night. He apologised straight away, as he always does, blaming his outburst on the stress he's been under lately. He keeps saying things will improve at work soon and he'll be able to relax a little more, maybe whisk me away on a romantic beach holiday, which he's been promising to do for almost eight years. It's funny, though; his so-called *stress* has been the reason for all his outbursts over the years. Just how much stress can one man be under at work?

As far as I'm aware, our finances are stable. We're not rolling in money, but we've always paid our mortgage on time, the bills are covered, and we have food on the table. But we've never been able to afford a holiday and I don't spend money on things like manicures or facials or new clothes. I've been wearing the same pair of jeans for ten years. My husband, Simon, says they look good on me, so there's no need to buy more, even though the hems are unravelling, and the knees are wearing thin.

I hadn't argued with him last night. I'd just happened to pour him a whiskey from the wrong bottle; the one he'd been saving for a special occasion that was worth a lot of money. How was I supposed to know that? They all looked the same to me, lined up on his special bar in height order. But then, if I hadn't poured him a glass, he'd have shouted at me for not getting him one in the first place. I can never seem to win when it comes to my husband. Treading on eggshells every day gets exhausting and confusing because there's never a clear trigger for him. Sometimes he can go months with no outbursts, and I've been lulled into a false sense of security on more than one occasion. But I never learn and he never changes.

Simon wasn't always like this. I guess he's always been protective of me, telling me he doesn't want me going out with my girlfriends because he doesn't trust them, or telling me I don't need new make-up because I look perfect without it. Small things at first. Things I barely even noticed were having an impact on my life, but it got worse.

The first time he hit me was on our first wedding anniversary eight years ago. Before that, we'd been together almost six years and he'd never hurt me. He was so appalled at what he'd done, he broke down in tears and begged for my forgiveness. After the first time, he didn't hit me again for almost three years. But the second time was much worse. I had to go to the hospital for stitches on my chin and I'd been so embarrassed that I lied to the nurse who stitched me up and said I caught my chin on the edge of a table, which was true because he'd shoved me against it, and I'd fallen badly. Whether she believed me or not I was never sure, but Simon had been very apologetic for months afterwards.

That's the thing about Simon. He's always sorry . . . until the next time.

'Lisa, you in there?' The voice of Jenna, my colleague, sounds through the door.

'Yes, sorry, won't be a minute.' I quickly finish applying the concealer, wipe a small tear from the corner of my eye, take a deep breath and then open the door with a smile.

'Everything okay?' asks Jenna.

'Yes, everything's fine. Lunch?'

Jenna nods. 'You bet.'

* * *

Five minutes later, we buy a meal deal and settle ourselves onto a bench outside the shopping centre. It's better than sitting in the back of the store where there are no windows. Plus, it's a beautiful spring day and my lunch break is the only chance I get to sit outside in the fresh air. The birds are singing, the sun is shining, and people are milling about in light jackets rather than bundled in thick coats for the first time in months. I love people watching and coming up with random storylines for their lives.

There's a young mum alone with a small baby who can't be more than two months old. She looks so happy and is smiling on the outside as she picks up her bundle of joy and rocks them in her arms, yet I can tell by the way her shoulders are hunched and her hair is unbrushed that she's exhausted. But her smile tells me how much she loves her child and I know for a fact she's a great mum. I hope her boyfriend or husband or whoever is nice. She deserves happiness.

I take a bite of my ham and cheese sandwich as I check my phone. There's a message from Penny in the group chat entitled: The Bitches.

Me, Penny and Holly.

We've been best friends since we were seven years old. We met at a ballet class our parents forced us to go to and have been inseparable ever since. Back then, we lived in the same area near Manchester. We didn't go to the same school, but twice a week we attended Tiny Dancers and had the best time messing around and learning a few dance moves. When we grew up a bit and entered the more advanced class, we began to lose interest in dancing, but we kept going to class anyway because otherwise, we wouldn't see each other. It wasn't until we left for different universities that we began to see each other less and less, but we continued to stay in contact, and have done so until this day.

Now, we're in our early thirties and have been through it all together, despite living far apart and only meeting up once a year (if we're lucky). Every time we try and set a date to meet up, something always comes up. Penny has two kids and runs her own business so it's usually her who struggles to find time. Holly is busy in Edinburgh working as a personal trainer. And I'm almost at the opposite end of the UK from her in Cornwall.

I don't have any other close friends. Not like them. We tell each other everything. Well . . . almost everything. They don't know about Simon and his stress at work. They don't know he hits me, and they don't know I suffered a miscarriage two weeks ago when he accidentally tripped me and I fell down the stairs, cracking a rib or two in the process. I went to the doctor for the blood that poured from between my legs, but not for the pain in my ribs. As far as the doctor was concerned, I'd suffered a tragic miscarriage, just like approximately one in five women experience.

I'm not sure why I don't tell my friends about my horrible husband. Maybe it's because I don't want them to worry and it's not like they could do anything to help me anyway. They have their own lives and problems to deal with. They are my best friends, though. I'm just not sure they'd understand that I really do love my husband, and it's probably my own fault he hits me.

Jenna is engrossed in a phone conversation with her husband, so I don't feel guilty for checking the group chat on WhatsApp. I love catching up on the events of the day with the girls. Penny sends lots of voice notes. She talks fast anyway and it's easier for her to do a voice note than typing it all out. She's also often very crude and has a spill-all approach to sharing, which I always enjoy listening to at 2x speed.

Penny: *Hey, bitches. Okay, so you're not going to believe what happened last night while Drake and I were having sex. There we were, doing it doggy style and he says, "Hey, babe, can I cum on your face again? I really enjoyed that last time. And call me Timothy." I mean . . . what am I supposed to say to that after almost seven years of marriage? I don't want fucking cum on my face, thank you very much. I just want the ordeal to be over. You know what I mean? But that's not what bothered me the most. He said 'again' as if I'd let him do it before, which I haven't, which means either he's got me confused with someone else or he had a sex dream about doing it to me and he's got confused between dreams and reality. Which one do you reckon is the truth? Anyway . . . How are you both? Ooh, I found a cute skirt the other day. I'll send you a pic!'*

I stifle a laugh because only Penny can talk about her husband cumming on her face and finding a cute skirt in the same message. Penny's always been the one of us who speaks her mind. She's honest, blunt and takes no shit from anyone, and I love her because of that. I bet if her husband hit her, she wouldn't let him get away with it. She'd most likely hit him back. I know she does karate lessons once a week.

I type a reply.

Lisa: *Okay, that's weird and kind of gross. And who's Timothy? I'm sure he just had a dream about you. Drake loves you. I'm okay. Just on my lunch break xx*

I hit send. The truth is, I don't know Penny's husband well at all, but from what she tells us, he's a doting husband and father. Although he does like it a bit kinky in the bedroom.

I immediately see three small dots and Penny's reply arrives seconds later. I bring the phone up to my ear and listen.

Penny: *'Timothy Grant is a name he likes to be called in bed sometimes. It's a role-play thing he came up with years ago. I don't know why. It is so gross! He's never cum on my face for the entire time I've known him. So why did he ask in the first place? Did he think I was someone else? Oh my God, he's cheating on me again, isn't he? My husband is cheating on me with some slut who lets him cum on her face. I know he's a bit kinky and once asked me to call him Daddy while he spanked me, but . . . oh shit, that's weird and gross too, isn't it? Who the hell am I even married to?'*

19

I go to take a bite of my sandwich but find my appetite has gone, so I put it back in its wrapping and take a sip of water instead.

Lisa: *Maybe he saw it in a film and wanted to try it.*

Penny types her response this time.

Penny: *So, he watches porn. Great.*

Lisa: *I didn't say that, but you know what men are like. They're very visual. Plus, I'm pretty sure even married men watch porn from time to time.*

Penny: *Gag.*

Lisa: *Lol*

Penny: *Where's Holly? Why isn't she weighing in on the whole cum-on-my-face story?*

Lisa: *I think she's probably in the gym training.*

Penny: *That girl makes us look bad with the amount she trains.*

Lisa: *It's her job. What are you up to now?*

Penny: *On a break from doing inventory. As much as I love being self-employed, it sucks that I have to do all the work, but at least I have a nice view.*

A few seconds later, a photo arrives of rolling hills with the sea beyond. Honestly, if I didn't know any better, I'd think Penny was a movie star. Her huge country house is only a few miles away from the beach and is worth at least a million pounds. If I didn't love her so much, I would constantly seethe with envy.

Lisa: *Wow*

Penny: *Wish you girls were here.*

Lisa: *I wish I was there too. Instead, I'm sitting outside on a tiny bench eating a sad sandwich on my lunch break.*

Penny: *Sucks to be you, babe . . . kidding! Love you!*

I smile and take a deep breath as I look up at the blue sky. She has no idea just how much it does suck to be me. I wish I could be anywhere else, be anyone else. How did I let it get this far? How did I let it happen?

Holly: *Um . . . why have I just opened the group chat and listened to messages about Penny and her husband cumming on her face?*

Penny: *Ah, she lives! And, for the record, he did NOT cum on my face.*

Lisa: *He just asked her if he could do it.*

Holly: *He's cheating on you again.*

Penny: *I knew it . . .*

Lisa: *Let's not get ahead of ourselves.*

I lower my phone as Jenna nudges me. 'You ready to go back in?'

'Um, yeah. Give me a minute.'

'See you in there.'

I watch as Jenna walks inside. We don't talk a lot. At least, not about important things. I know she notices the way I wince every time I lift a heavy box and I know she looks at me funny when she thinks I'm not looking, but she never says anything. She never asks me if everything is okay. The thing is, even if she did ask me, I wouldn't confide in her. I don't confide in anyone. Not even my two best friends.

I glance down at the group chat again, which has now exploded with messages. I need to get back to work.

Lisa: *Sorry girls. Gotta go. I'll catch up later.*

Penny: *Bye, babe.*

Holly: *Later!*

I dump my uneaten sandwich in the nearest bin and head inside. As I walk past the baby aisle, my heart misses a beat, and a wave of nausea threatens to overwhelm me. My eyes are drawn to the cute babies on the side of the packaging and the array of tiny socks that could easily fit a doll.

I glide my hand across my empty stomach and sigh. Maybe it was for the best that I lost the baby. I wouldn't want to bring an innocent child into my abusive marriage. I doubt having a baby would change Simon. I couldn't risk him hurting the baby too. I love him, but I know I need to get out of this situation. Do I really want to be in this marriage for ever? Where would I go? What would I do?

There was a time, back when we'd only been dating a few months, when we were the happiest couple on the planet. I know we were. I could tell because I laughed all the time. I laughed at his jokes and the way his hair would stick up in weird directions no matter how much gel he'd use. We'd hold hands constantly, as if we were afraid to let each other go, as if not touching the other person would physically hurt us. I remember I once watched a film about a woman in an abusive relationship. I can't remember the name of it now, but I do remember the thought that popped into my head.

What a silly woman. What self-respecting woman would stay with a partner who abused her?

That's what I'd thought. And here I am, all these years later . . .

I guess that means I'm a silly woman. A silly, silly woman who deserves the treatment she gets.

I find myself thinking back to the film as I wander to the back of the store ready to start my final shift. The woman in the abusive relationship did eventually get away from her husband in the film. But to be free, she'd had to kill him. She'd stabbed him eighteen times with a kitchen knife after making him a beautiful dinner and pouring him a glass of wine. As he'd sat there eating and drinking, she'd taken a knife from the side drawer and gone to town on him.

The last scene was of her with a smile across her face as she'd been led off to jail.

And she'd never looked so happy and free.

CHAPTER FOUR

Penny
Now

The laptop screen is flickering again, making my eyes ache as I try hard to concentrate on my work while ignoring my sick compulsion to pick at the scab on my arm. It's driving me insane. I've said goodbye to the girls via WhatsApp for now, aware we all have lives and jobs to be getting on with, but now I'm staring at the screen, attempting to sort out this fucking invoice, and all I want to do is pick, pick, pick at my skin just to relieve the tension that's building.

I've looked it up and it's a common disorder, funnily enough, called skin picking disorder, or dermatillomania or excoriation disorder, both of which I can't even pronounce properly. It's extremely normal to pick at a scab or a loose bit of skin on a nail, but I take it too far, to the next level. I pick a scab over and over until it bleeds and leaves a permanent scar. I dig at the skin around my nails until it cracks and bleeds. Hell, I even scratch at the skin on my arms and legs so much that I create a wound and then continue to pick at it until it gets bigger.

I've not seen a professional about it, even though I know I should. My husband doesn't notice I do it because he wouldn't notice if a plane landed in our garden or if the house caught fire, but my six-year-old twins have begun to ask me why I pick at my skin. And that's what's made me realise how serious it is because it's not just a small habit now. It's taking over my life, causing me to become distracted and now it's leaving scars all over my body, making me look like a fucking leper.

The thing is, I don't have time to go and speak to someone about it because I know what the doctor will say and do. They'll arrange for me to see a therapist and start some sort of behavioural therapy, and who the fuck has time for that these days?

There are the children to look after. The school run to do. The errands that need running. The shopping, the washing, the cleaning, the tidying, the ironing, the cooking. Plus, I work a full-time job running my own business, so when am I supposed to find the hours in the day to take myself to the doctor and then have therapy once or twice a week? It's not happening. I barely have time to go to the hairdressers every eight weeks. With my dark skin and naturally afro hair, I have to pay a lot of money to have my hair tamed and straightened every few months. It's always a treat to go to the hairdressers where I can sit in a chair and relax for a couple of hours and drink a cup of strong coffee without it going cold. Sometimes I take my laptop and get some work done, but often it's nice to chat to the hairdresser, who basically is like my own personal therapist.

I'm not lonely because I have a whole circle of mum friends who I somehow manage to see on Saturday afternoons for our weekly catch-up (although more often than not, I can't make it because of one thing or another), but I miss The Bitches. Holly and Lisa are my people. They get me. I tend to say the wrong thing or talk too much or embarrass people (especially my husband and kids) regularly, but they never care. They take me as I am. The foul-mouthed, straight-talking bitch. That's me.

It's been too long since I've seen them. Yes, we chat every day via WhatsApp without fail, but it's not the same. The thing is, we haven't lived near each other since we left home around the age of eighteen. We're in our early thirties now and the fact we've remained close friends all these years is, quite frankly, a miracle.

As soon as we moved away from our hometown of Manchester, we seemed to spread to the furthest areas of the UK. It wasn't by choice, either. Holly got accepted into Edinburgh University and she's lived up there ever since. And Lisa's husband, Simon, moved her down to Cornwall almost as soon as he physically could. I originally lived in London with my then-boyfriend-now-husband, but then moved to St Davids, because my Aunt Silvia is there and she's the only family I have left.

My husband, Drake, works as an insurance broker in one of the top companies in America and, because of that, he frequently travels over there to work, so is barely here. Our million-pound house is often empty of life during the day apart from little old me in my home office, a small pod at the end of the garden where I hide away. It's my haven. Yes, there's a large office in the house, but I prefer to work in my pod. It has a lock on the door and only I have the key.

I designed the house myself. Had it built from the ground up. I was the project manager during the build while my husband watched from the other side of the world via Zoom. I planned all the decorations and furniture myself with the help of an interior designer; marble worktops, ornate banisters, a state-of-the-art oven and a fridge which automatically adds anything we've run out of to my online grocery shopping list. The sofas are quite possibly the most expensive items in the house, along with the four-poster bed in the master bedroom, which cost thousands. I did all of this while juggling twin babies/toddlers.

I'm very house proud. And why shouldn't I be? I earn a decent wage too, so this was paid for using my money as well as my husband's. He doesn't care about the house or what's in it. He's never been into material things, which is odd considering he earns so much money. My home business took off five years ago when the children were babies. I make and sell personalised accessories, from notebooks and book-marks to hairbands and clothes. It's called Personalise Me, and thanks to lockdown, my small hobby turned into a huge busi-ness almost overnight. I went from earning roughly £100 per month to hitting six figures in two months. I've had to upscale massively, and thanks to outsourcing most of the work, I don't have to do a whole lot now, apart from keeping on top of the books and paperwork. I do have my own warehouse, though, which stores all of the items, and a team of people who sort, pack and post them. I pop over there every few weeks to check on things, but I let my staff run the packing and distribution of the products, while I run the social media, paperwork and administrative side of the business.

I lean back in my leather swivel chair while picking at the scab on my arm. I miss the girls. I should try and get us all back together. It's been too long.

It's as if a lightbulb has just flicked on inside my head.

It's no secret that it's always me who struggles to set aside time for my friends. I see the women who live down the street and whose children go to the same school as mine, but my two best friends whom I grew up with, experimented with alcohol for the first time, went through our first boy crushes (and girl crushes) with, I never make time to see.

It's time that changed.

I grab my iPad, navigate to my work calendar, and check out my schedule. Thanks to running my own business, I can take holidays whenever I want, but whenever I do I get a nag-ging feeling that I should get back to work.

Earlier this year, Drake booked for us all to go to Disney World on the spur of the moment. I was not impressed and had to cancel a load of work. Not only did it cost us dearly, but the kids didn't even enjoy it. He dragged them on all the rides (the ones they were old enough for) and they ended up puking their guts up on most of them. He told them to grow up and have fun and I spent the whole time there glaring at him, wishing I'd picked a better husband.

Because Drake's not perfect. Far from it. And I'm not saying I am, but at least I didn't ask my spouse to cum on their face on their anniversary. I shudder just thinking about it. Seriously, what had he been thinking? Maybe I'm right. Maybe Holly's right. Maybe he is cheating on me, and it was a slip of the tongue and he thought for a moment he was shagging his mistress . . .

It's happened before.

I hate myself for it, but back when we first got married, before the kids came along, Drake cheated on me with a woman who I don't even know. We'd been married for three months. I kicked him out of our London townhouse, told him to go and curl up in a ditch and die, and then began divorce proceedings. I am not one of those women who accept cheats, but then I started puking my guts up.

I was pregnant with Lori and Luca.

So, I swallowed my pride, allowed my cheating husband back into the house and pretended like we were a happy family. I still haven't forgiven him. I'm not sure I ever will, and he still has never told me the woman's name. It wasn't like I found out by accident either. He actually admitted it to me and apologised, saying it would never happen again. Did I believe him? Not really, but so far I haven't noticed any suspicious behaviour, apart from the cumming on the face comment.

I crane my neck from side to side, attempting to forget about my cheating husband, and quickly type out a message to the group.

Penny: *Let's have a girls' weekend. I haven't seen you both for fucking years. What are you doing this weekend? My treat. I'll pay for the transport. You can stay with me. It's been too long and I'm betting you could both do with a change of scenery, am I right?*

Neither of them responds straight away. I'm about to put down my phone and finish my coffee when the phone springs to life. My husband is calling me.

I answer with my eyebrows raised. 'Bit early for you to be calling, isn't it?'

'It's nine a.m. on the East Coast, babe.'

'Right. I forgot. What's up?'

'What's your mother's maiden name?'

'Why?'

'It's a security question for our new life insurance.'

'It's Pauls . . . and what new life insurance? What was wrong with our old one?'

'I'm changing it.'

I sit up straight, a frown on my face. 'Why?' I ask him, elongating the word. It's fucking typical of my husband to do things without telling me.

'I've got us a much better deal. I've also changed my will. If you cheat on me, you get nothing, which I think is fair enough. Also, if I die unexpectedly or go missing then you get everything, and vice versa, plus $250,000.'

I can't help but accidentally release the cough that forms in my throat. 'Seriously?'

'Yeah, pretty good deal, huh?'

'What about if you cheat on me?'

A laugh erupts through the phone, and I have to fight the urge to throw it across the room, imagining I'm hurling it at my husband's head. 'Babe, you don't have to worry about that.'

'Fine. Whatever. What if I kill you? Do I get the money then?'

Another laugh. 'Fat chance. If you kill me, you get nothing.'

'Really? There's an actual paragraph in there that says that?'

'No, but it's implied. However, technically, if someone else killed me then you'd be set.'

'Okay, that's good because I fear every day for your life, that someone will jump out at you with an axe and chop you up into little pieces and drop you in plastic bags in the ocean.'

My husband tuts. 'Now, now, you can't go dropping plastic into the ocean, you know that. It's bad for the environment.'

'Right. Well, thanks so much for consulting with me as usual before you make a big, life-altering decision. By the way, my friends will probably be visiting this weekend, but that's okay with you, right, because you're not even going to be here?'

'Of course, babe. Whatever you want. Love you. Bye.'

He hangs up before I can say 'Fuck you' so I say it to the empty room instead.

CHAPTER FIVE

Holly

I don't get home until eight on Wednesdays due to leading an evening spin class, which means my husband will have eaten dinner by himself, drunk a beer (or three) in front of the television all the while wearing the baggy trousers he's probably been festering in for over a week. Sometimes he cooks for me, sometimes he doesn't. It's a dinner lottery. Some days I hit the jackpot, but more often than not, I don't, which means I always have a quick and easy Gusto meal ready to go for when I get back and am starving after a busy day at work.

Will is a very good cook when he sets his mind to it and puts the effort in. Back when we were first dating at university, he'd make meals for me all the time. Then, when we moved in together, he'd surprise me when I walked in from work with a glass of wine and a three-course meal. But now he's just lazy. However, his chorizo and prawn linguine is still a firm favourite of mine. About a year ago, we went through a bit of a rough patch and decided to spruce up our relationship by having monthly date nights. He'd make the linguine dish, or we'd end up going out to a restaurant in the city centre or ordering in a takeaway. But that routine didn't last long, and we haven't had a date night for at least six months now, so I really should try and bring the idea up again, just so it looks as if I'm making an effort with our marriage, even though I'm perfectly happy to not be around him.

As far as he knows, we've been trying to get pregnant for six months, but so far, no joy. And that's because I still have the coil fitted. He brought up the whole idea of having a baby and to shut him up, I agreed, but when I went to have the coil removed, I actually went and had my nails done. Some people might call me a bitch for lying to my husband, but those people don't know the truth, nor will they.

However, lately, Will keeps throwing out comments like, 'You're not getting any younger' and 'Maybe you need to get yourself checked out'. He hasn't suggested it's anything to do with him. It's not like I'm forty-eight and even if I was forty-eight, it still wouldn't be the end of the world because loads of women have babies later in life. It just might take them a little longer to get pregnant. As it happens, I'm in my early thirties so I don't see what all the fuss is about even though the whole concept is moot because of the coil he doesn't know about.

Will always says I work too much and am clearly putting excessive stress on my body by continuing to exercise when I should be resting and preparing my body to become pregnant. Plus, apparently, I drink too much, and I should be cutting out alcohol altogether while trying to get pregnant. I notice he's not prepared to make any sacrifices, so until he stops drinking every night of the week, I'm not going to stop either. I've always found it ironic that men expect women to give up everything to have a child, but they won't even consider it. It's a strange world we live in.

Again, it's moot.

I dump my gym bag on the floor, making a mental note to put my used gym clothes into the wash before I go to bed, and head straight to the fridge where I know there's a half-empty bottle of pinot grigio left over from last night waiting for me. The tinny noise from a football game echoes through the thin walls. I despise football. I cannot watch a single minute without getting fed up, annoyed or bored. I blame myself. I should never have married a football fanatic. It's the price I must now pay for my own stupidity. I could have chosen a man who enjoyed tennis, a more sophisticated sport, but no, I had to choose a football hooligan who has been known to get into fist fights after a big match when the result didn't go his way. And don't even get me started when the World Cup comes around. I basically lose my husband for a month (which honestly isn't all that bad in hindsight).

As I lean against the counter and take the first sip of tangy wine, the long day starts to melt away. My shoulders relax and I inwardly sigh with relief. It might be the middle of the week, but it feels like it's still Monday. The rest of my day went by without further incident, though. Jenna and I didn't see that woman again, the one whose hairdresser was found dead. But we did find out that the hairdresser, Leanne Somebody, had indeed been murdered. It wasn't a suicide. She was strangled last night while walking home from her evening bar job and then dumped in the river. The killer hadn't even tried to hide her body, as if they wanted it to be found.

I shudder, my calmness at enjoying my wine now gone. The truth is even I'm afraid to walk around the city in the dark by myself, which doesn't happen often, but when I do I keep an extra grip on my bag and ensure I have my keys clenched in my hand, ready to poke in some guy's eye. It's something I've always done ever since I was a teenager and seeing the young girls on the news who get raped when walking back home. It's a sobering thought.

It's why I'm glad we live in Roslin in a quiet cul-de-sac where not a lot happens. We have a semi-detached house with three bedrooms, two bathrooms, a lounge, dining room and a decent-sized kitchen. It's not elegant or grand, but it's home. The building next door isn't occupied. It's been empty for years, which suits me just fine, even though the garden is severely overgrown and often attracts foxes. But I don't care about that either. In fact, it works in my favour.

'Hols?' The tipsy voice of my husband echoes through the halls.

I stay where I am. He knows I'm home. He can come and talk to me. I turn and begin to get out the ingredients to make a quick pasta carbonara. I place my glass on the side and chop an onion.

'Hey, good day?' he asks me.

I don't turn around, but continue to slowly chop the onion with the sharp knife. Sometimes the sight of him makes me feel queasy. 'Yeah, not bad. You?'

'Was okay.'

'How did your interview go?'

'It was fine. I should hear back by the weekend.'

I nod, the grip on the knife increasing. The truth is my husband doesn't work at the moment. He was *let go* from his previous job as a plumber four months ago because he was caught stealing from a client's house. Because of that, he wasn't given a reference and now is struggling to find a job, but I have a horrible feeling he doesn't even want a new one. He seems perfectly happy lounging about the house every day in a dirty T-shirt while attempting to grow his beard and hair as long as possible. It's one of the reasons looking at him makes me queasy. He looks like a homeless person right now and doesn't smell much better either. Apparently, since he lost his job, he's lost the ability to wash himself too. He's not depressed. He's just lazy.

I don't even know how he spends his time. I'm ashamed of him for the first time in our marriage and I haven't told the girls he lost his job. I know I tell them everything, but there are some things I can't tell them, like my husband being a thief and a lazy twat. It's embarrassing.

I can't support us both on my salary for ever. As a personal trainer, I'm mostly freelance so it's up to me to find the clients at the gym. If I don't train people, then I don't get paid. It's a tough gig sometimes. I have a few scheduled classes which I teach (spin and body combat), which I get paid for each week, but otherwise, I'm dependent on my clients to pay me. The gym itself also takes its cut. If I had money, I'd buy my own space and set up a training business so I could work independently away from the gym, but I don't have that luxury, especially now my husband is out of a job. The money I earn doesn't seem to go far enough these days, thanks to the crippling state of the economy. However, I have a plan in place to secure some funds soon. Hopefully.

He thinks I haven't noticed he uses my bank card and then slips it back into my purse. He assumes I don't know he likes to go on those online gambling sites. I keep getting emails from them and I know for a fact I never signed up for any. Maybe he thinks he's outsmarting me. But there's one thing he doesn't know about; I've got myself a locked box in the house with almost £5,000 in cash. I know it's a bit old-fashioned to keep cash in the house, but it's my rainy-day money. In case anything goes wrong. Sometimes my clients slip me tips because they know the gym takes a cut of my earnings, so instead of spending it, I store it away.

Will's arms slip around my waist, and he nuzzles his furry face into my neck. This move used to turn me on (mildly), but now I find the hairs on the back of my neck stand up and I have to fight the urge to flinch away from him. I know this isn't normal, but ever since he stole from a client's house and lost his job, I've lost respect for my husband.

'You smell funny,' he says.

'I haven't showered yet,' I reply, as I continue to chop the ingredients. I bite my tongue just in time to stop myself from telling him he smells like stagnant sweat. I love the smell of sweat usually, but not when it's wafting from my husband mixed with body odour and beer. 'What time did you get in last night? You were dead to the world when I left for work this morning.'

'Ah, yeah, it was a late one. Me and the guys went to Juniper Green to that pub by the river.'

I stop chopping. 'Juniper Green?'

'Yeah.'

'How did you get home? That's a bit of a walk.'

'Erm . . . Oliver dropped me off.'

'What time was that?'

'What is this, twenty questions?' Will releases his grip around my waist and stomps back to the lounge to watch the football, leaving me frozen on the spot.

My brain ticks over at record speed, unable to focus on a single thing other than the words that have just come out of my husband's mouth. He never goes to Juniper Green because it's too far to walk. Oliver lives in the opposite direction and, for the entire time I've known Will's best friend, he's never once been the designated driver. Oliver likes to drink. A lot.

That pub by the river he said he went to is right next door to a hairdresser's . . . and a hairdresser was murdered last night and found in the water in Juniper Green.

A lump forms in my throat as I continue to slice the onions, but I'm not focused on what I'm doing. The knife slices into one of my small fingers on my left hand like butter and I yelp, yanking my hand away from the sharp edge, immediately bringing it to my mouth, sucking the wound.

The tangy taste brings instant relief and I suck as much blood out of my finger as I can. It's weird, but at least it calms me down.

I leave the ingredients on the side and grab my bag, fishing around inside with my uninjured hand for my phone. I ignore the dozens of messages from the girls and type out a message to Oliver.

Me: *Hey. Thanks for dropping Will back last night. He must have got pretty wasted.*

It's not read straight away so I continue to suck my finger, the sting of pain making my eyes water. I stare at my phone,

36

praying it flashes up soon with a new message from Oliver. But it doesn't. There's no point standing around waiting, so I head back to the counter and continue making my dinner, taking a big gulp of wine while I'm at it.

* * *

After my meal and a hot shower, I can finally relax, so I settle myself on the sofa as far away from Will as possible. Thankfully, football has now finished, and he's switched to watching a home improvement show, which I can just about cope with. I've got dressed in my pyjamas and fluffy socks, and tuck my feet under my bum while scrolling through my phone.

There's nothing much on social media so I enter the group chat and my eyes widen in surprise when I read the message from Penny asking if we're free this weekend to come and visit. It's rather out of the blue, but I can't think of a good enough reason to turn her down. It has been three years since we've all been together.

But I can't just book a weekend off work at such short notice. I'd lose hundreds of pounds. Sometimes Penny doesn't get that Lisa and I don't have as much money as she does. Nothing against her, but she's always been very flamboyant with her spending. When she showed us the plans to build her house, Lisa and I had to hold our tongues. It was far too big for a family of four. Then again, if I earned what she did, I probably would be flamboyant too. Between her and Drake they must easily take home half a million pounds a year. Penny's business took off over lockdown once I taught her how to use TikTok properly. I'm happy for her, really, I am, but I've always thought she could do more with all that money.

I'm about to type out my response that I'm sorry I can't make it, but maybe in a few months when things have settled down when another message pops up.

It's from Oliver.

I click on it and my whole world turns upside down.

Oliver: *Holly, what are you talking about? I didn't drop Will back last night. I wasn't even out with him.*

I slowly raise my eyes and look at my husband, who scratches his balls and burps loudly. Why would he lie to me? What's he hiding? A cold tingle of fear creeps over me, making me shudder.

'You cold?' Will asks me as he pulls a blanket off the side of the sofa.

'Yes, thank you.' I take it from him and drape it across my legs, attempting to cover the fact they're trembling.

My husband has lied to me about where he was last night. What else is he lying about?

CHAPTER SIX

Lisa

By the time I walk through the front door of the small flat I share with my husband at half past five, I can barely breathe. My eye still throbs, providing small jolts of pain every time I blink, but it's my broken ribs that have been causing discomfort all day and not even the Paracetamol and Ibuprofen concoction I've taken is taking the edge off. It feels as if I'm being constantly stabbed in the ribs over and over and taking a breath is causing me to almost black out.

There's no point in going to the doctor. I know they won't be able to do anything for broken ribs, except strap me up and ask questions I'm not prepared to answer. As a pharmacist, I know the best course of action is to take painkillers when needed, rest, and use ice compression around the ribs. Unfortunately, I can't take time off work to rest, so painkillers and ice will have to do.

I don't have my own car, so I walk twenty-five minutes back and forth to work each day. On normal days, I don't mind, but for the next six weeks, while my ribs heal, I know it's going to be torture. The fresh air does me good though, and the walking often helps my stiff and aching muscles. I sometimes wish I were more like Holly, who practically lives in the gym and exercises every day, but I've never had time for structured exercise. Plus, I don't have the energy and Simon always tells me he doesn't want me going to the gym so other blokes can ogle me in my gym wear. But walking has always been a favourite pastime, even on the days I'm off from work, when I'm not severely injured, I still walk into town or along the seafront, allowing the rough winds to buffet around me like a cocoon.

I spend as little time at home as possible. It feels like my personal prison, a living hell on earth. As soon as I step over the threshold, my whole body tenses as if it senses danger, preparing for an impact I know is going to come sooner or later. I'm constantly on high alert, ready for the flight or fight response to kick in. Although I don't do either of those things. I just stay in one place and take it because it's easier and will be over quicker that way. I have so little respect for myself that I don't care anymore. I know I should, but Simon's slowly but surely beaten the life and the fight out of me.

The front door always sticks, so I shove my shoulder against it, wincing as pain flashes through my ribs. Simon is moving about in the kitchen, so I quickly hang up my jacket and put my bag down on the floor, scooping my phone out from the front pocket. I walk into the kitchen with a smile on my face.

Simon is in a pair of grey jogging bottoms and a black T-shirt, his hair damp from a shower. Despite what he did to me last night and the broken ribs he gave me, I'm still attracted to him. He's always been handsome. It's what drew me to him in the first place. I know it's shallow of me, but I was swept up in his beauty back then. He knew it too, but I always assumed he wasn't interested in me. I've never considered myself attractive, but he's always told me how beautiful I am. That's why he wants to keep me all to himself.

He spins around as he hears me enter the kitchen. 'I've missed you! How's your day been?' he asks as he wraps his large arms around me, lifting me off the ground. I almost shout out in pain as the breath leaves my lungs. He squeezes me too tight, but I don't fight against him. I bury my face into his shoulder and inhale his scent, almost passing out from the stabbing pain.

'I've missed you too,' I stutter.

'How was work?'

I blink back tears as I say, 'It was fine, thank you. How was your day?'

Simon plants me back on the ground and I stumble slightly but catch myself against the worktop. I cannot show weakness, or he'll sense it like a hungry hyena.

'Busy,' he says. 'We had a large shipment come in and were a staff member down, but we managed to get it all unpacked and done.'

'That's great.'

Simon works for a packaging and delivery company, transporting goods all over the country. Luckily, he doesn't do a lot of driving but spends most of his time at the large warehouse taking note of stock and inventory. He doesn't find it a glamorous job, but he seems happy day to day and hardly ever complains about his work.

We have a good thing going. We both work full-time and are happy with our lives on the outside, but I could never tell him how I feel; that I'd rather be anywhere else but in the same room as him. I wish every day that an opportunity would arise for me to escape, but I know he'd find me. If I left him, he'd hunt me down. I know it. There's no escaping my husband.

Often, our marriage vows come back to haunt me. 'To have and to hold until death do us part.'

Simon smiles as he reaches out and strokes the side of my face. 'Ooh, your eye looks sore. I'm so sorry I lost control last night. You know I didn't mean it, right?'

My throat constricts as I fight back a cough. If I cough, then it's even more painful than breathing. 'I know.'

Simon frowns and takes a small step closer to me and I focus all my energy on not shaking or flinching away from him. 'You need to put more make-up on it tomorrow otherwise people might notice at work.'

'I will do,' I say.

'Good. Now, why don't you go and have a nice hot bath and I'll finish dinner. I'll even bring you a glass of wine to enjoy. How does that sound?'

'It sounds wonderful. Thank you.'

Simon leans forward and plants a kiss on my forehead. 'I love you, Lisa.'

'I love you too.'

* * *

Once I'm safely locked in the bathroom, I delicately run a make-up wipe across my eyes and over my face, cleansing my skin and removing the layers of foundation it's taken to cover my black eye and bruising. I look at the dirty wipe and then up at my gaunt face in the steamy mirror.

How did I let things get this far?

I light a sweet-smelling candle and glance at the glass of wine Simon poured for me, which now rests on the side, the condensation sliding down the stem and pooling at the bottom, causing a water ring.

Turning back to the mirror, I turn my head to the left and then to the right, studying the contours of my face. In the flickering candlelight, the bruise looks darker and more foreboding than it does in the light and the shadows under my eyes make me look like a living corpse.

I'm pathetic.

The tangy odour of sweet and sour sauce drifts through the closed door. It's not a shock to me that Simon is acting so nice. It's what always happens after he loses his temper. All I can do is enjoy the next few days while he showers me with love and affection before he hits me again. It could last a week or maybe more. It's the not knowing that kills me, that takes away a little piece of my soul every day. He used to go years or months between attacks, but now they're more regular. One day, I fear he might actually kill me.

Until death do us part.

My phone is resting on the side, and it keeps lighting up with incoming messages from the group chat. I haven't checked in with the girls since I've been home, but now I just want to be alone and sink into the warm water, covering myself in bubbles. As I lower myself into the bath, I run my fingers across my sensitive ribs and look down. They are bruised too, and I gasp as the hot water takes my breath away and causes a shooting pain to ripple through me.

I lie down, taking it an inch at a time, and allow the water to become still, watching as the levels rise and lower in time with my shallow breathing. Then, I hold my breath and wonder what it would be like to never breathe again.

* * *

Forty-five minutes later, I've finished my glass of wine and watch as my husband pours me another while setting my plate down in front of me. I lean forward and inhale the delicious and tangy aromas, even though it immediately turns my stomach.

What if he's poisoned it?

'Wow, this smells amazing. Thank you,' I say as I take the glass from him. Our fingers lightly touch for a moment, and a jolt of electricity shoots through my hand, up my arm and spreads around my body. I used to think it was a spark of love, but now it's something very different.

'Why did you just flinch?' he asks.

'I–I didn't.'

'You did. You flinched when I touched you.'

I smile, setting the glass down. I take both his hands in mine, squeezing them. 'I'm not flinching now.'

43

Simon purses his lips and then leans down and kisses me lightly. 'Eat up,' he says.

I look down at the delicious meal on the table and pick up the cutlery. I take a bite, pretending that it tastes yummy when in fact it tastes like plastic. I watch Simon wordlessly from across the table. His attention is on his phone, absent-mindedly scrolling through a social media app while shovelling food into his mouth, ignoring me completely.

I take a large gulp of wine in the hope it will steady my nerves. I've already read the message from Penny, asking if Holly and I are free this weekend to visit her, all expenses paid. I want to go more than anything in the world. To see my two best friends again after so many years, to squeeze them tight, to never let go, to forget about my marital problems for a long weekend. Maybe I will never come home. Perhaps it's the escape route I've been waiting for.

But the thought of asking Simon is enough to make my stomach perform flips and my mouth turn dry. Should I even ask him? Or should I just get up and leave? I'm not sure which is a worse idea. I keep licking my lips and squirming in my chair. I clear my throat, decision made.

'Penny has messaged to ask if I'd like to visit her this weekend,' I say in a cheery voice, all while attempting to hide the tremble in my words.

Simon continues to chew.

I clear my throat and try again. 'I said, Penny—'

'I heard what you said,' he says in a monotone voice, not even taking his eyes off his phone. 'I just assumed you were joking.'

'I . . . No, I'm not joking. I think it will be really good for me to get away. Penny will pay for the travel expenses, which is very kind of her and—'

Simon snorts. 'Great, so Penny now owns you.'

'Excuse me?'

'I don't want her thinking we can't pay our way.'

'She doesn't think that.'

44

'Look, Penny's just trying to control you. Why can't she come here?'

I lower my knife and fork, already knowing the battle is over before it's even begun. I'd rather stab myself in the eye than have my friends visit me here. 'Fine. I won't go.'

Simon slams his phone on the table and knocks over his wine glass. 'Don't be like that!'

I open my mouth but can't find any words.

'You love making me feel bad, don't you?' he snaps.

'I'm not trying to make you feel bad, Simon. I just want to see my best friends for the weekend. That's all. I have a few days of holiday left. We haven't got anything booked. You see your friends all the time.'

'That's because all my friends live just down the road.'

I sigh and look down at my food, my stomach grumbling in response. I'm hungry but I just can't face eating. I know I've lost a lot of weight recently. My clothes are hanging off my small frame and my hair is lifeless and limp.

The silence that fills the room is one I'm used to with Simon around. I dare not say anything else in case it pushes him over the edge, and I can't take two beatings back to back. I sip my wine and decide to risk lifting my head, and look at my husband. He's gone back to scrolling through his phone and eating his dinner as if the past conversation didn't even happen.

I guess that's that then.

End of discussion.

* * *

After dinner, I stand at the sink and wash the dishes, staring straight ahead and not paying attention to what I'm doing. I feel as if I'm in a trance most days. I'm looking forward to crawling into bed and closing my eyes against the hideousness of today. I haven't responded to Penny yet, but I know I must soon. Maybe I should just leave without telling him.

Simon walks into the kitchen and I hear him take the bottle of wine out of the fridge and top up his glass. 'You can go.'

I stop scrubbing a dirty plate and glance over my right shoulder. 'What?'

Simon sighs as he calmly walks to me, puts his glass down and wraps his arms around my shoulders, one forearm straight across my neck. He's tender and gentle, but I know with one swift movement he could have me in a chokehold.

'You're right. It's been too long since you've seen the girls. I know how much they mean to you. I'm just a bit worried what they'll say about your bruises.'

'I'll put extra make-up on, I promise. If they say anything then I'll say I had an accident or something.'

Simon tightens his grip as he plants a kiss on the side of my head. 'Then have fun, won't you?'

I only let out a breath once he releases me. 'Thank you,' I say.

This is it.

This is my chance to escape. Whether I tell the girls the truth about him, I haven't decided yet, but I could stay with Penny for longer than the weekend. He doesn't know where she lives. I could hide out with her for a while.

CHAPTER SEVEN

Holly
Fourteen years ago

It's weird being away from home for the first time in her eighteen years of life. She doesn't like it, and her mum only left her here half an hour ago. She's moved all the way from Manchester up to Edinburgh University to study Fitness and Personal Training, along with Management and Business on the side. She doesn't even know why she applied to this university. She thinks, at the time, she wanted to be as far away from her parents as humanly possible without moving overseas, but now she wishes she'd applied to the same university as either Lisa or Penny, or maybe stayed in Manchester.

Being so far away from her best friends is torture. They've basically grown up together and have always lived less than ten minutes away since the age of seven. What if they meet other people and become best friends with them? What if they forget about her? They promised each other that they'd talk every day on the phone or via text, but friends always say that. It's easy to say they're going to stay in contact, but when it comes to making the effort when they're so far away, it's much harder. She misses the girls already. She wishes they were here with her. Why hadn't they applied to the same universities? She knows the real reason why: because they wanted to do different courses and no one university did all three. They're growing up and they have their own lives to lead now, but it's terrifying. She doesn't want to live her life without them. They're her people.

She's standing in her tiny bedroom in halls, looking around at the boxes and suitcases, wondering where the hell to start. How is all of this even going to fit in this shoebox of a bedroom? There's a freshers' fair this week and apparently, it's mostly about getting stupidly drunk, meeting people and settling in, but she doesn't want to do all that stuff without Lisa and Penny. They should be doing this together. The thought of making new friends fills her stomach with butterflies and not the good kind that are pretty and glittery, but the ones that are black and mouldy and dying.

She's wearing her favourite jumper that she couldn't bear to leave behind. It's purple and sparkly and she's had it since she was eight, so it's now more like a cropped jumper, showing off her bare midriff. But she loves it, and it reminds her of home.

There's a knock at the door, and she freezes. This is it. The start of her new life. She has to meet new people, make new friends and start down a new path without her girls. She holds her breath as she opens the door.

A boy stands in front of her, holding a bottle of vodka in one hand and a packet of cigarettes in the other. 'Uh, hi,' he says. 'You're the only person I haven't met on this floor yet.'

He's cute, in a weird sort of way. Not overly attractive, but not bad either. His hair is super short on the sides, but longer on top, and his dress sense is somewhat muddled, a mix between hippy and posh. She can't quite work it out.

'Um . . . hi, I guess. I'm Holly.'

He holds out the vodka and packet of cigarettes. 'Welcome gifts.'

She takes them with a smirk. 'My favourite. How did you know?'

'Lucky guess. What are you studying?'

'Fitness and Personal Training, plus business management.'

He raises his eyebrows. 'Ah, a fitness freak.' His eyes suddenly notice her left hand and he winces. 'Oh, gee, sorry . . . I didn't mean . . .'

'It's fine. I'm used to it.'

'No, but . . . I didn't mean to call you a freak. You're not. I mean . . . Can we start over?'

She nods, used to people behaving awkwardly around her disability. 'Sure. You haven't actually told me your name yet.'

'I haven't?'

'Nope.'

'It's Drake.'

Now it's her turn to raise her eyebrows. 'Interesting name.'

'Thanks. So . . . you fancy smoking those up on the roof and getting wasted? It's like a rite of passage or something. Do you have a boyfriend?'

His abruptness takes her by surprise. 'No. Do you?'

'No. And no girlfriend either,' he adds with a smirk.

'Good to know.'

He steps backward and beckons her to follow him 'Come on. Let me introduce you to the rest of the floor.'

She glances back at her room full of boxes. She really should make a start on unpacking, but there's only one chance to make a good first impression at university. As much as she already misses the girls, she knows she has to be brave and do this without them, just like they're doing without her, possibly at this very moment.

She follows Drake up to the roof, and doesn't remember much after that.

CHAPTER EIGHT

Lisa
Fourteen years ago

Everything hurts. Even parts that shouldn't hurt. She had a lot to drink earlier in the night, which numbed her mind slightly, but not her body. She wishes the pain would go away. She'd always dreamed her first time would be special, but this wasn't special at all. Her attacker hadn't cared she was crying or bleeding or shaking from fear. At some point during the ordeal, her bladder had released, and he'd spat on her face and told her she was disgusting, but it hadn't stopped him.

He only stopped when he was finished. Then, he left her on the damp ground with her skirt shoved up to her waist, the whole lower half of her body exposed to the cool night air. He took the thong he'd ripped from her as a souvenir after smelling it and then laughed as he ran off. He'd been nothing but a blurry, black shape. She couldn't remember anything about him.

After a few minutes of lying still, wondering if he'd come back, she sits up, testing and stretching each limb to bring some feeling back into them. Her head spins and then she vomits onto the grass beside her before wiping her mouth with the back of her hand. She pulls her skirt down, but as it's so short, it barely covers her modesty, and now she has no underwear to protect her. She's bleeding. Not a lot, but enough to trickle down her thighs. Why hadn't she worn trousers? Would that have stopped him? Had she invited him to do this to her by wearing such a short skirt? Was it her fault? She never usually wore such revealing clothes, but it had only been this once. She'd just started university a few months ago and all the other girls were wearing short skirts.

She knows it's normal to bleed after losing your virginity, but he was too rough, and she knows it shouldn't feel as painful and uncomfortable as this. She tries to stand, but her legs are like jelly and unable to support her, so she crawls across the grass, unsure which direction is the best option. Maybe she should go back the way she came, back towards her friends' house, but she doesn't remember which way that is.

She wishes she'd stayed at her friends' house now. She wishes she'd stayed and gone out partying like they planned, but they'd had an argument, something that very rarely happened. Too much to drink maybe. She wishes she hadn't stormed out and taken a shortcut through the dark park. She wishes she hadn't drunk so much so she could have fought back harder. She wishes a lot of things. But wishing won't change what's happened to her.

She needs help, but it's late. Or early. It's gone one o'clock in the morning, she knows that because that's the time she left the house, but she has no idea how long her attacker was raping her.

She freezes and stops crawling for a moment.

Rape.

That's what's happened to her. She'll now always be known as a rape victim. People will blame her for wearing her skirt too short, for drinking too much alcohol, for walking alone at night. They'll say she was asking for it. That's what he'd said, wasn't it? That she'd asked for this by wearing such revealing clothing. Is that what other people will think? Is that what her parents will think? She remembers her father looking at her once when she was younger and shaking his head at what she was wearing before she'd left the house for a party. But he wasn't here now, and she thought it would be okay.

Maybe if she hadn't worn a short skirt, this wouldn't have happened. Or would it? Whose fault was this?

She cries as she begins crawling again, calling out for help. She doesn't have any way of contacting anyone. She has a mobile, but who would she call? All her university friends are drunk and out partying by now. She needs to get back to halls. It's not far. Maybe she can crawl there, but her knees already hurt and have cuts all over them, stones embedded in too deep.

'Help,' she squeaks.

Her voice is gone.

Then, footsteps approach, and she stops, terrified that it's him coming back for more.

CHAPTER NINE

Penny

The twins came home from their play date with Tracey, their best friend, full of sugar and about a million questions because, apparently, Tracey told them that babies came from mummies and daddies having sex. Naturally, my twins asked me what that was as soon as they got in after Tracey's mum dropped them off, extremely red-faced and after apologising profusely she scurried away with her tail between her legs. I then spent almost an hour explaining in a simple yet honest way what sex was, by which time they'd got bored and asked for a packet of crisps each. So I gave up explaining and gave myself a mental high-five for dodging that bullet for maybe another year or two.

Bedtime is a raging success as always . . . Not!

Lori refuses to brush her teeth. Luca decides to run around the house naked while shouting 'I have a penis!' at the top of his lungs. They both throw a tantrum when I tell them I am too tired to read them a seventh bedtime story. Who knew six-year-olds could still throw a tantrum? Then I'm overcome with mum guilt for not reading them a seventh bedtime story, so I cave and then they want me to read another. By the time I'm able to escape both of their rooms, it's gone nine and a small migraine is forming behind my eyes. I've read eleven different books and they've each told me in detail the events of their day, even though I stopped listening after the first five minutes and merely nodded my head and said 'Oh, wow' and 'That sounds fun' in all the right places. It's a skill I've mastered over the years.

Having kids is hard work, but having twins is an honest-to-God slow torture method. They gang up on me when I least expect it and they can turn from gentle, loving angels who adore each other one minute, to conniving, evil psychopaths who want to rip each other's throats out the next. There is no in between. I stupidly and naively thought that having two would make things easier in the long run. They could entertain themselves and play with each other, right? Wrong. Having twins of the opposite sex is like having any other siblings. They are as different as chalk and cheese.

Lori hates anything to do with Luca. She hates his toys, his clothes and his haircut. Luca is happy to play with her toys sometimes but refuses to breathe the same air as her most of the time. When there are times of calm, I hold my breath because I know even the slightest thing will set them off again.

Drake told me to hire a nanny right from the start, but I told him to go and suck a lemon. Yes, we can afford a nanny and yes, it sure as hell would make things easier around here, but I don't need help with the kids. I can do it all myself. I'm not the perfect mother and I don't pretend to be, but I'm not going to stick them with a nanny like my mother did with me and pretend like they don't exist.

I love my kids. I do. But sometimes they can be proper dickheads and I'd easily swap them both for a puppy in a heartbeat.

When I finally sit down with a glass of well-deserved red wine, I open my phone and then the group chat, hoping for some good news. I haven't had a chance to check for updates since I sent the message asking the girls to come for the weekend. Work got in the way and then the twins came home and utter chaos and devastation ensued.

Lisa: *I'm in!*

Holly: *Screw it, I'm coming too. I never do anything on the spur of the moment. Plus . . . I really need to talk to you girls about something.*

Penny: *Yay! Omg, I'm so fucking excited. I'll book your train tickets now. What's going on, Hols?*

Holly: *I can't say now. It's more like something you'd talk about in person over a glass of wine . . . a big glass!*

Lisa: *Hope everything's okay.*

Penny: *Yeah. Sounds serious. To be fair, I need to tell you girls something too.*

Holly: *You're not pregnant again, are you?*

Penny: *Ha!*

I attach a picture of my wine for proof.

Penny: *No, Drake has changed his life insurance. It's complicated. I'll explain when you girls get here. Bring swimsuits. The pool is lovely and warm.*

Holly: *Woohoo!*

Lisa: *Yay!*

I say goodnight to the girls after they tell me the best times to catch their trains on Friday morning. I book their journeys, using my husband's credit card (he won't notice) and ensure they both are seated in first class on all their connections. It's the least I can do as the train takes several hours for both of them. I want to treat my girls.

55

After the journeys are booked, I send them their itinerary and a list of stations they need to change at and then I go to bed. My migraine is getting worse, and I know from experience the only way I'll feel better is to lie down in a dark, quiet room. Unfortunately, having six-year-old twins and a full-time job means that rarely happens, so I take the opportunity while I can.

I peer in each of the twins' rooms to check they're still breathing (force of habit from when I first read about cot death, which scared me so badly I bought one of those cot alarm things that alert you if your kid stops moving or breathing) and then creep to my room, avoiding the squeaky floorboard because if I step on it, it's almost guaranteed one of them will hear it and wake up, and then demand a snack or ask to come to bed with me.

I pop a few painkillers and wash them down with the dregs of wine before slipping under my silk sheets. I pick at the scab on my arm while I wind down as a cool breeze blows in from the open window. It feels wonderful against my clammy skin. I hope I'm not coming down with something. I rarely get sick. I don't remember the last time I was unwell. The kids get ill all the fucking time, but I somehow manage to fend off their germs and battle through. It's my superpower. Although, I did get sick once with their horrible germs, and I felt so awful that I couldn't even get out of bed without vomiting. To this day, I don't know how I survived because Drake was away and the kids were still potty training. Fun times.

Eventually, I fall asleep and have a bad dream where my husband tries to kill me by poisoning my wine and then I never drink wine ever again. Such a horrible nightmare! Imagine never drinking wine ever again . . .

* * *

The next morning, my migraine is gone, and the twins are up extra early, ready and willing to start my next one. I down my second coffee of the morning so far, leave them to finish their breakfast of toaster waffles and cereal, and step under the hot jet of water in my shower. This shower is worth every single penny I spent on having it installed. It has fifteen different jet variations, five light settings and various strengths of water pressure and temperature. There's even a sound system with noises of the rainforest, whale song and whatever else takes my fancy. I could stay in this shower all day.

I drip water all over the tiled floor as I walk into my bedroom naked. Thanks to having hardly any time to eat, my figure is trim for someone who does little to no exercise. I do Pilates and yoga and sometimes a body combat class, but I'm not very consistent, despite paying a fortune for my gym membership at the nearby leisure club, which is very exclusive. I fight the urge to check myself out in the floor-length mirror and pull on a set of matching loungewear that I saw Stacey Solomon wearing a few weeks ago in her Instagram stories. I'm a sucker for anything she wears or promotes, which is why my entire house is filled with her Asda home range.

That's when I notice something different about Drake's side of the room. We each have our own dressing rooms and en suites but share the same room and bed. His side is also very tidy, hardly an item out of place, from his rows and rows of aftershave to his immaculately lined-up shoe collection. Since he's never here, it doesn't take a lot to keep his side of the room tidy.

I'm about to walk out of the room because I can hear my children arguing again, but the fact his dressing-room door is open catches my eye. It's never open. But I can't remember if it had been open last night when I came to bed because my migraine had distracted me. I hadn't turned on the lights either, using only the moonlight to see my way across the room as I'd undressed, ready for bed.

But his door is open now.

Ignoring the twins' shrieks of 'I hate you!' and 'Muuuum!', I creep towards the open door and peer inside, flicking on the light switch. At first glance, nothing looks out of the ordinary. His dozens of suits are lined up perfectly in colour order. His ties are neatly rolled up in drawers behind glass, and his trousers are expertly draped over hangers in their correct places.

But something is amiss.

My eyes find it after a few seconds of searching.

A single drawer is slightly open as if it had been closed in a hurry and forgotten about.

I tiptoe across the floor, knowing if my husband knew I was in here, he'd freak. He never likes me going into his dressing room. To be honest, I'm mildly surprised he hasn't been hiding something dodgy in here, but other than the partially open drawer, there is nothing.

My fingers brush the edge of the drawer.

And I slowly pull it open.

I raise my eyebrows when I see what's inside, barely believing my own eyes.

CHAPTER TEN

Holly

When I tell my husband that I'm going to visit the girls, he responds with a single grunt, which either means he's heard and he doesn't care, or he hasn't heard me but nor does he care what I've said. Either way, I couldn't give a crap because I'm going. I need to get out of this house and away from my husband otherwise I fear I might stab him in his sleep or maybe strangle him during one of our less-than-adequate sex games. Last night he woke me up when he finally crawled into bed and fell asleep the instant his head hit the pillow and began to snore so loudly, I swear the walls started shaking. I couldn't get back to sleep and it was all I could do not to grab a pillow and suffocate him. We need some space. He needs to get his act together and find a job. He's not the man I used to know.

When I met him, he had his whole life planned out. He was successful and determined and I was attracted to him because of that, but now he's different and I don't like the person he's changed into. I know a marriage takes work and often people fall out of love with their spouses for one reason or another, but this feels different and that's because it is different. I don't respect him anymore. It's the biggest turn-off for me. Plus, there's the added issue that he may or may not have murdered a woman . . .

Friday morning can't come fast enough, but I do spend the whole of Thursday worrying and stressing about that dead woman and my husband. Surely, they can't be connected. I'm just seeing connections that aren't there. My husband doesn't have the skill or mental capacity to murder someone. There's also the small issue of . . .

No, it doesn't matter. I've changed my mind. I've decided not to fixate on it. I have other things to worry about and they are much more important. The dead woman isn't my business or priority right now.

I cancel the few clients I had booked in for the weekend and rearrange them for the following week, schedule myself a deluxe manicure and dig out my suitcase from the attic. It smells a bit musty, but it's time it got some air. I can't remember the last time I went away by myself without my husband. We took a long weekend break last Christmas to a gorgeous country cottage in the middle of the Peak District. Honestly, I never wanted to leave. I switched my phone off and it was bliss . . . other than the fact Will was there, ruining my bliss and demanding sex every night, like it was some written rule that married couples have to have sex while on holiday.

Since Edinburgh is over four hundred miles away from St Davids, I first have to take a flight to Cardiff Airport and then get a train from there, and then change, which still takes over four hours. Penny says she'll pick Lisa and me up from Haverfordwest. Honestly, I hate living so far north. Not only that, but none of my family lives anywhere near me, not that I speak to them regularly. It's just my mum and dad, who don't bother to call me unless they want something. Once, my mum called me to ask me to design her a workout programme, which I did, and we spent a while on the phone going over some things and then I didn't hear from her for six months until she was ready for an upgrade. It's up to me to call them but to be perfectly honest, I have better things to do with my time than hear about my dad's latest ailment or my mum's fascination with vegan wax melts. I'm sure if anything drastic happens, I'll get a call from them. I'm sticking with the idea that no news is good news as far as my parents are concerned. I'm an only child, thank God. I couldn't be dealing with siblings. Lisa and Penny are my true sisters. It doesn't matter that we aren't related by blood.

* * *

I'm bouncing up and down on the balls of my feet, trying to catch a glimpse of the departure board. The number of my gate should be appearing any time now. The waiting area is bustling with people all hell-bent on reaching their gates on time. I just want to get on the plane. I was up stupidly early this morning to grab a taxi to the airport, as my husband refused to drop me off. He barely said a word to me when I left. I expect he's happy he gets the house to himself for a long weekend. Not that I expect him to do much with his time. I gave him a short list of things that needed doing around the house last night, like the curtain rail in the bedroom needs fixing and the bathroom needs a decent clean. I highly doubt he'll get around to doing it because he'll be so busy sitting on his butt, drinking with his friends and maybe murdering women . . .

Nope, I'm not going down that road again.

It's not a long flight and I'm not a nervous flyer, but I just want to get going. I want to see my girls. I'm not sure which one of them I'm looking forward to seeing more.

I love Penny, but she can be a bit overbearing at times and I have a weird feeling that Lisa isn't totally okay at the moment. Whether it's to do with her life, her work or what, I don't know, but I'm hoping a few drinks will loosen her tongue and she'll open up to us like she used to do. I've noticed she's become more closed-off since she married Simon. I've never told her this, but I'm not keen on him. The guy is downright creepy. He's too nice and overly helpful whenever I've seen him, and I don't trust him. At my first wedding anniversary party, he made a huge scene by declaring his love for Lisa in front of everyone and honestly, it just looked like she wanted to crawl into a ditch and die of embarrassment. She's never been into huge displays of affection or being the centre of attention and if he knew her at all, he'd know that and wouldn't have put her through such an awful and traumatic ordeal, especially at my party. I hadn't been impressed, to be honest, but at the time I'd just laughed it off and pretended it was mega cute, while inside I was seething that he'd distracted from my day. I hadn't asked for much. I'd just wanted my anniversary to be about me, that's all. Oh, yeah, and my husband. We hadn't had a proper wedding ceremony, so our first anniversary was our chance to have all of our loved ones together.

Anyway, I've never liked Simon since.

Today, I'm dressed in my most sophisticated outfit of loose slacks and a sheer blouse, which nips in at the waist and enables anyone who looks to see my bra. My husband told me it looked a bit slutty when I first bought it, so today I've opened the top two buttons to emphasise my cleavage, which isn't extravagant by any means, but I'm proud of the girls anyway.

I still haven't been able to forget about the other night. Will's blatant lie has been eating away at me ever since. Oliver was adamant he didn't go out drinking with him on Tuesday and I believed him. I've been trying to squirrel more information from Will, but as soon as I mention that night he starts clamming up and gets all stroppy, so I dropped it. But it doesn't mean I've stopped thinking about it.

I'm doing it again . . . I'm thinking about it when I know I shouldn't.

Finally, my gate is announced, and I begin my walk. Penny has very graciously booked me a seat at the front of the plane with the most leg room. She said she would have booked me a first-class ticket, but as the planes are so small flying within the UK, there's no such thing as a first-class lounge. I had to laugh. Oh, how the other half lives!

Lisa and I are meeting at Cardiff train station and then travelling together from there, so at least I'll get to spend some time with her alone before we arrive at Penny's.

* * *

The flight is uneventful, and I find myself drifting off, but in a little over an hour, we're already getting ready to land. I make it through baggage claim and head to the train station, the butterflies in my stomach fluttering at the thought of seeing Lisa. I don't even know what she looks like now. She hardly ever sends us pictures of herself, and she doesn't have social media, which is a right bummer.

She was always very pretty, though. Plain, but pretty. I remember her having amazingly straight teeth, and her smile often lit up the room.

'Hollllyyyyyy!' An ear-piercing shriek makes me jump while I'm waiting on the train platform and I spin on the spot to see Lisa jogging towards me, dragging her case behind her. The first thing I notice is the fact she's lost about two stone in weight, and the second thing is she looks a little stiff and is protecting her left side. As a personal trainer, it's easy to spot these things. I often study the way people move and can see their misaligned posture before they even know about it.

'Lisa!'

We half-drag and half-carry our cases along before dropping the handles to the floor and flinging our arms around each other, screaming and shrieking like we're teenagers at a Busted gig (yes, we were/are fans). We jump up and down still clinging onto each other as if our lives depend on it.

Lisa breaks away, wincing, and leans awkwardly, clutching her side. 'Ooh, sorry,' she says.

'What's wrong?'

'Ah, I . . . had a little car accident the other day and the seat belt bruised some ribs.'

'But you don't drive.'

'Right. Simon was driving.'

I nod my understanding, but immediately red flags start popping up in front of my eyes. She grins from ear to ear and hugs me again, a little less enthusiastically this time.

'Oh my God, it's so good to see you. I've missed you so much.'

I smile back at her, but it's a little forced. Something's not right, but now isn't the time to bring it up. 'It's been fucking years! Come on, let's go get on the train and grab a drink.'

'Let me just message Penny to say we've arrived. She said to let her know when we met up.'

I watch Lisa type out a quick message, studying her body language and what she's wearing. She's got on an oversized grey hoodie and black leggings, hiding her slim body shape underneath, but I can tell by her pale skin and sharp cheek-bones that she's lost a lot of weight. I don't like what I'm see-ing. She's still smiling, with her perfect teeth, but she's hiding something much darker.

We find our first-class seats on the first train and order an alcoholic drink as we set off. Lisa tells me about her job, mainly. I know she's a pharmacist in Boots and she says she enjoys the work, but other than work, she doesn't tell me any-thing about what she gets up to. Does she go out with friends? Does she have a hobby? Why haven't I realised this before? Another thing I notice about Lisa is that despite wearing over-sized clothing and looking like she hasn't made an effort, she's wearing a full face of make-up. Mostly foundation, which, all credit to her, is the perfect shade for her skin tone, but I can see it caked around her eyes as if she's layered it up too much.

I try and push all of these red flags out of my mind. I need to speak to Penny about this. Maybe Lisa would open up more if it were both of us because right now, she seems in complete denial about everything. She's laughing and making jokes, but her body language doesn't match her cheery exterior.

'Wow,' says Lisa, a few hours later as she leans against her seat. 'This first-class carriage is amazing. I've never travelled in one before, so this is a little spot of luxury for me.' We're on the last train now, due to arrive at Haverfordwest in fifty minutes.

'This is a little bit surreal,' I say as I sip my wine. We've had a few already and I don't know about her, but my head is deliciously fuzzy.

'Just how much money does Penny have?' asks Lisa.

'Um . . . I'm not sure of the exact figure, but I'm thinking . . . a lot. Her business is doing well and I know Drake earns a lot too.'

I check my phone as the train assistant walks past, asking if we need anything else. 'No, this is all wonderful, thank you.' I settle against my seat and read a message from Will, which I've been ignoring for the past two hours.

Will: *My credit card's not working. Can you give me your details? I've forgotten. Thanks. Love you! Hope you're having fun xx*

A loud groan escapes my mouth.

'Everything okay?' asks Lisa, as she applies some lip salve from her bag.

'Yeah . . .' Then I sigh. 'No, not really.' Maybe if I open up a little to Lisa, she'll do the same.

'Tell me.'

'Will is gambling again.'

If Lisa is surprised, it doesn't show on her face. 'Oh, gosh. I thought he got help a few years ago?'

'He did, but . . . it's sort of started up again recently.'

'Have you spoken to him about it?'

'No, because he hasn't even told me. He just keeps using my card or spending my money and thinks I don't notice.'

Lisa reaches over the arm of her chair and squeezes my arm. 'I'm so sorry.'

I give her a weak smile. 'Thanks. I don't know what to do.'

'You need to speak to him about it.'

'I know I do, but . . . there's other stuff too.' I toss my phone on the table and run both my hands through my hair, then rub my eyes. 'Urrggh! When did life get so complicated?'

'Around the time we got married, I think.'

I laugh. 'That's true. Do you ever regret it? . . . Getting married?'

Lisa tilts her head to the side. 'Sometimes, but Simon used to be a good man, so I can't ever forget that.'

I want to say more. I want to ask her a dozen questions, but I don't. I know the vague story of how they met, but she very rarely talks about it. I get the feeling she hasn't told Penny and me the full details when it comes to Simon. Then again, there's a lot I haven't told the girls too.

A voice comes over the Tannoy system, announcing our arrival at the next station, which promptly makes us forget what we were talking about and move on to another topic.

CHAPTER ELEVEN

Lisa

It's so lovely to see Holly again. She looks so good, her eyes bright and wide. Her skin and hair are healthy and vibrant. Her body is toned and sculpted, and I would kill for her rounded butt. It makes me feel sick to think about my pale, thin body under my baggy clothes. Simon told me to dress this way early this morning. He doesn't like it when I wear clothes that show off my figure. Not that I have any sort of figure to show off, but even so, he likes me to stay hidden behind frumpy clothes. He says my body is just for him. Once upon a time, those words filled me with exhilaration and pride – that he loved my body and didn't want anyone else to see it – but now it makes me feel . . . invisible. And like I'm an object to him and not a living, breathing person with feelings and values.

Holly mentions several times during our journey that I look tired, but she doesn't pry too much, which I'm thankful for. I don't want to have a complicated and awkward conversation about my appearance on the train, surrounded by strangers. Because I know my friends will mention it at some point this weekend. It will inevitably happen, and it's why I wanted to come. I might not have the guts to tell them of my own free will about what's going on in my marriage, but if I know Holly and Penny, they'll see something is wrong and reach out to help me. I know I'm a coward, but it's the only way I can ask for help without actually asking for help.

With still forty minutes to go on our last train, Holly says it's okay if I want to shut my eyes for a while. We've had a few glasses of wine each, which have gone straight to my head, so I'm grateful for the chance to have a snooze. We fall into comfortable silence and my head naturally leans on her shoulder as we listen to the sound of the train gliding along the tracks, the hum of passenger chatter and the doors opening and shutting at each station.

It's not long before I drift off. I don't often sleep on public transport, so when Holly gently shakes me awake, I jolt upright in shock.

'Sorry, didn't mean to startle you. We're about ten minutes out from Haverfordwest,' says Holly.

I yawn and stretch my arms, but then flinch as a sharp pain stabs me in the ribs.

'Your make-up is a bit smudged,' says Holly.

My stomach drops as I realise what she means. 'I'll just go and freshen up in the toilet,' I say, grabbing my handbag which has my make-up in it and squeezing past her into the aisle. 'I'll be quick.' Ignoring Holly's quizzical stare, I stagger along the train as it rocks side to side to the small toilet cubicle. I assess myself in the mirror. This toilet is small, but posh, especially for a train. Holly's right. My make-up is smudged, and the foundation has worn away, probably smeared from leaning against her shoulder while I slept. The bruise around my left eye is more noticeable than it was yesterday. It's darker, but from past experience I know that means it's healing.

'Fuck it,' I mutter. I sigh heavily, grab a make-up wipe, and remove all traces of foundation from my face. I don't want to keep hiding, especially from my best friends. It's about time the truth came out. Plus, wearing so much foundation makes me feel claustrophobic and hot. I want to allow my skin to breathe.

Every lie that comes out of my mouth when I defend my husband is slowly eating me alive, and I can't do it anymore. I can't keep defending his actions and thinking it's okay and that I deserve it. I know I need help, but the thought of telling the girls my husband abuses me is enough to make my stomach churn. But it has to happen. It must or I'm going to die eventually because he's going to end up killing me. What will they think of me? Will they silently judge me for allowing it to carry on for so long? I wouldn't blame them if they did. I blame myself.

A loud rap on the door jolts me back to reality. 'Lisa, we have to get off in two minutes.' It's Holly. I didn't realise I'd been in here so long.

I wipe a tear from my injured eye, take a deep breath and open the door. I look straight into Holly's eyes and my head automatically dips down, trying to avoid her gaze.

'We have to talk later,' she says matter-of-factly, and then she walks away back to her seat to collect her bags.

I nod, grinding my teeth together as the train jolts again.

* * *

Holly and I see Penny at the same time. She's standing in the station entrance holding a homemade sign that says, HEY, BITCHES! Her whole face lights up as she shrieks like a banshee when she sees us, jumping up and down on the spot before barging through the crowds, accidentally bumping into an elderly couple in her haste. Holly reaches her first and they hug and cry and do a silly little dance that they made up about seventeen years ago. I never learned it; it was their thing. I catch up, still in pain from my ribs.

Penny lets go of Holly and runs to greet me. She attempts to hide her shock upon noticing my black eye, but expertly

brushes past it and embraces me in a hug, albeit not as enthusiastically as the hug she gave Holly. Has Holly messaged her
separately from the group chat and warned her about my eye
and possible broken ribs?

'You okay?' she whispers in my ear.

I nod again, fighting back tears. 'Let's talk later.'

'You bet.' Penny turns, grabs Holly, and pulls us all
into a three-way hug. 'Bitches! We're back together! Let's get
shit-faced!'

***

Two hours later, I'm sitting in a comfy chair in a tiki hut by a
beautiful outside pool, complete with a hot tub at one end and
a slide at the other. Penny has a fire lit inside the hut, which
also has a bar. The sun is beginning to set, but I could honestly
stay inside this hut for ever. As soon as I saw it, I asked if we
could sit in it for the evening rather than inside the house.

Penny is plying Holly and me with drinks and snacks,
fluttering about, ensuring we're comfortable. She's already
made us cocktails and has an array of finger foods laid out
on the bar.

She showed us around her house when we first arrived
and I'd stared in utter awe, gobsmacked at the sheer size and
splendour. We even have private bedrooms and en suites in
the guest part of the house. It shocked me to hear Penny
doesn't have a housekeeper or a cleaner. How does she have
the time to run this place, work a full-time business and look
after her twins? From what I gather from our group chats,
Drake isn't around a lot, and hasn't been for a long time. She's
a superwoman.

I sigh happily and sip my pink cocktail. I'm not sure
what's in it, but after the buzz I'd had on the train and now
this, my head is beautifully foggy. I'm a world away from my
life in Cornwall and for the first time in a very long time, I
feel safe. He can't reach me here. He can't.

My eyes close against the ambient glow of the crackling fire and I listen to the soft background music Penny has put on. It's coming from the surround-sound speakers situated around the pool and the hut. Holly has gone inside to use the bathroom.

'So,' says Penny, taking a seat next to me. 'How was the journey?'

'Long, but it was lovely. Thank you so much again for paying for the tickets and letting us travel in first class. It was an amazing experience.'

'It's my pleasure. I should have done it years ago. I can't believe we've let it go so long. If we didn't live so far apart then we'd see more of each other.'

'You have a beautiful home. This is like paradise.' I gesture at the gorgeous hut, pool and the dimming view of the countryside. I know further beyond the trees is the sea, which I'm excited to go and visit tomorrow. 'You're living the dream here.'

Penny smiles. 'Yes, but sometimes dreams can turn into nightmares.'

I take hold of her hand and squeeze it. I'm not sure what she means by that comment. Holly joins us and perches on the seat next to mine. There's silence for a few moments before I say, 'Where are the kids, Pen? I'm so excited to see them again.'

'At a sleepover with their mates. Do you think I want the twins running around here while I'm getting smashed with my friends? They'll be back tomorrow, don't you worry, and then you'll regret wishing they were here.'

'I can't wait to see them. I can't believe how big they've grown.'

Penny downs the rest of her drink in one big gulp. 'Yep, before I know it, they'll be teenagers and off having sex and taking drugs and doing God only knows what.'

Holly snorts. 'Kind of like what you did as a teenager, you mean?'

'Yep. Dreading it. Honestly, people tell you that as a parent it will be so hard and your life will never be the same again, blah blah blah, but what they don't tell you is how much you'll worry about them and the mind-numbing, gut-wrenching fear you have of them growing up and having lives of their own. I'm terrified. What if I didn't teach them right? What if they make the wrong decisions and end up getting hurt? What if some other person hurts them?'

Holly and I share a look. Neither of us can truly relate because we don't have kids, but I can relate a little. Only last week I had a child growing inside of me and already felt the strong maternal instinct to keep them safe, yet I'd already failed them as a mother. I'd lost them before they were even born into the world.

A bubble of nausea rises in my throat and I swallow it down.

CHAPTER TWELVE

Penny

It's been so long since I've hosted anyone at my house, other than my children. I don't, however, consider myself as their host, more like their eternal slave. I used to host a monthly book club, but that fizzled out after the rest of the people in the group decided to take a trip to the pub instead. It's now no longer a book club, so I quit. I can drink wine any day. I do read, but I can't remember the last time I picked up a book. Usually, I'm too tired to focus on reading in the evenings, so I end up binge-watching Netflix shows instead.

However, it's wonderful to be hosting my best friends. They haven't visited my house since it's been renovated. Any weekend where we have got together as adults has usually been in a city, sandwiched somewhere between the three of us, a spa weekend or city break. Once, we flew to Rome for a long weekend, but that was before I had the twins. It was during our university days. Holly flew over from Edinburgh and Lisa and I met her in Rome. Funnily enough, that's when she first told me about Drake, the strange boy who gave her fags and vodka the first time he met her.

73

Holly was good friends with my husband at university. He lived in her halls of residence. The first time I met him was at her university graduation ceremony. Lisa and I flew up to support her and then we all went out for drinks afterwards and Holly introduced me to Drake. She always said nothing happened between them, that they were just friends, and I believed her, because Drake is not Holly's type at all. Drake and I started chatting that night, and he asked for my number.

We dated for three years, were engaged for two years and married for three months before he cheated on me and I started picking at my skin. That's what started the insane habit and now I can't stop. We had a good run. Holly never forgave him for what he did to me, and she hasn't spoken to him since. Luckily, her friendship with me meant more to her than her friendship with him. Drake doesn't speak about his time at university much, nor does he mention Holly. Anyway, all that was so long ago now. We're different people.

There's a niggling cloud of exhaustion threatening to ruin this night, so I yawn once and then pour another drink. I stayed up far too late last night once the kids had gone to bed before the girls arrived, making homemade sausage rolls and googling recipes for cocktails. Who the hell am I? It's about time I put the bar in the tiki hut to good use, though. Usually, I sit out here during the evening with a glass of wine, which takes little to no time to pour. Now, though, I've got lemon wedges, cucumber slices, ice cubes, tonics, mixers and all the varieties of spirits behind the bar. Drake's a big drinker and he's the one who keeps the bar stocked, despite never using this outside space to its full potential. Ah well, you snooze, you lose.

When the darkness draws in, I turn on the fairy lights which brighten the space in the most magical of ways. It's so cosy and welcoming. It's made me fall in love with this hut again. I used it solidly for a few weeks after it was originally built, but then life got in the way, and I became too busy to sit and enjoy the silence once the kids had gone to bed. I vow to myself I'll do that more now. Fuck work. It will still be there in the morning.

I don't know what time it is, but I do know it's about time Lisa started explaining why she has a massive fucking bruise over her eye. It took me less than a second to notice it earlier, and Holly gave me a quick look that said, *I see it too.* I think we went past the point of being drunk an hour or two ago, so it's the perfect opportunity to bring up a serious topic. Or maybe not. Alcohol and serious talks are never a good combination, but we don't get to do it in person very often. It's about time she told us the truth.

Holly and I had spoken briefly earlier, and I said that I'd start the conversation, but at the right moment. Not that there is ever a good moment to bring up the fact one of our best friends has a black eye.

But, as it turns out, I don't have to bring it up because, eventually, we find ourselves in a quiet moment just staring up at the stars and listening to the ocean waves (on the sound system, because the sea is a little too far away to hear properly except on a particularly choppy day).

'Go on, then. Out with it,' says Lisa. 'Let's get it over with.'

Holly takes a deep breath. 'Why do you have a black eye?'

'And why are you walking as if you've shat yourself?' I add.

Lisa bursts out laughing at my crude question, which then sets us all off giggling. I know it's inappropriate to do so, but if laughter makes it easier for her to talk to us then so be it. She needs to be able to trust us.

Lisa sets her drink down and manages to compose herself. I can tell this is difficult for her. 'A few days ago, my husband hit me, and I fell down the stairs a few weeks ago too.' She opens her mouth to say something else, but then closes it and lowers her eyes to the floor.

In the flickering light, I see her bruise even more now. It's practically glowing. I get the feeling she has more to tell.

75

My skin tingles with anger, and I can't stop the words flying from my mouth. 'Was this the first time?'

Lisa shakes her head.

Holly sucks in a breath and holds it. 'How many times?' she asks.

'I've lost count.'

'Shit. That many?'

I spring to my feet, my fists clenched. 'Lisa, what the fuck? Why the hell didn't you tell us? We could have done something. We could have helped you. Why would you keep this a secret from us for so long?'

Lisa's body language turns from open to closed and she wraps her arms around herself, guarding against my vocal attack. I immediately shake my head.

'I'm sorry. I didn't mean . . . I'm not angry at *you*.'

'You're wondering why I never told you.'

I sit down next to Lisa. Holly gets up and joins us on the same seat, so we are on either side of her. We wrap our arms around her, protecting her, even though we're about ten years too late for that. She's never told us the full story of how she and Simon met. One day, she just told us that she was seeing someone and we didn't meet him for several years.

'We've been worried about you for a while, but we haven't said anything,' I say. I blame myself. The truth is I should have said something, but I was always too busy or too preoccupied. Some fucking best friend I am.

'We knew something wasn't quite right, but were afraid to bring it up,' adds Holly.

'We're bad friends,' I finish.

'The worst,' says Holly.

Lisa grabs one of our hands in each of hers and squeezes them tight. 'You girls are my best friends in the whole world, and I'm a bad friend for not confiding in you. We should be able to tell each other everything. We used to, right? We grew up together. We all got our first periods in the same month. We told each other the minute after we lost our virginities. Hell, Penny gave us a minute-by-minute replay of her delivery of the twins, including all the graphic stuff. We should be able to share other stuff too. I'm sorry I kept it from you.'

I have to physically fight back the urge to shudder. I've been hiding plenty from both of them too. How had we let it get this bad? Lisa is right. We had grown up together and shared so much over the years, from the ups and downs of reaching our teenage years to the broken hearts after being dumped by our first crushes, to attending universities and having to make other friends outside of our close trio. It had been a tough time, but we'd got through it together, despite being so far apart.

When had we started lying and keeping important things from each other? When had we stopped trusting each other with the truth? I would die for these girls, just like I'd die for my children (my husband, not so much), but the point is I'd do anything to ensure their happiness.

'We need to make a plan of action,' says Holly. 'We can't let this continue.'

It's funny how sober we've all become during the last couple of minutes, although our words are still slurred a little around the edges.

'Yes,' I say. 'For a start, you're going to report Simon to the police and kick him out of your house immediately.'

'I can't . . . the house is in his name. It's legally his. And he says if I ever call the police then he'll kill me.'

'Then you move out. I'll pay for whatever it costs. Hell, stay here for as long as you need.'

Lisa chuckles. 'Thanks, but it's a little far to commute to and from work.'

I sigh. 'Oh yeah, I forgot about work. Damn adult responsibilities . . . Why don't you quit? Again, I'll pay.'

'Penny, I love you, and thank you so much, but I can't accept your money for ever.'

'I'm not talking about for ever. Just until you get away from your husband and get set up somewhere else.'

'He'll find me. I'm terrified of him. You don't know what he's like.'

Holly clears her throat. 'Do you think he'd actually come after you and kill you?'

'Yes. I have no doubt. He's very controlling. He wouldn't take me leaving him well at all. He'd find it humiliating.'

'Has he always been like that? I remember you telling us that he was amazing at the start.'

'At first, he was. He was like my saviour, but over the years he . . . changed.'

Holly and I look at each other for several seconds.

'They always do,' answers Holly with a sigh. 'Lisa, I'm so sorry for what he's put you through, but you can't keep putting him on a pedestal just because he used to be nice to you at the start. He's abusing you, babe. You need to leave him. We'll do whatever it takes to help you.'

We sit in silence for a while. Lisa's body is shaking, but I don't think it's due to the chilly night air. I hate seeing my friend in so much pain. But maybe there is a way I can help her. A plan is forming in my mind. It's completely crazy, but it might just work.

I can't stay with my husband either; not after seeing what was in the box I found in his wardrobe. The thought makes me sick. Even thinking of him touching me again is enough to send nauseating shivers up my spine and make my skin crawl. He makes me want to pick at my skin until I peel it off.

I need to get out.

Lisa needs to get out.

And Holly can help us.

'I have an idea,' I say. 'But I need you girls to hear me out and trust me. Yes, I'm drunk, but I'm not that drunk. What I'm about to suggest is nothing short of crazy. I know that, but just hear me out.'

Both girls turn their heads and stare at me. I have their full attention. They know when I'm being serious. I'm known for being the joker, the silly one, the crazy one, but this isn't a game. It isn't anything like the truth or dare game I made them do when we were kids. This is real life, and this is as serious as it gets.

'We should kill our husbands.'

CHAPTER THIRTEEN

Lisa
Fourteen years ago

She doesn't know whether to shout for help or crawl under the bramble bush next to her, risking slicing her pale skin to pieces, and hide. What if he's come back for round two? But what if it's someone who can help her? She does the only thing her body will allow her to do at that moment and that's to collapse with her face against the dirty ground and sob loudly.

She just wants this to be over. She doesn't even care anymore. She has nothing left. No fight. No strength. Nothing. That monster, whoever he was, has taken everything from her. Her dignity, her virginity and her life because she knows she'll never be the same girl again. She can already feel herself changing. She's no longer an innocent young girl, but damaged and used. Maybe she deserves this. Maybe she deserves to be treated this way. Out of all the girls the monster could have chosen tonight, he chose her. Did that make her special? She didn't feel special. Why her? Why not anyone else?

'Oh God . . . are you okay? Miss . . . shit . . . what's happened?' It's a male voice; deep yet soft.

She senses him kneeling beside her and then he lays a hand on her back and she screams, her body frozen and unable to flee. 'Don't touch me!'

The stranger leaps back. 'I'm so sorry. I'm sorry. I just want to help, okay? You can trust me. I'm here to help you. I'm going to call an ambulance, okay?' He stands up. The panic is clear in his voice.

'Don't leave me!' she shrieks, tears cascading down her cheeks, mixing with the dirt and grime on her skin. At some point, she's bitten almost completely through her lip and it's bleeding badly.

'I'm not leaving you. I promise.'

She cries softly as she listens to him on the phone, calling the emergency services and giving them the details. That's when she rolls onto her back, tugging her skirt down as far as she can to hide herself. She looks up at the man above her, his eyes full of concern. He's young, older than her, but no more than twenty. It looks as if he's been out partying, as he's dressed in a posh shirt with the sleeves rolled up and jeans, which fit him perfectly. His hair is slicked back and he smells heavenly.

He hangs up and kneels next to her, keeping his distance. 'The ambulance is on its way, and so are the police. You'll be okay. I wish I had a jacket I could give you to keep you warm. What's your name?'

She can't form any words. Not even her name. He seems to understand and smiles. 'My name's Simon. I'll stay with you for as long as you need me to. I won't let anything bad happen to you, I promise. I'll keep you safe.'

And that's when she knows he means it. She is special. At least to Simon. And he's just saved her life. She owes him everything and she knows in that moment she'll do anything to make him happy and never wants him to leave her alone ever again.

He is her saviour.

CHAPTER FOURTEEN

Holly
Fifteen years ago

She and Drake become the best of friends during their time at university. He's doing some boring accountancy and business degree and eventually starts hanging around with posh, rich boys, but he doesn't let it change who he is at the core. Despite being good friends, she and Drake have never gone any further than a drunken snog one night, after which they both laugh and pretend like it never happened the next day. The truth is he's a good-looking guy, but not someone she wants to settle down with. But she reckons he'd get on well with Penny, so she introduces them when Penny comes up to celebrate her graduation. She's delighted to see that they like each other and after that, Drake seems much happier and the weirdness between them disappears. Not that things were weird, but . . . It does start getting a bit weird when she meets Will.

She graduates from Edinburgh University with a second-class degree. She has a job lined up in a local gym and plans on taking further courses to enhance her skills, but a lot of the courses say they won't be able to adapt to her disability, which annoys the hell out of her. She'd not planned to stay in Edinburgh, but she met Will a few months ago and he asked her to move in with him. She said yes without hesitation because she thought she loved him, but now she's having second thoughts. Not about him, but does she really see herself living and settling in Edinburgh?

Will is a plumber and they hit it off at a nightclub after being introduced by a mutual friend. That's when Drake goes weird with her, commenting that he isn't good enough and that she can do better.

After she finishes university, she and Will move into a small, rented flat in the centre of the city, which is stupidly expensive. They plan to save as much as possible to be able to buy their own house, but there's no way they'd be able to afford one in the city, so somewhere in the surrounding countryside would be perfect.

She and Will decide to get married after a few months on the spur of the moment in a little remote chapel with a couple of witnesses and the celebrant. Holly handles everything, even choosing the witnesses. She doesn't tell her parents, but she does tell Penny and Lisa, hoping they'll understand and won't be too disappointed that they won't get to be bridesmaids at her wedding. They do understand, even though Penny mentions that it's very quick, but she supports her decision.

She is happy, but there's something missing in her life, and she knows exactly what it is. Her best friends. She hates that they've been separated. Penny and Drake are a proper couple now and Lisa has met some guy called Simon, who has moved her away from Manchester and down to Cornwall, which is the furthest away she could possibly move and still be in the UK. Holly doesn't like Simon, but she keeps her thoughts to herself. There's something about him that isn't trustworthy. He's overly nice. She likes to think she has a sixth sense about these things, but as long as Lisa is happy then that's all that matters.

She wishes the three of them lived closer. She doesn't know how their lives are going to pan out, but maybe one day they can all be together again, like they used to be when they were growing up. Those were the best times.

CHAPTER FIFTEEN

Holly

Penny has said some outrageous stuff over the years I've known her. She once told us, at age fifteen, she wanted to apply for a space mission to the moon, despite getting motion sickness if she travels in the back of a car for more than fifteen minutes. She even suggested we sleep with each other's boyfriends because she was bored and wanted to do something fun and stupid. The woman is known for her crazy ideas, sharp tongue and wit but the words that have just come out of her mouth are, by far, the craziest yet. There's no hint of humour in her voice and no suggestion she's playing a joke. This isn't the time to play a joke anyway, not after what Lisa has just told us.

But the words slip from her mouth effortlessly and without hesitation as if she's merely suggesting we take a trip somewhere or make a pact to lose five pounds each.

In the distance, a weird noise pierces the darkness around the hut. It sounds like a pair of cats fighting to the death. It creeps me out and Penny must notice that I've heard it because she quickly says, 'Ignore that. It's just a couple of foxes. They like to the raid the bins around here.'

I frown at her, confused at how in one breath she can suggest killing our husbands and in the next talk about foxes raiding her bins. Because that is what she said, wasn't it? About our husbands? I hadn't misheard her? I know we're all a bit drunk, but surely, as she said herself, we're not *that* drunk.

'Penny,' I say. 'How much have you had to drink?' I glance at her empty glass. I'm pretty sure she's had the same amount as me, which, come to think of it, is at least four cocktails. And they're strong too. Penny doesn't believe in measuring shots. Her single shots are more like doubles, plus a little bit more for good luck.

Penny stands and paces up and down in front of us as she speaks while Lisa and I sit on the seat, huddled close, wondering why our best friend has suddenly lost the plot and wants to murder our husbands – although I'm pretty sure she's not talking about Will in all this because he may be lazy, but that doesn't warrant him deserving a death sentence. Even so . . .

'Right, before you jump to conclusions, I said to hear me out, okay? What I'm about to tell you cannot leave this house, you got it? I'm serious. It will ruin my family. It will ruin everything I've worked for. You know how I said the other day that Drake asked me if he could cum on my face during sex and you, Holly, suggested he was cheating on me—'

'Yeah, but Penny, that's no reason to kill the guy! I mean, I know he cheated on you a few years ago, but—'

'Shhh! Just listen,' she snaps. 'I don't care that he's cheating on me. I couldn't give a fuck. It just means he's cumming on someone else's face and not mine, which is a relief in itself. I found out he's doing something worse. Much worse.' She takes a deep breath and holds it, composing herself. 'You remember I told you he changed his life insurance so that if he died of natural causes then I'd get everything? Well, it also means I get everything if he's killed or goes missing.' Penny stops talking for a moment, probably expecting one of us to interrupt. I can't seem to find any words to say, so I wait for her to begin again.

Lisa clears her throat. 'Penny . . . what has Drake *done* exactly?'

Within seconds, Penny's eyes fill with tears. I don't think either one of us has seen her cry. Not since we were kids, anyway. She's always been the strong one, the one who shows little to no emotion; even when her mum died five years ago, she barely stopped to accept it. She wasn't close to her mum, having grown apart since leaving home, but even so, Penny didn't cry in front of us. I don't know if she broke down behind closed doors; she's never told us otherwise.

But seeing her broken and crying now, something must be seriously wrong.

Lisa leaps to her feet and wraps her arms around Penny, who's shaking so badly she can barely stay upright. I don't know what to do. I'm not great with shows of emotion, especially when it's Penny who's crying. Does she want to be held? Does she want a strong drink? Does she want me to make some lame joke to make her laugh? A slap across the face, maybe?

I stand and approach her. I lock eyes with Lisa who appears as shocked as I do. I can't imagine Drake doing anything that bad, but, then again, I never expected him to do a lot of things I know he's done, most of which Penny doesn't know about, and I'd rather keep it that way for a while longer. He's changed a lot since university. I barely know the guy anymore. At least, I do know the old Drake. The new Drake sounds like a right twat.

'Penny . . . what has Drake done?' Lisa asks again, talking slowly, pronouncing every syllable.

Penny sniffs loudly then lifts her head off Lisa's shoulder, wiping her nose on the back of her hoodie sleeve, leaving a wet streak. Her make-up has smudged and for the first time in a long time, I see a vulnerable woman who has had to hold herself together for too long the same as Lisa.

What the fuck is wrong with me? How have I not noticed my two best friends have been going through hell while I've been dealing with my pathetic excuse of a husband who steals money from me and his workplace? It's a small drop in the ocean compared to what Lisa's husband is doing to her and, by the sounds of it, Penny's as well.

'He . . . I found . . . pictures,' stutters Penny. She takes a deep breath. 'I found a laptop hidden in a drawer in his wardrobe. It's not usually locked or anything because it's just a wardrobe, but I didn't realise he hid a laptop in there. It's one I haven't seen before. Anyway, I logged on using his usual password and had a look around . . . and there were pictures . . . on a folder on his home screen.'

'Pictures of what?' I ask.

Silence.

'Penny . . . pictures of what?' asks Lisa.

Penny's bottom lip wobbles. 'K-kids . . . pictures of kids . . .'

The breath in my lungs escapes out of my mouth in a garbled cry and I quickly clamp a hand over my mouth to stop from swearing. Because it's clear these pictures aren't just innocent photos of kids.

Lisa looks as if she's about to be sick.

Penny glances from one of us to the other. 'My husband is a paedophile, and he has photos of young kids on his fucking laptop in his wardrobe.'

Then she pushes Lisa away from her, sprints into the garden and vomits onto a nearby flowerbed.

Lisa jumps forward, and grabs Penny's long black hair, pulling it into a ponytail away from her face as she heaves her guts up. Lisa looks up at me as she uses her other hand to rub circles on Penny's back.

'Holly, can you get some water, please?'

I nod, astounded that Lisa is holding herself together so well after only a minute ago revealing she's been physically abused by her husband for most of her adult life. How did the evening take such a dramatic and dark turn? I can't even think straight as I make my way to the bar. I fill a glass with water, my hands trembling. I can't believe any of this is happening. Drake, a paedo? How is that even possible? Has he always been one? Even at university?

Penny and Lisa come back inside the hut. Penny sits down on the seat and smiles weakly as she takes the glass of water from my hand.

'Thank you,' she says before taking a sip. 'I'm so sorry . . . I don't know what came over me. I've been in a state of shock since finding the photos and I didn't know what to do or how to react, so I didn't react. I just put the laptop back and left it there. That was two days ago.'

I swallow a lump in my throat. 'I'm assuming you haven't confronted him about it?'

Penny scoffs. 'Hardly. What am I supposed to say? "Oh, sorry, darling, but I noticed you accidentally left a drawer open in your wardrobe and there was a laptop in there which I knew the password to. I found pictures of naked children on it. Care to explain?"' She takes another gulp of water and shudders as if someone has walked over her grave or she's swallowed something vile.

'But what you said before . . . you said you wanted to kill him . . . I mean, there are better ways of dealing with this, don't you think?' Lisa shoots me a stern look, but I ignore her as I continue. 'For a start, you can go to the police. He'll be arrested and jailed.'

'Yes, and then what? I know my husband. He won't let me have his money. I'll be left with nothing. And what about the twins? I don't think I could live with myself if they found out their father likes to . . . to . . . fuck, I can't even say it. No. It's the only way. I can't live like this. I can't live knowing what he is, and I won't let him get away with it. He deserves to die. I don't love him. Not anymore. I don't think I ever really did. I wanted to leave him before I even got pregnant. I wanted to leave him when I found out he cheated on me the first time. After that, nothing was ever the same again between us. Three months, my happy marriage lasted. Three months.

It's now six years later and I'm fed up with living a lie.' Penny picks at her arm, aggravating a wound.

I can understand where she's coming from, but her rationale makes no sense. How is murdering her husband going to help anything?

A long silence fills the night air. I don't even know my best friends anymore. Then Lisa steps forward.

'I'll do it.'

'What?' I say, almost choking on my tongue.

Penny jerks her head up. 'You will?'

'On one condition . . .'

'Name it.'

'You kill my husband too.'

CHAPTER SIXTEEN

Lisa

How much have I had to drink for my mind to even conjure up such a crazy, dangerous idea? Have I seriously just asked for help in killing my husband and agreed to off Penny's too? I'd come here with the hope of asking for help to save me from my marriage, but after talking it through, it was never going to work. Simon will find me, no matter where I hide and I can't keep running away from him for the rest of my life, constantly worrying if he'll show up unexpectedly while looking over my shoulder. I wouldn't put it past him to send dangerous people after me, maybe even have me killed. He's never said it, but I know he would kill me to stop me from leaving him.

The only way I'll ever feel safe to live my life is to know that he will never come and find me. He can't just be locked up in jail either because I know him. He'll find a way to get to me and hurt me. He has friends who'd do anything for him. The only way is for him to be dead. Dead. Dead. Dead.

I know it's risky and stupid and will probably never work, but why not kill two birds (or husbands) with one stone? A smile appears on my lips at the irony of the phrase. I'm not sure how we've managed to go from talking about my husband abusing me to Penny revealing her husband is a paedophile, to now agreeing to kill them both, but somehow it makes perfect sense in my mind.

Penny raises her eyebrows at me. 'Are you sure?'

'Yes,' I say, 'I've never been more sure of anything in my life.'

Holly jumps to her feet, throwing her hands up in the air. The movement makes me jump. 'This is fucking ridiculous. I can't believe what I'm hearing right now. This is all a joke, right? Are you girls playing a joke on me? Haha, very funny. Let's all kill our husbands. But let's stop now. Enough.'

'Does it sound like we're joking?' asks Penny, rising to her feet and squaring up to Holly, who shrinks back at her tone of voice. It's a bit scary when Penny puts on her serious voice, and I don't blame Holly for stepping backwards.

Holly's mouth drops open. 'B-but we're talking about murder here. *Murder.* You're talking about killing your husbands. I can't . . . I can't deal with this right now. This is not happening.' She throws her hands up in the air for the second time and storms out of the hut and into the house, leaving Penny and me alone.

'We need to get her on our side,' says Penny after a few beats of silence.

'I know, but what if she doesn't agree to it?'

'Then we'll do it without her. I'll kill Simon and you kill Drake. We'll have to plan this carefully to ensure there are no holes in our plan or any way for the police to suspect they were murdered. We need to make their deaths look accidental, otherwise, it won't work. I'll look after you, Lisa. I promise. The money I'll get from Drake's death, I'll split with you, and Holly, if she agrees to help. I'll look after my girls and, if for any reason we get caught, then we'll all go down together.'

I nod, but my eyes fill with tears at the realisation of how serious this situation is or could get. So many things could go wrong. People will notice when the men go missing or die suddenly. They have parents and colleagues. They're both healthy and fit. We have to tread carefully. Even conspiracy to murder is a serious offence, for crying out loud.

Penny reaches over and grabs my hands, pulling me into a tight hug. 'We can do this. We won't let them rule our lives anymore. They are horrible men who deserve to die. Say it.'

'They are horrible men who deserve to die.'

'Good girl. Come on, let's go and talk to Holly. I managed to convince her to streak down the road naked once, completely sober. I'm sure I can convince her to do this.'

We find her in the living room, curled up on the sofa with a blanket over her legs and a glass of clear liquid in her hand. I have a feeling it's not water. Penny sits on her left and I sit on her right. She continues to stare ahead, unwilling to meet our eyes.

'Hols, look at me,' says Penny.

Holly blinks and takes a sip of her drink. She shakes her head vigorously as she swallows. 'There's nothing you can say that will make me change my mind. Murder is wrong.' Even as she says it, I can sense the hesitation in her voice, almost as if she doesn't quite believe what she's saying. We all know murder is wrong, but some people deserve it.

'You're right,' says Penny. 'Murder is wrong. But so is physical abuse and paedophilia. Our husbands are not nice people, Holly. Surely, you see that. We'd be better off without them, and so would the world.'

'I'm not disagreeing with you on that,' replies Holly, taking another sip. 'But there are other ways . . . *legal* ways that they can be stopped.'

'If we do that then Drake won't allow me access to the money.'

'So, this is all about money for you? Don't you have your own money?'

I can tell Penny is fighting the urge to snap at Holly. I've always hated confrontation and the few times they've fought over the years have always been awful and stressful.

This situation hasn't turned into a full-blown argument yet, but I can see it brewing under the surface, bubbling away, ready to explode.

'No, it's not all about money and yes, I have some money of my own, but not nearly enough to look after us all. Look, there's stuff I've never told you about my marriage. Drake made me sign a prenup, and that's another reason why I couldn't divorce him once I found out I was pregnant.'

'Really?' I ask. 'What were the terms?'

'If I ever cheated on him, I'd get nothing. If I ever initiated a divorce, I'd get nothing. And . . . any money I made would be his.'

'What the fuck? Surely, that's not even legal. Why would you sign something like that?' asks Holly.

'Because I was stupid and in love, that's why.'

'I always wondered why you decided to stay with him.'

'Well, now you know. I swallowed my pride and took him back. I didn't want to be left with nothing. I didn't want to raise the twins by myself. I did it so they'd never have to want for anything and there was no way I was letting him take them away from me. This way, they'd always be secure. I did it for them. And now, he's taken out this new life insurance policy and I'm completely screwed . . . unless he happens to die from natural causes or is accidentally killed, like in a car accident or something. Plus, now I don't feel that my kids are safe with him around. I feel guilty I've let that sick monster live under the same roof as my children all these years when God only knows what he's . . . I . . . I can't think about that, about what he might have done.' Penny grasps her throat and gags.

Holly gulps back the remnants of her glass. 'This is royally fucked-up.'

'Tell me about it,' replies Penny, taking a deep breath, composing herself.

'And Simon . . .' Holly turns to me. 'You really believe there's no other way?'

I shake my head. 'He won't let me leave. He'd track me down and find me, I know he would. And he . . . when he pushed me down the stairs, I was eight weeks pregnant. A few hours later, I lost the baby.'

Penny gasps and covers her mouth. Holly lowers her eyes. 'Oh God, I'm sorry.'

'It's okay. To be honest, even though I was very sad, I think it's for the best. If I got pregnant, he'd have had an even greater hold over me and I wouldn't want to bring a child into an abusive home. I need to get out. I don't see any other way, I'm sorry.'

Holly squeezes my hand. 'Okay . . . you know I love you both more than anything, right? There's no fucking way I'd agree to do this if it were anyone else asking.'

Penny straightens up. 'You'll help us?'

'Yes . . . but on one condition.'

Penny tilts her head. 'Don't tell me you want us to kill your husband too?'

Holly smirks. 'No, but . . . I do need help finding out if he killed a woman near where we live.'

Penny and I stare at her in bewilderment.

'What?' I ask with a gasp. 'Are you serious?'

'I don't have proof. I just have a hunch. Also, my husband is a lazy twat, and he lost his job a few months ago because he stole from his clients. He's also stealing from me, so . . . I guess we're all hideously bad at picking decent men to marry. But . . . let me get this straight . . . Will doesn't deserve to die. He used to be a good guy.'

'Got it,' says Penny.

'Out of interest, why haven't you gone to the police about this? You know, about Will's stealing and your hunch about him killing a woman.'

'Because that's all I have. A hunch. It's not enough, is it? Nowadays, the police want solid proof before they'll even lift a finger,' answers Holly.

'But you will leave him, right?' I ask. 'I can't believe he's been stealing from you.'

'Hell, yes. I'm not staying married to him, especially if he killed someone.'

'Technically, if he did kill that woman . . . he deserves to die too,' adds Penny.

'Let's just deal with one thing at a time, okay?'

'So, it's settled . . . we're really going to do this?' I ask.

It's a huge risk for all of us, but especially Penny. If she goes to prison, then the twins are without a mother, and could be left in the hands of a paedophile. Penny's always been a strong woman, always stood up for her friends, but we're not just talking about murder here. We're putting the steps in place to commit it. It's the biggest and riskiest thing I've ever done. Once we start, we can't back out either. It's going to take all the courage we have, rolled up into one. But despite being terrified of what could happen if anything goes wrong, I'm more afraid of what could happen if we don't do this.

Penny stands up, goes to the nearby bar, and pours each of us a drink. We stand up and join her and hold our glasses up together.

'Here's to our horrible husbands,' says Penny. 'May they get what's coming to them.'

We clink glasses and drink.

CHAPTER SEVENTEEN

Penny

I'm not sure what time it is when we finally call it a night and stagger to our beds. I remember seeing 1 a.m., but after that, my brain is a bit foggy. When I wake up with my eyes fused together by dried mascara, I feel worse than I did after four cluster-feed nights in a row when the twins were newborns. And that had nothing to do with alcohol. God, how much did I drink last night? A lot, I'm guessing. The exact details are a little blurry around the edges due to lack of sleep, and shots (I don't remember doing shots, but I can taste tequila, which I only drink in shot form), but the general idea is still there.

We made a deal to kill each other's husbands so that I can get Drake's money and look after the girls and ensure my children are safe. Well, two of our husbands anyway. Plus, find out if the third is a killer and if he is then possibly bump him off as well.

I'm not sure how the three of us turned into contract killers overnight, but after finding those awful photographs on my husband's laptop, a switch has been triggered inside me. My children are not safe with that man, and I don't want him even in the same room as them, which is going to be tricky to accomplish, but nothing I can't handle. I hope he's away with work for the foreseeable future. If he came home, there is no way I'd allow the twins anywhere near him. My maternal instinct has kicked in big time, not only for my children but for those he has decided to pay attention to. Every time I think about those pictures, I want to hurl. How did it start? Has he always been this sick? Has he ever looked at our children and . . .

I clamp a hand over my mouth and sprint to the en suite, barely making it before hurling my guts up. How am I supposed to act like nothing is wrong? I thought I hated the man before I found out, but now I'd like nothing more than to tie him to a chair, cut off his balls with a blunt knife and make him eat them with a sprinkling of sea salt.

As I clutch the rim of the toilet, waiting to see if anything else will appear, my fingers scratch at the wound on my thigh. Somehow, last night, I'd managed to get dressed into my shorts and T-shirt I sleep in. I scratch and scratch and scratch until the wound peels, bleeds and stings with the sweet release of pain.

Once satisfied, I wipe my mouth with the back of my hand, flush the toilet and pull myself to standing, leaning against the sink for support as I wash my hands with soapy water. My fingernails are now caked with blood, so I scrub them until they are clean.

I know the girls will be counting on me to lead this . . . this . . . whatever *this* is. Vendetta? Plan?

I am the one who must take control. It's my idea. I must be the one to see it through and ensure nothing goes wrong. Because so many things can go wrong. I can end up in prison and lose my children to a paedophile. There is no way in hell I am letting that happen. That's why the plan must work. That's why it is going to work. No matter what.

I don't know what time I eventually emerge from the shower. I spend a long time under the jets, scrubbing my skin until it's bright red, having another cheeky scratch at another wound on my other leg. I feel dirty every time I think of my husband touching me.

When I finally surface, clean on the outside, but not inside, I head to the kitchen where bacon is sizzling on the Aga. Lisa's tending to it while Holly is slouched on a stool at the breakfast bar looking a little green. She has a large cup of coffee in front of her, but it doesn't look as if it's been touched yet.

'Morning,' says Lisa. 'We didn't want to wake you.'

Holly grunts a hello.

'Morning,' I reply, sliding onto the stool next to Holly. 'You look worse than you did the morning after my hen party.'

'Urrggh, don't remind me. You look surprisingly good. What gives?'

I shrug. 'I drink most nights, so I'm used to it, but you should have seen me an hour ago. The toilet bowl was my best friend.'

'We can't drink like we used to, can we?' asks Lisa, as she turns the bacon with some tongs.

'We can . . . It's just the morning after where it all goes to shit. How are you, Lisa? Thanks for getting breakfast started.' The woman is a machine. Not only is breakfast on the go, but she's unpacked the dishwasher, laid out plates and got the coffee brewing.

Lisa places a coffee cup in front of me. 'I'm okay actually, other than a headache. I feel as if a weight has been lifted from my shoulders now I know I'm finally going to be free from him.'

I grasp the cup and warm my hands around it. 'Good, I'm glad.'

'Oh, so last night did happen, then. It wasn't some messed-up dream. We really did plan to kill both your husbands.' Holly takes a slurp of coffee, grimaces, and dry heaves.

I pat her gently on the back. 'Yep, it happened. Now, I think we need to spend today coming up with a scheme. I did have other things planned while you were here, but I think this takes precedence over getting our nails done and going to the beach, am I right?'

'Absolutely,' says Lisa.

Holly merely nods, probably too afraid to open her mouth in case she vomits.

'Let's enjoy breakfast as best we can and then I'll get the whiteboard from my office. If we're going to do this, then we're going all *CSI* on this motherfucker.'

Holly lifts her head from the crook of her elbow. 'I think you'll find that in *CSI* they never set out to murder people. They solve murders.'

I shrug. 'Whatever. The point is this is not something we can do on the spur of the moment.'

'So, Lisa's not going to attack your husband when he gets home with a kitchen knife?'

I turn to Holly, my lips pursed. 'I'm going to let that slide because clearly, you're feeling a little worse for wear. Are you still in on this thing? Because if you've changed your mind, then say now.'

Holly lowers her head to rest on her arm again. 'Yes, I'm still in. Will you hurry up with the bacon so I can soak up some of this tequila that's still in my system? Whose stupid idea was shots anyway?'

'Yours,' Lisa and I say together.

'That's what I was afraid of.'

Lisa picks up the tongs, fishes the bacon out of the pan, and lays it on a plate on the breakfast bar in front of us. She adds a plate of buttered bread.

'Eat up, bitches. We've got work to do.'

* * *

An hour later, Holly looks a little better. The colour is back in her cheeks and after two rounds of bacon sandwiches and three rounds of strong coffee, we're ready to head to the office pod. My husband never goes in there. I always keep it locked too because the twins will often go in and raid the pen drawer; I've never given Drake the key. I set up the small sofa and the whiteboard in front of it. I feel like a teacher but have no idea what it is I'm supposed to be teaching.

'Right, we've got two hours before the twins get dropped off from their sleepover and chaos resumes, so . . . let's get started.' I grab a marker pen and approach the board, then write *The Plan* at the top, underlining it twice.

I spin around and face my audience. They stare back at me with blank expressions as if it's their first day of school.

'This shit just got real,' says Holly. 'Where the hell do we even start to plan this kind of thing? Have you guys seen the show *How to Get Away with Murder*?'

'No, is it good?' asks Lisa.

'Oh my God, it's so good. It's got that kid from *Harry Potter* in it, but he's all grown up and is strangely hot.'

'Daniel Radcliffe?'

'No, the other one.'

'Rupert Grint?'

Holly huffs. 'No, the tall one who snogs Ginny. Cute smile.'

'Oh, him. Dean Thomas.'

'Yes, but that's not the actor's name—'

'Girls!' I snap, clapping my hands. They both jump and turn to face me. 'Can we stop talking about *Harry Potter* actors and focus, please?'

'Right, sorry,' says Holly.

I take a breath. 'Okay . . . let's think of the big picture. It's my husband who has the money, right? But he's only just changed the life insurance over, so if he suddenly drops dead it's going to look a little suspicious, isn't it? But . . . I refuse to let him anywhere near the twins, so that means I need him out of this house as much as possible for the foreseeable future.'

'Does he have a lot of work on at the moment?' asks Lisa.

'Yes, but it's not guaranteed he'll have to work away from home. The first thing I need to do is get in contact with his boss and ensure he gives him lots of work where he has to travel.'

The girls nod, so I turn and make a note on the board.

Contact Drake's work.

'Will his boss not ask questions about why?' asks Holly.

I turn and twiddle the pen around my fingers. 'Maybe, but I'll make something up. I don't see it being a problem. Okay, so that's Drake away from my kids for a while . . . but I think the next thing we need to do is decide whether we're going to kill Simon first or investigate Will.' At this point, both girls lean forward and open their mouths to speak, but I cut them off, my mind already made up and running at a million miles a minute. 'I think we should kill Simon first, then Lisa is free to help us with the rest of the plan. Then she's safe.'

Lisa smiles weakly and Holly nods. 'That makes sense, but I have a question.'

'Go for it.'

'How are you supposed to run around killing people when you have two kids at home, and you don't have a nanny or anyone to look after them?'

The pod falls silent.

'Fuck,' I say. 'I forgot about my kids.' Okay, I didn't forget about them, but still . . .

Holly has made a good point. A murder spree with my best friends isn't exactly a kid-friendly activity. I can't give them an iPad and say, 'Here, watch *Minecraft* while Mummy goes and kills Daddy.' My own mum's dead, and my dad's out of the picture. He left when I was young, and I haven't heard from him since. My only living relative who I'm close to is my Aunt Silvia who lives about twenty miles away on a smallholding. She's my mum's sister and I used to go to her for the summer holidays every year. It was amazing. The wide-open spaces, the rivers and hills and fresh air. It was the perfect place to be a child.

It's the Easter holidays now, so it makes sense to take the kids away somewhere. Aunt Silvia was a big support to me when my mum passed away too, and she always jumps at the chance to see the kids.

It wasn't like I was a child when my mum died, but it had still hit me hard, despite not being particularly close to her. We didn't have that mother-and-daughter relationship where we told each other everything and were like best friends. I have my actual best friends for that.

'Okay, here's what I'm going to do. I'll drop them off with Aunt Silvia for a few days. She'd love to have them.' I turn and write a note on the board.

Contact Aunt Silvia. Drop kids off.

Lisa clears her throat. 'So . . . how are we actually going to do it? Are we splitting up or something? I go and kill Drake. Penny goes and kills Simon?'

'I'm not sure splitting up is a good idea,' says Holly. 'I understand that we need to have alibis, especially you, Penny, who needs to be nowhere near Drake when he's killed, but I don't like the idea of going off on our own.'

I nod. 'I think you're right. We need to be in this together but ensure we're nowhere near our own husbands when it happens. Let's take them one by one. We're killing Simon first, right? Lisa, is he highly allergic to anything?'

'No, nothing.'

'How about a car accident?'

'I don't want to risk anyone else getting hurt.'

'Tell us about his daily routine. Walk us through it. I'll make notes.'

Lisa takes a deep breath and begins. She explains how he starts the day with a superfood smoothie (gross), then takes a long, hot shower, using up all the hot water (dick). Next, he trims his beard and then makes himself breakfast. At this point, Lisa goes to work, so she doesn't see him again until he gets back, so she can't explain much more of his daily routine, but when he gets back from work, he takes another shower, eats dinner, then sits in front of the TV until bedtime. On Mondays, Wednesdays and Thursdays, he goes to the gym after work, so is home later. In which case, he eats dinner when he returns home.

'What about poison?' suggests Holly once Lisa has finished. 'We could poison his superfood smoothie.'

'Possibly,' I say, 'but risky. Too little poison and he'll just get sick. Too much and it will look suspicious, and he might have a post-mortem toxicology report done on him.'

Holly and Lisa look at me with blank expressions.

'I binge-watched *CSI* throughout my pregnancy when I was bedridden, remember?'

'Ah, yeah. You were talking about dead bodies and autopsies for weeks,' says Lisa.

'We were a bit concerned,' adds Holly. 'Now we know we had reason to be.'

I shake my head. 'Okay, so poison is out. I'm not sure whether either one of us is strong enough to take him on one-on-one like with a knife or anything because that would look like murder and there's a risk we would get hurt.'

'What are we left with?' asks Lisa, sounding a little downhearted.

I turn and write one word underneath Simon's name. *Suicide.*

'How are we supposed to make it look like he took his own life?' asks Holly.

'Easy. Get him drunk or sedate him with something. Put him in the bath and drown him.'

'Just that easy, is it?'

I roll my eyes at Holly. She isn't being very helpful at all. She seems determined to question me at every opportunity. I know she isn't enthusiastic about the idea, but I need her on board . . . and fast. She's the loose wire when it comes to this plan. Lisa looks calmer than I thought she'd be. I choose to ignore Holly and look at Lisa instead.

'What do you think?' I ask her.

She squirms in her seat for a moment. 'It could work. What would we sedate him with?'

'Does he do drugs?'

Lisa lowers her head. 'Yes. He does. I've never told you girls because I was ashamed of him. He doesn't do it a lot. Just every month or so with his best friend.'

'What kind of drugs?'

'I'm not sure. Cocaine, I think.'

I nod again, spin around, wipe the word suicide off the board and replace it with *Overdose*.

Lisa shrugs. 'It could work, but do any of us know how much cocaine someone has to take before they overdose?'

We all swap looks. It appears none of us does.

'I know some people,' says Holly. At that comment, Lisa and I raise our eyebrows. 'What? I do. I have friends outside of this threesome, you know.'

'What kind of friends?' I ask, narrowing my eyes.

'Just . . . *friends*.'

'Best friends?'

'No, more like . . . good friends. And don't worry, I won't tell them anything. They may be good friends, but I don't think they'd go as far as killing for me.'

'No, because only best friends would do that.' I smile at her, and she smiles back. The tension, while still palpable between us, is beginning to ease and I can see the fun-loving Holly returning.

Not that this plan is going to be fun, but it has been a long time since the three of us have done anything together. The last time we'd all met up was for a long spa weekend at Champneys in Surrey. When we said goodbye, we promised to meet up again soon and do it again.

I'm not sure this is what any of us had in mind, though.

CHAPTER EIGHTEEN

Holly

This is surreal. What the hell is happening? Here I am, sitting with my best friends, talking about how we're going to kill each other's husbands. And it's their idea! The weirdest part is that it makes complete sense. Either Penny is a master at mind control or she's one hell of a spokesperson. She certainly has a knack for making this strange ordeal feel relatively normal, as if we are planning on throwing our husbands a surprise birthday party, not a surprise murder spree. I'm getting swept up in the process, yet the fundamental fact is we're talking about murder.

Murder!

Not only that but murdering a man who I used to consider a friend. Drake may have changed a bit since university, but he's still the guy I once shared a spliff with, and who held my hair back while I vomited into his wastepaper bin.

Penny is leading the room like a general in charge of a battle. The next two hours are spent going over every detail. We look at what could go wrong, where things could take a bad turn, and all sorts of different scenarios and make a list of who's doing what and when. Once it's all written down on the board in black and white it feels so . . . so . . . real. So final.

Shit. We're doing this. We're going to kill two men. Granted, they deserve it and I hope they rot in hell for what they've done. Although, by the sounds of it, I'm not going to be doing any of the killing. That's Lisa and Penny's job, so it's not like I'm taking a knife and plunging it into a man's heart and watching as blood spurts out, but I am involved in their ultimate demise, and I'm not sure how I'm going to sleep for the rest of my life after this is over.

Maybe better. Maybe worse.

At least Lisa will be safe. And Penny's children will be protected from a horrible monster. I'd do anything to keep them all safe. I hope Penny knows that. And that's what I keep telling myself because I would honestly die for these two women. I would, but, as it turns out, I'd also kill for them, and do a lot more. And that makes me their best goddamn friend in the entire world because only a best friend would plot to kill their best friend's husband for them.

We're pausing for a coffee break and chatting in the kitchen when two six-year-old children run into the room, screaming at the top of their lungs, 'Mummy!'

Penny bends down level with them and wraps her arms around both, squeezing and kissing them. It's clear she loves them more than life itself and a lump forms in my throat at the thought of them being hurt or abused in some way by their father. I hope to God he hasn't . . . The thought makes my stomach roil. How could I have ever been friends with that man? How could I . . .

'Luca, Lori, you probably don't remember, but these are Mummy's best friends. This is Holly and Lisa. They've come to visit me for the weekend.'

The twins step away from their mother and turn to me and Lisa, who immediately waves and says, 'Hi! It's so lovely to see you both again. You've gotten so big!' Whereas I remain standing awkwardly, unsure how to interact properly with people their age.

This is another reason why I still have my coil fitted. I can barely say hi to a couple of kids. I'd be a terrible mother. Thank goodness I no longer have to worry about getting pregnant. Once Will is out of my life, I can focus on the two people who mean the most to me: Penny and Lisa.

'Hi,' I squeak.

'I like your hair,' says Lori, coming up to me. 'It's pretty.'

I touch my short black hair, tucking a strand behind my left ear. 'Thank you. You have very pretty hair too.' She really does. It's gorgeously long and blonde. She has beautiful blue eyes and a cheeky little nose dotted in freckles. Her brother has darker hair. It's strange to think of them as twins because they look nothing alike.

'How long are you staying?' asks Luca.

'Just for the weekend,' replies Lisa. 'Your mum's told us all about you.'

'I need to talk to you both a little later, but for now why don't you unpack and then tell me all about your sleepover, okay?' says Penny.

'Okay!' They both give their mother another hug before running from the room. The loud thumping of their footsteps, like a small herd of elephants, sounds throughout the house as they stomp up the stairs to their rooms.

Penny turns to us. 'We'll have to do the rest of the planning tonight when they're in bed.'

'That's okay,' Lisa says. 'Means we can spend some decent time together and not talk about . . . you know . . .'

'Another coffee?' Penny asks.

'Please,' I say. My hangover is just about gone, but one more cup should do the trick, even though I feel as if my whole body is vibrating from a caffeine overdose.

* * *

The next few hours are spent lounging by the outside pool, chasing the kids around with a water pistol and sunbathing, although whenever the sun dips behind a cloud, the temperature drops by about five degrees, so I have to keep taking my hoodie on and off. It's honestly the most fun I've had in a long time. Penny keeps scratching at a strange-looking scab on her arm and I keep meaning to ask her about it, but I don't get the chance.

Penny lent me a book to read so I settle on a sun lounger. It might be early spring, but it's delightful to sit outside. My phone vibrates beside me. I haven't given it much thought since we've been here and then I remember I never messaged Will back after reading his message about the credit card.

Shit.

I hope he hasn't bombarded me with more messages or freaked out. I click on the text, silently hoping it's nothing bad.

Will: *Don't worry about the previous message. Hope you're having a good time. Love you xx*

I frown. Why shouldn't I worry about his previous message? Does that mean he's remembered my bank details or no longer needs them? A sinking feeling in my gut makes my lips dry as I type out a reply.

Me: *Having a great time!*

Then I snap a quick selfie of me by the pool and send it. The sinking feeling doesn't go away, so I scroll to my banking app, input my login details, and hold my breath as it loads . . .

My bank account is empty.

There's not one single penny in it.

What the fuck!

I breathe in through my nose and out through my mouth several times, attempting to quell the panic and sheer anger at what I'm seeing. There's a child only a few feet away from me playing so I know I can't do and say what I want to do and say because it would be inappropriate for young ears.

My hands tremble so badly I have to put my phone down before I drop it.

Okay . . . okay . . .

Calm down.

It's not that big a deal . . .

I squeeze my fists together and grind my teeth so hard I see stars in my eyes.

'Hols . . . what's wrong?' asks Lisa. She's walking towards me and takes a seat at the bottom of my lounger. She places a hand on my leg. 'Tell me what's happened.'

I make some sort of strange whimper, all the while attempting not to shout expletives into the air. I shove my phone towards her with my foot and watch as she picks it up and scans the screen, her eyes widening as she realises what she's seeing.

'Oh my God,' she whispers.

I take a deep breath and hold out my hand. 'I need to check the joint account.'

Lisa hands me the phone and watches me while I log into our joint account.

I'm met with the same thing.

It's empty.

The last transfer was into his personal account yesterday evening. All £3,145.87 of it.

Gone.

Plus, the £1,254 from my personal account.

Luckily, he doesn't know about my separate savings account because it's with a different bank and I never shared the details with him, but that's not the fucking point. There's also the cash hidden in my locked box. It wouldn't surprise me if he's taken that too, but I'm pretty sure I've hidden it well enough for him never to find. My husband has stolen money from me, and he hasn't even tried to cover it up.

I slam the phone on the lounger, and it bounces off and onto the patio. Neither of us makes a move to pick it up. We sit in silence for several moments.

'I'm going to kill him,' I mutter.

At this point, I don't know if I'm speaking literally or figuratively, considering what's happened in the past twenty-four hours.

'Why has he taken all the money?'

'It's got to be because of his gambling or paying off his debts. I can't think why else he'd do it, but he didn't even ask me. He hasn't told me anything about his gambling and debts, but he's not even trying to keep it a secret.' I stand up and storm into the house. Penny is in the kitchen making one of the kids a sandwich. 'Penny, please can I use your laptop? I need to do some research.'

'Of course. I'll grab it for you. Does this research have anything to do with our special project? I'd rather you didn't leave an online trail.'

'No, this is a personal research project,' I seethe through gritted teeth.

'Is everything okay?'

At this point, Lisa joins us. The three of us stand in the kitchen while we wait for Lori to leave with her sandwich. Then, I keep my voice low.

'My husband has just drained my bank account and our joint account of every single penny.'

Penny gasps. 'No!'

'I'd now like to find out what the hell is going on and see if there's an update on that woman's murder.'

'You don't honestly think he did it, do you?' asks Lisa, picking up a piece of cut apple from the plate that Penny had prepared for the twins, but neither have touched. The crisps and biscuits went quick, though.

'I don't know, but I need to find out if he's hiding anything else. Then, when I have the proof I need, I'm going to confront him and have him thrown in jail. I'll probably never see that money again, but I don't care. No one steals from me. No one lies to my fucking face and gets away with it. Certainly not my lying, dickhead, lazy sod of a husband who I should never have married.' Penny and Lisa look as if they're holding their breaths, waiting for me to finish my rant. 'Okay, I'm done,' I say.

They both exhale loudly. 'Wow, I don't think I've ever seen you so riled up. You're kind of scary,' says Penny. 'Let me get you the laptop.'

* * *

One hour later, I'm still shaking. It could be from shock and anger, but it could also be the three cups of strong coffee I've had. Honestly, I need to calm down on the coffee. I must have had at least six cups today. Lisa joins me in the office pod while I sit hunched over Penny's desk, my eyes glued to the laptop screen, the only part of me moving are my fingers, which type and navigate furiously. Lisa has been jotting down notes and dates and pieces of information regarding the murder of the woman found in Juniper Green, only down the road from where my husband said he was the same night.

Her name was Leanne Prince. She was twenty-nine years old. She was a hairdresser. Her hair was short and black, she weighed roughly the same as me and her eyes were the same colour. The similarities between her and me are scary . . .

Apparently, she only cut her hair short and dyed it black two days before she was killed. Before that, she had long brown hair. That was the picture used on the news bulletin, which is why I didn't notice the similarities between us before.

'This can't be a coincidence,' I say as I reread the online article.

More information has been released about her death. She was strangled using a very thin, strong wire, which cut through the skin on her neck, leaving a nasty wound. She was also roughly thirteen weeks pregnant when she died. Bile bubbles at the back of my throat.

'I don't know what else to look for,' I say to Lisa.

She looks up from making a note on her writing pad. 'You should make a list of each time he's taken money from you. Do you know his online banking details or his email login?'

I nod slowly as I navigate to the email login screen. I hope he hasn't changed it recently, although knowing my husband, he's not that smart, considering he's not making any sort of effort to hide his transgressions. Does he just think I won't notice or care? Does he think I'm a complete idiot?

I type in his email and his usual password.

Bingo.

I spend a few minutes reading through his emails. It's clear he's using a multitude of online gambling sites because most of the emails are from them. Quite a few are reminders about payments and warnings saying his account will be locked until he can pay. Maybe he has other email addresses I'm not aware of and uses them to create new accounts. I wouldn't put it past him.

The thing is, I've known about his gambling for a long time. On our first date he told me he had a small problem, but it was under control. I believed him and it never became an issue between us. He's only started stealing money from me since he's lost his job. Before that, I didn't know anything. I didn't even realise he was still gambling. It was one of those things about him that I shoved under a hypothetical rug because it wasn't a problem in our lives.

Now, it most certainly is. In fact, it's tearing us apart and has been for a long time, but I've been too blind and naive to notice.

Is it my fault? Have I driven him to this? Am I so unapproachable that he doesn't feel he can come to me with his problems?

And what about this murdered woman? Does she have anything to do with Will and his gambling? It doesn't seem likely, but that niggle of doubt won't leave me alone.

'Did Leanne Prince have a husband?' asks Lisa.

I scan through the online articles. 'No, I don't think so.'

'Boyfriend?'

I shake my head. 'It doesn't say. It just says her parents are devastated at the loss. No mention of a husband or boyfriend.'

'Then who got her pregnant?'

A lump forms in my throat. 'One-night stand?'

'Possibly, but . . . she was twenty-nine, not twenty-one. I'm not saying women of twenty-nine don't have one-night stands, but it's less likely.'

'What are you saying?'

'She was clearly sleeping with someone. Check her Facebook and other social media pages.'

I nod again. 'You know, you're good at this research thing.'

Lisa smiles. 'Not my first time.'

I want to ask her what she means by that and to elaborate, but it's at that moment I find Leanne's Facebook profile. It pops up straight away, so I click on it and begin scanning down her page. She doesn't have any security settings, so I can see most of her photos without being friends with her. There are lots of posts to her page sending well wishes to the family and messages of support and love.

None of the pictures jumps out at me other than her comparison photo of her with long hair and then her with short black hair. It really does change her whole persona. Why such a sudden change? There's nothing on her profile about her pregnancy, which must mean she was trying to hide it from her friends and family. She was probably planning on telling them soon, or maybe she didn't even know yet.

I cast my eyes casually over her friends list.

A profile photo jumps out at me.

It's a man who has dark brown hair, a strong, chiselled jaw, brown eyes, and perfectly straight teeth.

His name is Malcolm York.

Except it isn't . . .

Because the man in the photo . . . the man who is friends with Leanne Prince . . . is my husband.

CHAPTER NINETEEN

Lisa

I've taken a break from making notes for Holly and am looking at my phone when Holly lets out a garbled whimper, covering her mouth with her hand. My head jerks up. She's found something. I place my phone face down on the table next to me, ignoring the fifteenth call from Simon, and rush to her side, leaning over her shoulder to see what she's found.

'Oh my God,' Holly whispers. 'Will knows her.'

Holly's staring open-mouthed at the screen, too shocked to react, so I reach forward and take control of the laptop, clicking on Malcolm York's profile. His security settings are locked down tight, so all we can view is his profile picture. There's nothing else to see, but it's Will for sure.

'What the hell does this mean?' snaps Holly, pushing herself to her feet. She paces up and down by the desk. 'Was he cheating on me with her? This is a clear link to that murdered woman.'

I don't know how to respond. That's what it looks like. I've always been the type of person to give someone the benefit of the doubt, but it's not looking good for Will.

'I need to get back home and find out more,' says Holly.

'You can't confront him about this.'

'Why the fuck not?'

'Because then we could lose the element of surprise. I mean, Will's not even attempting to disguise that he's gambling and owes a lot of money, but he's certainly going to a lot of effort to hide the fact he's possibly been seeing another woman,' I say. 'I don't mean to accuse him, but . . . if Leanne was thirteen weeks pregnant, then where was Will around that time? Do you remember?'

Holly laughs. 'I barely remember what I had for dinner last week, let alone what my husband was doing thirteen weeks ago.' I watch her while she checks her phone planner. 'Fuck.'

'What?'

'Thirteen weeks and three days ago, Will went out for the night with his friends to that same pub in Juniper Green. I had it in my diary. That's what he told me anyway. I never questioned him about it because it was a normal thing for him to do. Not to go there, but to go out with his mates. I remember thinking it was strange he was going to Juniper Green, but I didn't think any more about it because I was looking forward to having a night in to myself.'

'Did any of his friends corroborate his whereabouts?'

She stares blankly for several seconds. 'N-no, I didn't ask them . . . Shit. You think he met up with Leanne and . . .' Holly looks genuinely nauseous. 'God, what if he met up with her again the other night and she told him she was pregnant, and he killed her . . .'

I sigh. 'We have no proof so let's not—'

'Oh, stop it, will you?'

I flinch, aware I've hit a nerve with Holly. 'I'm sorry.'

'You're always doing that. Always trying to look on the bright side and not accuse people. Well, sometimes it's not bright and light and happy. Sometimes it's fucking dark, okay? And people do bad things. Not everyone is as perfect as you.'

The words hit like a punch to the gut. I know Holly's hurting, but . . . and there I am doing it again. Making excuses

114

for Holly saying nasty things. Maybe she's right. I am always doing that and it's about time I stopped. Maybe I don't want to be the nice one anymore.

As soon as Holly spits the words out, she drops her eyes to the floor and shakes her head. 'I'm sorry, I didn't mean that. I take it back.' Tears flood her eyes, and she sobs as she covers her face with her hands and turns away from me. I rush up to her and wrap my arms around her shoulders. I don't say a word, just hold onto Holly as the emotion pours out of her, and her body shakes with the effort.

Penny opens the door and peers around it, catching my eye. I give her a weak smile and nod, telling her I've got our friend; she'll be okay.

But I don't know that for sure. How can I? How can any of us know it'll be okay, and things will work out in the end? All there is left to do right now is for Holly to cry and get it all out of her system, just like I did yesterday and Penny too.

'We'll find out the truth,' I say, giving Holly a gentle squeeze. 'And one by one they will pay. This isn't just about us anymore. This is about all women, and how we're fed up with evil men being in control and hurting us and others.'

Holly nods, while clinging onto me. She wipes her nose with the back of her hand and looks up. 'We will. And if I find out Will has killed that woman . . . then he'll be the last of our husbands to die.'

* * *

To my delight, the twins ask me to read them a bedtime story that night. They have their own rooms but take turns to snuggle on one of their beds before one gets off and goes to their room. It's the cutest thing I've ever seen, and my heart swells with joy as each child sits next to me, leaning over to look at the pages of the book I'm reading.

Penny warned me earlier there are often squabbles and the twins argue over which book to read or how she does the voices, but tonight they are perfectly behaved, hanging on my every word. When I've finished the book, I close it and let out a satisfied sigh. The children smell lovely and clean after having a bath, like shampoo and something sweet.

My body aches for the baby I've never even met.

'Auntie Lisa, how come you don't live closer to us? You could read us lots of stories if you lived closer,' says Lori.

'Ah, well, you live in Wales, and I live in England. It's a long way, isn't it? Your mummy used to live in England too, but she moved here when you were very young.'

'Can't you move here?'

I smile. 'I wish I could. I'm sort of . . . trapped at the moment, but maybe one day we'll all live closer together.'

'I'd like that.'

'Me too,' says Luca.

'If I could, I'd move away from here, then we wouldn't be close to Daddy,' says Lori, taking the book from my grasp and gently turning the pages to look at the pictures.

The sentence takes me off guard as I realise what Lori has said. I don't want to overstep the mark, but something tells me to keep the child talking. 'What do you mean? Don't you like living with your dad?'

'He's never here,' says Luca. 'He works a lot.'

'And I'm glad,' answers Lori.

'Why's that?'

Lori lowers her head and shakes it. 'He can be mean sometimes to Mummy. And . . . never mind.' The child scoots forward off the bed, then turns, leans in, and gives me a hug. 'Goodnight, Auntie Lisa. Thank you for the story.'

'Goodnight, Lori.' I watch the girl leave the room, feeling an overwhelming urge to wrap my arms around her and never let her go. I get off the bed and tuck Luca in. 'Goodnight, Luca.'

'Lori doesn't like Daddy,' he says.

I attempt to keep my face as normal as possible. 'I'm sure she does deep down.'

116

Luca shakes his head as he lies down. 'I don't think she does.'

'Do you like your dad?'

'No, but only because he can be mean to Mummy and Lori, especially Lori.'

Bile rises at the back of my throat as my stomach clenches. I can't. I shouldn't. I should fetch their mother, but I can't . . .

'W-what did he do to Lori?'

'Lori told me never to tell. We're twins and twins never break their promises to each other.'

I nod. 'I understand. That's a very lovely thing to say, but sometimes we have to tell our secrets in order to protect the ones we love. Do you understand?'

Luca nods but doesn't expand.

The answer is slipping out of my grasp. If I find out Drake laid a hand on Lori or touched her inappropriately or did anything relating to what was in those photos, then I'll grab a knife and stab him myself. I want to keep asking Luca to tell me more, but I don't want to push him. I'm not his mother. I don't have any right to pry.

My eyes swim with tears as I smile and flatten down a piece of his hair that is sticking up. 'You're a wonderful brother. I hear you and Lori argue a lot. Why's that?'

'Because she's annoying and she's a girl.'

A little giggle escapes my lips. 'I'll leave you to sleep now. Goodnight.'

'Goodnight, Auntie Lisa.'

I plant a light kiss on his forehead, stand and leave the room. I creep towards Lori's bedroom and peer around the open door. The girl is in bed, her duvet pulled up around her chin. I want to go in, to wrap my arms around her, to comfort her, but I shouldn't.

Penny and Holly are watching television when I enter the lounge. 'Both in bed without a fuss,' I say.

Penny turns to me. 'Okay, that's it. I'm officially hiring you as their nanny. What the hell? Bedtimes usually take over an hour. What's your secret?'

I shrug. 'I'm not sure. Your children are wonderful.' I sniff and fight back the tears.

Penny smiles. 'Thank you. They drive me crazy, but they're my babies and I'd do anything to keep them safe.'

I sigh as I think, *Me too*.

118

CHAPTER TWENTY

Lisa
Fourteen years ago

He stays with her while she cries. He tries his best to reassure her that she'll be okay and she's safe now, but how can he know that? Will he protect her for ever? Will he promise to stay by her side and fend off anyone who could hurt her for the rest of her life? She doesn't even know him, and he doesn't know her, so how can she believe him?

Simon. That's his name. She's always liked the name. And it suits him. He's a very handsome man, and she's awash with humiliation when she thinks of how she must look, but all she can do is cry and tremble. Her body is numb. She's not even cold. Just numb.

Simon stands up as footsteps approach. She screams and shuffles backwards towards the bush, hoping it will hide her. He's back.

'No, it's okay. It's just the paramedics,' says Simon.

She nods her understanding, but her body continues to tremble. She shouldn't even be here. It's all happened so fast, too fast for her to understand where it all went wrong.

A female paramedic with dark hair rushes towards her while a male paramedic talks with Simon. They use hushed voices, but she catches a single word. *Raped.* It's a word that will haunt her for ever. The female paramedic kneels in front of her, reaching out her hand as if she were approaching a stray dog.

'It's okay. I'm here to help. Can you tell me your name?'

She whimpers and shakes her head.

'Okay. Are you hurt?'

She looks down at her bare legs. The paramedic has a small head torch and shines it on her skin, highlighting the blood smears and dirt.

'It's okay. I'm not going to hurt you. We're going to get you into the ambulance and take you to the hospital. I expect the police will come and ask you some questions so we can try and catch the person who did this to you, okay?'

She can only nod. She looks past the paramedic at Simon, who is standing just off to the side with a frown on his face. The paramedic notices her looking at him.

'Is that your boyfriend?'

She shakes her head.

'Was he the one who found you?'

She nods.

'Okay. Let me help you stand up. The ambulance is only about a minute's walk away. We parked as close as we could.' The paramedic takes her arm and helps her to stand, but her legs can't take her weight and she collapses. It's like her body has given up.

'Bill, I'm going to need you to fetch the stretcher from the ambulance,' the paramedic says to the other.

A few minutes later, the paramedic returns with the stretcher, and she shuffles on to it.

Simon stands back, watching.

'Do you want Simon to come with you?' asks the paramedic.

She nods once and lies back against the stretcher as the two paramedics lift it up and carry her to the waiting ambulance, Simon following at a distance.

CHAPTER TWENTY-ONE

Penny

It's another long night, fuelled by more alcohol, hot pizza and eventually coffee and cold pizza. The kids fall asleep surprisingly quickly after Lisa put them to bed, and they don't even wake up at midnight, asking for a snack. Lisa seems abnormally quiet and a little pale, but she's fully committed to killing her husband first. It's going to be tricky, though, because she can't have any involvement in the actual murder. That's the idea, anyway.

This plan reminds me of a book I read many years ago called *Strangers on a Train*. There are, however, various differences. For a start, Lisa, Holly and I aren't perfect strangers, so even if I'm the one who ends up killing Lisa's husband, I'm still connected to him in some way because I'm best friends with his wife. I know our plan isn't foolproof, but the more we talk about it, the more convinced I am that we can pull this off. Even Holly gets more and more invested in the idea and has come up with some brilliant insights, as well as helped to iron out some potential problems.

Aunt Silvia called me back earlier, ecstatic that I'd be dropping the kids off with her for a few days. I didn't mention it would more than likely be a week. According to the plan, it will only take four days, but we have to ensure there is time for any disruptions. There's a lot of travelling involved, thanks to us all living so far apart, and there's 'getting rid of the bodies' to deal with too.

Holly pointed out that maybe it's best we space the murders apart because two deaths so close together would look suspicious to the police, especially when they find out the two men are connected via their wives. There's a chance this whole thing could blow up in our faces, but if we ensure we're careful and don't leave evidence or incriminate ourselves in any way, then there's a chance this could work.

Therefore, the first part of the plan is to kill Simon. Then, we'll wait for my husband to return home from his work trip and kill him. I have no idea when that will be. He's on the other side of the world, and it's not like the three of us are going to traipse across the ocean and kill him. He can come to us. We don't want to leave any sort of trail. Therefore, even though I've estimated it will take four days, that time frame could be spread out over several weeks or months, which will probably work better in the long run.

I'm getting into bed when my phone springs to life and my husband's name flashes across the screen. I contemplate ignoring it because I don't want to hear his voice, but I need to keep things as normal as possible, and I'm hoping he's calling with good news.

'Hey,' I say as I shuffle under the sheets.

'Hey, babe. How's it going with your friends?'

'Fine. Good. Great.' I thump the palm of my hand against my forehead.

Use full sentences!

I clear my throat. 'Yeah, it's going great, thanks. It's so lovely to see them and the kids love them.'

'Cool. Look, I'm just calling to let you know that the life insurance is now in effect. You'll receive the papers in the post soon. Keep them safe. . . Don't worry about reading them. It's all boring stuff. And also, my boss emailed me and said I have to fly to New York tomorrow for four weeks.'

'Four weeks!' My voice comes out a little high-pitched. 'Sorry . . .four weeks? Why so long?'

'I don't know. He mentioned something about a client not being happy and that I needed to build a relationship with them and ensure I stick to them like glue, which means a lot of late nights, drinks, meals out and money spent, so it's all good.'

'Sounds fun for you.'

'Yeah, it is. Plus, it means more bonuses come Christmas.'

That's the thing about my husband. It's always about the money.

'How are the kids?'

I swallow back my vile retort. 'T-they're great.'

'Good. I guess I'll see you in a few weeks.'

'Yes . . . you will.'

'Bye, babe. Love you.'

I bite my tongue hard as I force out, 'Love you too,' before hanging up and throwing the phone across the room.

Four weeks.

That's a decent amount of time. We can work with that. Gives us plenty of time to kill Simon and investigate Will too.

* * *

Sleep comes quicker than expected. Maybe it's the alcohol or the sheer exhaustion from planning my husband's death, but I fall asleep within minutes after hanging up. My dreams are full of uncomfortable and unpleasant sensations which have nothing to do with the murders, but my strange fixation on the scabs on my body.

I pick and pick and pick away at them until my skin peels away and I pull off my whole arm. Once it's gone, relief floods my body like a wave. When I wake up, my hands and fingernails are smeared with dried blood. I've been picking at the wounds in my sleep and the sheets are splattered with red dots where I've tossed and turned.

* * *

I find the twins already eating breakfast in front of the large television in the playroom the next morning. They're watching some sort of kids show. I've stopped being invested in what they watch ever since they grew out of watching *Bluey*. Honestly, that show used to make me bawl like a fucking baby. It also made me feel very inadequate as a parent when I didn't play feather wand with my kids every second of the day or allow them to create dens from all the sofa cushions.

When did my babies become so self-sufficient? There was a time, not too long ago, when they still wanted me to check their bums after they'd used the toilet and now, they make their own breakfasts. Granted, it's merely a bowl of cereal and there's spilt milk all over the counter, there's Coco Pops all over the floor, which crunch under my feet, and they haven't put the box of Coco Pops away, but still . . .

'Good morning,' I say to them. 'I'd like to have a chat with you both this morning. It's important. Can you switch off the television for a moment?' I brace myself for an onslaught of whining and abuse, but it doesn't come. Luca switches off the screen and Lori turns her whole body towards me. I attempt to hide my shock. What's happened to my two argumentative children?

'Thank you. Now, as you know, your father is away with work. He called me last night and explained that he'll be away for a further four weeks.' I expect some form of response, but again, none comes, so I continue. 'Therefore, I think we should go on a little Easter holiday to visit Aunt Silvia. I used to spend many happy times with her on her farm when I was your age. What do you think?'

Luca's eyes widen and Lori's jaw drops.

'Really?' asks Lori.

'Cool!' says Luca.

'That sounds like fun,' says Lori. 'Does she have animals on her farm?'

'Yes. Lots. You have been there before, but I expect you don't remember.' Granted, it's been a while since I took them to visit her. I've always been too busy to visit, despite not living far away. I must make more of a conscious effort to be a part of her life. She was always a part of mine growing up.

'What will we do there?' asks Luca.

'Play in the fields. Make dens. Go swimming in the lake. Help Aunt Silvia muck out the pigs.'

'Ewww!'

'But it's all good for you, I promise. It will be nice to get away from technology for a while.' It's not that I don't agree with allowing six-year-olds to be babysat by their iPads (in fact, I wholeheartedly support it), but I think it's good for kids to get fresh air and play in the mud once in a while.

Luca's eyes narrow at me. 'What do you mean? I can take my games, right?'

'Yes, but while you're there it would be good for you to get some fresh air too.'

'And Daddy isn't coming?' asks Lori.

'No, he's not.'

Lori gets up from sitting on the floor, places her bowl of soggy cereal on the side and wraps her arms around my waist. 'Thank you,' she whispers.

* * *

Today is our last full day before we plan to travel to Aunt Silvia's. It's only twenty miles away and the idea is for me to drive the kids there on Monday morning, then come back here, pick up the girls and take them there too. My car isn't big enough to comfortably seat three adults, two children plus luggage. Aunt Silvia wanted to see the girls again and I thought it might be a nice way to end our long weekend on the farm. Then, we'd get to work.

Lisa helps Lori pack a suitcase while I help Luca and ensure he brings more than just his portable games console. The paperwork for the new life insurance comes via a delivery courier in the afternoon. I put it straight into my suitcase without reading it, but it's on my to-do list.

I cook a roast dinner while I watch my children interact and play with my friends. It dawns on me that I've been selfish for a long time. My children thrive on other adult interactions. I've tried to keep them to myself for so long. Yes, I let them stay over with their friends, but they don't have any sort of relationship with another adult other than myself. They're laughing and joking with Holly and Lisa, especially Lisa who they seem to flock to the most. Lori even grabs her hand and takes her on a tour of the garden, showing her all the flowers.

It's a beautiful yet heart-wrenching sight to behold, especially knowing what Lisa has lost recently.

I can tell Holly is keeping her distance and I don't blame her. She's always said she isn't the maternal type, and that's okay.

That evening, we eat our roast dinner and then pull all the cushions off the sofa and eat popcorn on the floor in front of an animated film. It's the most wonderful and best night I've had in a long time. And after that, I know it will all turn out okay in the end. It has to. Because there's no other way.

* * *

Monday morning with the kids around, we can't talk about the upcoming plan, but it's not too big a deal because we've gone over and over it. Maybe we should have waited a while longer before kicking off with killing Simon, but Holly and I agree there's no way we're letting Lisa go home to her husband knowing what we now know.

Simon keeps calling Lisa, but she refuses to answer, until finally relenting, just as I'm about to leave to take the kids to the farm.

I hear him shouting at her down the phone and it makes my toes curl. Other than my own husband, I don't think I've hated someone as much as I do him.

When she returns five minutes later, her face is pale.

'Everything okay?' I ask, even though I know it isn't.

Lisa glances at the kids briefly. They're in their own little world, hyped up on excitement. 'He's angry,' she says. 'I've been ignoring his calls all weekend. I'm glad I'm not going to see him again because I think he'd kill me if I went back to him now.' Tears fill her eyes as she attempts to shield her face from the kids in case they wonder what's wrong.

Holly grabs her hand. 'You've got nothing to worry about now. We're here and we'll look after you. He'll never hurt you again.'

Lisa nods and takes a deep breath. 'I know . . . but . . . oh God, you're right. I know you're right. Why do I feel so guilty?'

'Because that's what he's been training you to feel whenever he gets upset or angry with you. It's not your fault, okay? He's angry because he feels as if he's lost control of you, that's all. He's a pathetic little man, remember that,' I say matter-of-factly.

Lisa touches her eye, which is starting to look a lot better now the bruise is healing. 'He is,' she whispers.

'Can we go yet?' asks Lori.

'Yes, yes, we're going now. Go and get into the car,' I say to my children.

'Yay!' They race each other to the car.

'I'll see you both in a couple of hours.' I turn and join my children by the car where they are squabbling and hitting each other over who gets to sit on the left and who gets to sit on the right. Like it makes a fucking difference!

* * *

Forty-five minutes later, I turn onto the off-road track that leads to Aunt Silvia's farm. She's already got the main gate open and is standing in front of the huge farmhouse, waving like a maniac, a huge grin on her face. She looks the same as she did fifteen years ago; short brown hair (although I'm pretty sure it's a dye job now), muddy welly boots, dangly earrings and an oversized threadbare jumper I'm convinced she's owned since the mid-80s. She shrieks with delight when I stop the car. I get out and, before I unleash my children from their seats, throw my arms around her neck.

'Oh, my goodness, look at you!' she says.

'Look at you! Do you know something about an anti-ageing cream that I don't?'

'Pah! It's all the fresh air, my girl. Now . . . who are those two young adults in the car? They can't be the twins. They're too grown up!'

I turn and open the doors. Lori and Luca climb down and line up. Lori takes a brave step forward and extends her hand. 'Hello, Aunt Silvia. I'm six years and eighty-one days old.'

Aunt Silvia takes her hand. 'Lovely to see you again, young lady.'

'I'm three and a half minutes older!' pipes up Luca, giving his sister an elbow shove.

'Yes, I know. Nice to see you again, young man.' She shakes his hand.

Both twins grin from ear to ear.

'Weren't your friends coming too?' asks Aunt Silvia.

'Couldn't fit everyone in the car. If it's all right with you, I'll head back and get them now.'

'Don't you want a cup of tea first?'

'Sure. That'd be great.'

'So . . . this is exciting, isn't it?' said Aunt Silvia ushering the kids towards the main farmhouse. 'A girls' adventure!'

'I'm not a girl!' says Luca in a stern voice.

'Of course, young man. My apologies. You're here to keep us all safe, right?'

'No, that's not right,' says Lori. 'We don't need a man to keep us safe.'

My heart practically swells with pride.

Aunt Silvia's face blushes a deep red. 'You're very right! My, my, you kids are certainly like your mother, aren't you?' She flicks her eyes over to me and gives me a wink.

My body fizzes with energy and excitement as I step through the front door, carrying each of the kid's suitcases. I feel like a kid again myself. It's like the fake Penny is melting away, revealing the true Penny underneath. I've missed her more than I realised. The one who takes spontaneous trips and enjoys the mud and fresh air.

As soon as the twins enter the house, they run in different directions. They have been here before, but not since they were four, so this is an adventure for them. I don't call them back. I don't shout at them for being too loud. They are free here and my eyes fill with tears at the thought. Maybe I run too tight a ship at home. Maybe once my husband is out of the way, I can relax more.

Aunt Silvia walks up and stands next to me, listening as the kids shriek and laugh their way around the house.

'This place is massive!' Luca shouts as he rushes back into the room.

A black dog runs in, making a beeline for my son, but I don't care. It barks for joy as Luca begins to play with it, tickling its belly.

'Something tells me you're going to be staying here a while,' says Aunt Silvia.

I turn and smile at her. 'Can we stay for ever?'

'I thought you'd never ask.'

There will come a time very soon when Aunt Silvia will become suspicious. I need to speak with the girls first because if this plan is going to succeed, we need Aunt Silvia's help to keep the kids safe, or at least her silence and cooperation.

There's no getting anything past Aunt Silvia. It's always been that way, even when I was a kid. I'd tried smoking once and she'd caught me. I'd tried to sneak out in the middle of the night as a teenager during one of my stays to go and visit a local boy and she'd met me at the end of the lane with a torch and an extra coat, which she then gave to me and said, 'At least remember the basics when you're going to sneak out, girl.'

CHAPTER TWENTY-TWO

Holly

Once Penny's car disappears, Lisa and I head indoors. My stomach has been full of dancing butterflies all morning and my usual two cups of coffee don't help to dampen the anxiety. My forehead is sweating, and I feel like I need another shower, even though I stood under the hot jets for half an hour this morning. I do wish I had Penny's shower set-up.

'Everything okay?' asks Lisa.

I look up at her. 'Sure. Just . . . nervous, I guess.' Lisa's phone goes off again. 'Is he still calling?'

'He hasn't stopped.'

'Maybe you should turn off your phone.'

Lisa looks down at it. 'He must hate me.'

'Hey, stop that. He doesn't deserve your guilt or tears.'

'You don't know everything,' she whispers.

'Tell me, then. Tell me the exact details of how you met him. I know there's something you're not telling me.'

Lisa takes a deep breath. 'Do you remember when you and Penny couldn't get hold of me for, like, five days? We'd all gone to separate universities.'

I frown as the memory materialises. 'Oh, right. Yeah. I remember. You went for a night out and we didn't hear from you. We were worried sick.' I remember how she never let us know she'd got home safely. We made it a habit to always send a group text when we got home from a night out, even though we were miles apart, just so we knew one another was safe. The next day when we called, she didn't answer. We even called her parents, but they said they hadn't heard from her either. At one point, Lisa and I started making travel arrangements to go and look for her, but then she messaged us back.

'Well, that night I was raped in the park when I walked back to halls from my friends' house.'

'Wait . . . y-you were raped!' I almost choke on the word. A funny taste appears in my mouth, making me want to gag.

'I'm sorry. I know I should have told you and Penny sooner.'

'You think! What the hell were you thinking keeping something that awful a secret from us?'

'I wasn't thinking. I just . . . Look, can I finish the story of how I met Simon and then you can yell at me some more later?'

I sigh heavily. 'Fine. Continue. You told us that you were going to take a taxi that night.'

'I decided to walk instead. I thought the fresh air would help sober me up before I walked back to halls. I was very drunk. My friend and I had had an argument.'

'What about?'

'I don't remember. I don't even remember the girl's name. I guess it doesn't really matter now.'

'Okay . . .'

'Anyway, I left the house party and cut through the park. You remember the park I told you about? The one with the creepy trees and that homeless woman who always camped out under the bushes.' I nod. A dark, sinking feeling is settling in my stomach. 'Well . . . that's when it happened. He came out of nowhere.'

A sob escapes before I realise it. 'I'm so sorry . . . You must have been so scared. Why didn't you . . . Why did you never tell us?'

Lisa shakes her head. 'I was so ashamed. I didn't even tell my parents, or my classmates.'

'What? Why?'

'I . . . I just couldn't. I was so afraid of what they'd think of me. That it was all my fault because of how I was dressed that night. I was wearing that ridiculously short skirt that showed my butt cheeks with a thong and a low-cut top that even Penny wouldn't wear.'

'Okay, but how does Simon come into this?'

'After the man ran off. Simon was on his way home from a party too and walked through the park and found me.'

I couldn't stop myself from gasping. 'But you told us you met him at a café.'

'That was the second time I met him. Or the third. I can't remember. But he found me that night just after it happened and called an ambulance. He saved me. I owe him my life.'

I step forward and wrap my arms around my friend. She hugs me back, trembling slightly. 'I'm so sorry you had to go through all that. I wish you'd told us, though. We could have helped you.'

'I'm sorry. I know that now.'

'But Lisa . . . just because Simon helped you that night, it doesn't give him the right to treat you this way. You don't owe him anything. He's a bad man, no matter what good deed he might have done fourteen years ago.'

Lisa nods. 'I know that now. He's been holding that night over my head for years, telling me I'm not good enough for anyone else so there's no point in trying to make an effort with how I look. I've never realised just how much of a hold he's had on me since that night.'

'Did they ever catch the guy who did it? The guy who raped you.'

'No. I never took it any further. I have no idea who he is. He had a balaclava over his face, and he didn't say much.'

'Well, wherever he is, I hope he's paying for what he did. Thank you for telling me.'

'Thank you for listening and understanding.'

'What are best friends for?'

We hug again. 'Right, I think we have time for one last cup of coffee before Penny gets back and . . . wait . . . is that a car pulling up in the driveway? Is that her back already? She's only been gone fifteen minutes.'

I walk over to the window and peer out. I'm right about the fact there's a car in the driveway, but I'm wrong about who it belongs to.

'Oh fuck!' I duck down behind the windowsill.

Lisa looks up. 'What's wrong?'

I make the gesture for her to get down. She does. Terror has filled her eyes because she realises what's happening without me having to explain.

He's found her.

And we're in big trouble.

CHAPTER TWENTY-THREE

Lisa

Holly and I lock eyes and I know straight away what's happened by the way her face drains of all colour. I can feel it deep down in my bones, my soul. He's found me. He's driven from Cornwall to Wales for me, tracked me down and is here to drag me back. I should have done something. I should have answered the phone or switched it off. He must have a tracker installed on it. I've never thought to check. Even if I had thought to look, I wouldn't know what to look for. He's the one who sorts my phone payments and sets up my tariff plan. He's the one who checks my phone on a weekly basis for any sign I may have been texting someone I shouldn't. A tracking app of some sort is the only way he would have known where Penny lives because he's never been here before and doesn't know her address.

My body does what it's always done when faced with Simon and his wrath: freeze. Usually, people talk about the fight or flight response, but there's the freeze response; that moment when your body is trying to decide what to do and can't seem to make a solid decision. I literally can't move a muscle even though Holly is beckoning me to come with her. She's already duck-walking across the floor to the kitchen island, keeping low. She grabs a knife from the wooden knife block, and my stomach does a somersault.

A knife.

What does she think she's going to do with a knife?

This isn't what's supposed to happen.

We have a plan.

This isn't the plan.

Simon is supposed to die from a drug overdose in our house, but now he's here . . . and Holly has a knife in her hand, holding it as if she's about to head into an arena to fight to the death.

The knife looks huge in her right hand. She gestures with her left to come away from the window and join her.

'Lisa! Get your butt over here! This is serious!'

Finally, my body snaps into action, and my flight response kicks in. I shuffle over next to her. 'What are you doing with that knife?'

'Improvising.'

'B-but . . . we can't kill him with a knife. I'm not supposed to be anywhere near him. He's supposed to die of a drug overdose.' My voice is quaking, and my body doesn't feel like it belongs to me. This is all wrong. I can't stand by and watch Holly stab my husband with a knife. I can't let her do it. It would put her at huge risk. Our DNA is all over this house.

'He's kind of changed that plan by showing up here unannounced, hasn't he? I knew I should have checked your phone for a tracker. That dickhead has always known where you are at all times. This isn't right.'

'But we can't kill him in cold blood,' I reply, shaking my head.

'What choice do we have?'

'We could hide and message Penny to say he's here and then she can figure out what to do.'

Holly looks at me for three long seconds where time seems to stand still. That pause is interrupted by the sound of a car door slamming and feet crunching over gravel.

'Okay, call Penny and tell her to hurry. Then we'll hide, but I'm taking the knife with me for protection. If that bastard attacks us, I want to be ready.'

A loud knock at the door makes us jump. Holly grabs my arm and drags me through the house, keeping as low as we can, and we lock ourselves in the understairs cupboard, hiding amongst the various household appliances, an ironing board and shoe racks.

My phone vibrates in my hand as Simon calls again, but I ignore it and call Penny. My hands are shaking as I hold the phone to my ear.

'Hey, Lis, I'm just leaving now. What's up?'

'He's here,' I whisper.

'What? Who's here?'

'Simon. He's here. Holly and I are hiding. Hurry!'

'Motherfucker! I'm on my way. There are security cameras everywhere so I can keep an eye on him from my phone. Hang on. Okay . . . okay . . . He's circling the house and looking through the windows. Where are you hiding?'

'Under the stairs.'

'Okay, good. Stay there. If he's tracked you, he'll know you're in the house still.' I hear Penny in the background saying a rushed goodbye to the twins. Then the sound of fast breathing as she runs to the car.

The sound of a glass shattering echoes through the house.

'Fucking hell, he's just broken the utility-room window . . .' says Penny.

I let out a low sob and cover my eyes with my hands. Holly grabs the phone from me. 'Hurry, Penny. I have a knife, but I'd rather not use it and get blood all over your clean floor.' Penny hangs up. The light from the phone dies and the small space is plunged into darkness.

We hold our breaths, too afraid to make a sound.

Light footsteps signal he's now inside the house. He isn't calling out to me. He knows I'm hiding. I've hidden from him only once before in my life and it hadn't ended well. When he found me cowering in my wardrobe behind my clothes, he dragged me out by my hair and then forced me to give him oral sex by way of an apology.

Our whole plan has gone up in smoke before it's even begun, all because I hadn't realised my husband would be the type of man who'd track his wife's phone. Of course, he would! It explains so much. Whenever I'd arrive home late from work, he'd tut at me and say, 'It's a good job I trust you or I'd think the worst.' I've been so blind to him for all this time.

Footsteps approach. He's slowly searching the house. I'm not sure how exact his tracking system is, but it could lead him straight to this cupboard.

Shit.

We're sitting ducks.

My heart rate doubles in the space of ten seconds, and I can barely catch my breath as I grab the phone back off Holly and switch it off. But I know it's too late.

The footsteps get louder and then stop.

He's standing in the hall just beyond the door.

Holly grabs my hand and squeezes. 'When I say run, you run.' I nod, even though I know she can't see me.

'Come out, come out, wherever you are,' sings a male voice that sends shivers down my spine. Nausea clenches my gut and tears stream from my eyes.

It all happens in the blink of an eye.

The cupboard door is wrenched open.

Holly screams, 'Run!'

We bolt forwards at the same time, catching Simon off guard. He stumbles sideways as I barrel into him. I lurch to the side, free from his grasp, and start running, expecting Holly to be right beside me.

I hear a crunch and a thud behind me.

My foot catches on a low, uneven step and I crash to the ground, wincing as the pain in my ribs stabs me enough to take my breath away. Stars dance in front of my eyes as I push myself to stand, urging my weak body onwards.

But Holly's not with me.

138

I turn the corner and spin around just in time to see her slump to the floor after being punched in the face. The knife skids across the floor, but Simon doesn't pick it up. He's breathing hard, but otherwise looks unfazed.

Holly has sacrificed herself so I can get away and the thought makes my blood run hot with anger. I'm done being a victim. I'm done with taking his abuse.

A switch has been flipped. I'm not the only one at risk now. My friends are too, and he's just broken into Penny's home and attacked Holly. My friends. My *best* friends.

I peer around the corner and watch as Simon drags Holly into the kitchen. She's not completely unconscious, but I expect her head is spinning. I know exactly how hard he can hit. I take the brief opportunity to dart forwards and grab the knife from the floor.

A door slams. Maybe he's stashed Holly somewhere in a room.

It's time to play cat and mouse with my husband.

I dash into the nearest room and crouch behind a sofa. He's moving around in the kitchen, opening drawers, and slamming them. Maybe looking for something to use to tie Holly up.

How long's it been since Penny left?

It can't be much longer until she arrives, but what are we supposed to do when she gets here? It's three against one, but the plan was never to go up against him like this. He was supposed to die slowly and quietly of a drug overdose. Now, there's CCTV footage of him breaking into the house. It's all evidence.

We're so screwed.

'Lisa, it's time you and I had a little chat, don't you think?'

I remain where I am, holding the handle of the knife with both hands in front of me.

'Time to come out and play.'

He's in the same room now. There's nowhere for me to run. But I have to try. The room is eerily silent apart from his ragged breaths.

I shriek as I leap out from crouching behind the sofa and make a run for the open door to the hallway. He thunders after me.

But he's too quick and I'm too slow. The sudden movement makes my ribs explode with pain. He grabs my hair in his fists and yanks, then turns me around, punching me straight in the face. More pain erupts behind my eyeballs as my nose breaks. I taste blood as it trickles down my throat, making me gag.

I drop the knife.

'You fucking bitch,' Simon seethes into my face, his breath warm against my cheek. 'You think you can try and get away from me, huh? You went crying to your friends for help, did you? Let me get something through your thick skull once and for all . . . I *own* you. You are *mine*. You don't get to leave me. I'm the best you'll ever do, bitch, so you better get used to it and get back in line.'

Simon grabs a fistful of my hair again and pulls me along the hallway and into the kitchen. I can barely see straight as the room spins and red spots fly in front of my face. I'm going to pass out.

But I can't. Not now.

He's set up a chair in the middle of the kitchen floor. I can't see any sign of Holly, but I can hear banging from somewhere in the house.

He shoves me towards the chair, and I collapse onto it, using the seat to hold myself up. I spit out a mouthful of blood onto the sparkling clean floor, gulping in air through my mouth because my nose isn't functioning as it should. Sharp stabs of pain make it hard for me to keep my focus.

'I'll never come back with you. Never. It's over, Simon. I'm done.'

Simon laughs. 'Oh, you're done? You're not even close to being done, bitch.'

I turn and hold his gaze. His eyes are full of fire and rage. I've never noticed before how black his eyes are. Black exactly like his soul. How have I not seen it before? *But you have.*

140

Simon grabs a nearby tea towel and throws it at my face. 'Clean yourself up. You're a mess. Now, I'm not sure where the third one is, so we probably don't have a lot of time. I suggest you spend your time wisely and answer my questions.'

I use the towel to wipe the blood from my nose. A lump forms in my throat as I think of Penny and what she must be going through right now. She's probably seen most of it via the security cameras, which will hopefully give her an advantage when she arrives. My stomach contracts in a knot as I bend towards the floor. I'm trying not to allow the panic to overwhelm me, but Simon has hold of the knife and is expertly swirling it around his fingers. He even strokes the sharp edge with his thumb and smiles at me, enjoying every second of my torment.

'First question,' he says. 'Did you have a fun time with your friends?' I open my mouth, but the only sound that escapes is a small squeak. 'I'm sorry? You're going to have to speak up, my love.'

'Y-yes.'

'Good. Second question . . . did you or did you not tell them how you really got that black eye and broken ribs?'

He's baiting me. I know it. But I have to play along, because if I lie to him and he finds out, then there's no knowing what he'll do to me. I need to buy Penny the time she needs to get here.

'I–I did tell them.'

'That's a shame. A real shame because I think I remember you telling me once, no, *promising* me once that you'd never tell a soul about it. Did you or did you not make that promise, Lisa?'

'I did,' I say, wiping another drop of blood from my chin. My nose is screaming at me, and I have to keep spitting blood onto the tea towel, so I don't swallow it.

Simon sighs. 'And here I was thinking that you making a promise to me actually meant something.'

I know what he's doing now. He's trying to make me feel guilty. Make me apologise to him. Gaslighting me by making

141

me out to be the bad guy. Like I'm the one who's done something wrong, not him.

I fight the urge to scoff and retaliate with a list of all the broken promises he's made over the years, but I don't. There's the promise he made that he'd always put my needs ahead of his own. The promise he'd always respect, love and cherish me. The promise he'd never hit me ever again. He even made the promise that he'd rather die than see me cry over something he'd done to me.

All lies.

They all mean nothing now. Just empty words used to control every aspect of my life.

Even the promise he made that he'd never let anyone hurt me ever again. The one he made on the night we met when he rescued me.

'What are you going to do when Penny arrives?' I ask with a wobbly voice.

'I haven't decided yet,' he says. 'You three have really fucked things up, haven't you?'

My eyes flick over the knife again. He's now holding it with one hand loosely by his side. 'You broke into Penny's house and attacked us. It's all on camera. You're not going to get away with this.'

'You'll be surprised at what I can get away with,' he responds with a laugh.

I don't even want to think about what he means by that comment. Time is running out. I have no idea what Penny has planned for when she gets here. She might know what's going on in the house and she might not.

'Please, Simon. Don't hurt my friends. I beg you.'

'Begging has never suited you, my love. You begged me to stop the first time we met, and I didn't, so what makes you think I'll stop now?'

'What are you talking—'

Simon holds his hand up. 'Stop. It sounds like our host has finally arrived.'

I hold my breath as tyres crunch over gravel.

Simon flips the knife in his hand and catches it. 'I guess I'll go and say hello.' He points the knife at me. 'If you move from this chair, I'll gut Penny in front of you.'

I squeak as Simon storms from the room.

There's no time to lose. I launch from the chair and rush to the window overlooking the driveway, making sure to keep behind the curtains. Simon is nowhere to be seen. Penny is getting out of the car. I wave my arms to get her attention. She sees me and puts a finger to her lips before sprinting to the left and disappearing around the side of the house.

What the hell is she doing? She can't seriously be planning on taking him on one-on-one. Is she crazy? I know she takes a self-defence class from time to time, and she's pretty feisty, but even I wouldn't bet on her coming out on top when faced with Simon's fury.

Simon storms back into the kitchen. 'That bitch has run off.' He sees me by the window. 'Get back on the chair!'

'No.'

He points the knife at me. 'Now.'

'No. I'm done with being a victim. You may have saved me all those years ago, but you've slowly destroyed me ever since.'

Simon laughs again. 'Oh, Lisa. I've been waiting so long to tell you this. You've been so blind.'

I shake my head slowly. 'I know, but now I finally see who you really are.'

'Do you? Do you really?'

'Yes.'

'I don't think you do. You never did find out the identity of the man who raped you that night in the park, did you?'

And then everything clicks into place.

It was him.

143

CHAPTER TWENTY-FOUR

Penny

I don't take a proper breath during the twenty-one minutes it takes me to drive from Aunt Silvia's farm to my house. Every time I try to inhale, a shooting pain reminds me that my best friends are in danger, and I have to gulp back a sob and tell myself to hold it together for their sakes. I can't afford to fall apart right now because I feel responsible for them. Not only are they at my house being hunted by a sick, abusive bastard, but I'm the one who put the idea in their heads to kill him and put themselves at risk. I've almost called the police at least a dozen times as I navigate the narrow roads, hoping to God I don't meet a vehicle coming the other way because I don't have time to slow down or pull over, but I stay focused and remind myself that by involving the police, we'd lose everything.

It wasn't the plan for Simon to turn up at my front door, but we'll have to adapt. I set up the camera app on my phone on the dashboard so I can keep an eye on him as he searches the grounds. I see him break my window. I see him climb into the house. I see him search downstairs and find the girls in the cupboard under the stairs. I hold my breath as I watch them launch themselves out of their hiding spot. I see him grab hold of Holly and knock her out. I see everything, even if it is several seconds behind and slightly juddery and unfocused because of the mobile data strength.

I'm ready for him.

But none of the knowing helps to calm my racing imagination and the gut-wrenching feeling that I may be too late by the time I arrive. I skid the car to a stop in my driveway and fling the door open.

I see Lisa at the window and gesture for her to stay quiet as I race around the side of the house. Simon may think he has the element of surprise, but this is my house and I know all the different nooks and crannies and the various routes to get inside.

I just hope Lisa and Holly will be okay until I can get to them. But first, before I can help them, I need to get to my safe. I bet the bastard doesn't know about that.

I let myself in through the side door and slip into the house. Faint voices are coming from the kitchen, which means the coast is clear for me to enter the main office on the left. This used to be where I worked until I had the office pod built, but I still keep the desk and shelves set up. Eventually, the kids will use it to do their homework and studies as they get older.

I crawl under the large, mahogany desk and lie on my back, looking up at the underside. There's a small wooden knob in the corner, which I twist, revealing a moving panel, which slides away. Behind it is the safe. My husband doesn't even know about it.

He doesn't know what I keep in it either.

I remove the Glock from the safe, along with the silencer, which I screw into place.

It's already loaded.

No, it's not legal. No, I don't care.

I bought it illegally six years ago just before the children were born and hid it from my husband. I needed something to protect myself and my babies, and a knife wasn't going to cut it. I've never told anyone this, other than Holly and Lisa, but when I was eight months pregnant, a burglar broke into my London home and held me at knife point while he robbed us. Drake wasn't home. Due to the trauma, I went into early labour with the twins, and almost lost them. It was the reason I bought a gun. The man who robbed the house was never caught, and I live in fear of it happening again. I've never had to use the gun before, but I know how to use it as I take a few shooting lessons each year. Another hobby of mine that I keep from Drake. The girls know about it, even if they don't agree with me owning an illegal gun. I couldn't care less because if I had a choice between protecting myself and my children, or being fined over a gun I shouldn't own . . . The choice is easy.

I'm full of surprises.

Holding the pistol steady in both hands, feeling as badass as Lara Croft, I creep towards the kitchen. The voices are raised now. I can also hear Holly shouting from somewhere nearby. I don't worry about her because at least she's safe and alive, which is more than I can say for the dickhead who's broken into my house and attacked my friends.

I peer around the doorframe. Lisa and Simon are standing opposite each other.

'I-it was you . . . You raped me,' says Lisa.

'Bingo, my love.'

My breath catches in my throat. Raped? What does she mean? When did he rape her?

I step into the room, pointing the pistol at Simon's back. Lisa's eyes shift to me ever so slightly and her eyes widen as she spies the gun.

'Put your hands up right now,' I say.

Simon pauses and looks over his shoulder at me. 'Well, well, this is a surprise.'

'Give me one good reason why I shouldn't shoot you in the head right now,' I say, taking a couple of steps closer. 'You broke into my house and attacked my friends.'

Simon grins and it makes my stomach gurgle. 'This is true, but you have an illegal gun. If you shoot me with it, you're in big trouble.'

'I couldn't give a fuck. I knew there was something about you I didn't like. I'm sorry to say this, Lisa, but Holly and I have never liked your husband. We've always thought he was a creep. We just never realised how much of a creep he was.'

Simon laughs. He turns all the way around to face me. He now has his back to Lisa. He's holding a knife in his right hand. He takes a step towards me and I retaliate by raising the gun an inch higher.

'Take one more step towards me and I'll shoot you. That's your final warning.'

'No, I don't think you will.'

'How much do you wanna bet?'

'I've always liked you, Penny. Makes me wish I'd met you that night in the park and not Lisa.'

I frown. 'What are you talking about? What night in the park?'

Simon turns and looks at Lisa. 'Would you like to explain, my love?'

Lisa steps to the side so I can see her properly. 'The first time I met Simon, he rescued me after I was raped in a park on the way back from a party at university, but it was Simon who raped me.'

My mouth falls open. 'You were raped! What the fuck! Why is this the first time I'm hearing about this?'

Lisa lowers her eyes. 'I'm sorry. I just didn't want you to know the truth about how Simon and I met.'

'But Lisa, if Simon's the one who raped you, why the fuck have you stayed with him for all these years?' Too many questions are trying to spill from my mouth all at once.

'I didn't know it was him!' Lisa covers her face with her hands. 'I've only just found out. I'm such an idiot for not seeing it before. Simon found me afterwards and I thought he was there to rescue me. I never saw the face of the guy who

147

raped me.' Lisa sinks to the floor, head in hands. The sound coming out of her is more animal than human.

'You . . . sick . . . fuck . . .' I say slowly, grinding my teeth so hard that my jaw aches. 'You raped her, left her, then came back and pretended to be her hero? What kind of monster are you?'

Simon laughs like an evil villain.

I step forwards again, the gun still aimed at his chest. 'You're sick. Trust me, I'd like nothing more than to pull this trigger right now. No one will even hear it because of the silencer, and I can easily wipe the CCTV footage. Maybe I should kill you right now. It will be much easier than what we originally had planned.'

Lisa looks up at me. 'Penny . . . don't . . . I need answers.'

Tears stream from my eyes, distorting my vision, but I don't wipe them away. Both my hands are clenched around the handle of the gun.

A loud bang erupts from behind me.

I shriek and duck, shielding my head. Simon takes the split second of opportunity to lunge towards me while my focus is elsewhere. He piles into me, grabs the gun from my hand and hits me across the face with it. Pain explodes across my cheek, and I tumble to the ground.

Lisa screams, 'Noooo!'

Then I hear Holly's voice shout, 'Penny!'

She must have escaped and burst through the door.

Simon, in his effort to attack me, drops the knife. He now has the gun and is pointing it directly at my head. This is it. It's all over. I'm never going to see my children again. They're going to grow up with a paedophile for a father. I've failed them. I've—

Lisa throws herself against Simon's body. He loses his balance, and the gun is no longer pointing at me. I use the split second I have to kick him hard in his left ankle. A sharp crack erupts, followed by his guttural scream. The gun drops to the floor next to me and he topples over sideways.

I don't hesitate.

I grab it, aim and fire.

The bullet pierces straight through the side of his neck. Blood spurts across my face and half of the kitchen. The brightness of the blood against the cleanness of the white tiles makes it look as if it's glowing.

Lisa screams.

I'm still lying on the ground, holding the gun in both hands, pointing it in the same place as when I'd fired it. Simon's body is no longer there. It's on the ground. And a halo of blood is expanding at an alarming rate around his head and neck.

But he's not dead.

Yet.

He's pressing his hands against his neck, spluttering and gargling as blood pours from his mouth.

Holly appears above me, her face pale as she holds out a hand to help me to my feet, but I don't want to stand up. Not yet.

I drag myself over to Simon's body and grab his shirt, pressing my face close to his. 'I hope it fucking hurts, you bastard.'

Simon opens his mouth, but his vocal cords have been blasted to pieces. He has mere seconds to live. I leave him be and lean away from him. I'm completely covered in his blood.

Lisa bends down next to him. 'Goodbye, Simon,' she says before we all watch him take his final breath.

CHAPTER TWENTY-FIVE

Fourteen years ago
Lisa

Her body doesn't feel right. Everything feels . . . odd. Like parts of her body are doing their own thing without her control. In a strange way, she likes it, but she keeps remembering flashes of that night in the park. The man who raped her, he had a balaclava over his face and his breath stank. The only thing she remembers about his appearance is his eyes. They were dark, angry and empty.

An empty bottle of cheap vodka is lying next to her. She's slumped in the shower, her head rolling to one side as the torrent of water rains down, soaking her to the skin. She hasn't removed any of her clothes, so her white top is see-through. She bought the bottle from the corner shop and the pills she'd got from a friend who promised her they'd help her get a good night's sleep before her exam tomorrow. She didn't know what they were, but she'd swallowed them as if they were sweets. The exam doesn't matter. She can't even remember what it's about.

She's been in pain for days, ever since it happened. Sore and uncomfortable and she's only just stopped bleeding, but now she feels no pain at all. And it's bliss. She'll miss Simon, but she knows it's for the best. He was a nice man and all he'd wanted to do was help her, but she's beyond help now. Her university friends are out for the evening, not back for hours. She'll be gone by then. She can feel herself drifting into oblivion already.

At least, this way, there will be no more pain.

And she won't have to remember about the night in the park.

It doesn't matter now.

It's better this way.

She hopes no one else will ever have to go through the pain of what she's gone through. She's just not strong enough to keep going with her life. She can't face her parents or friends knowing that she was attacked in that way. No man will ever want her. Not even Simon. He says he wants to protect her, but he can't promise that.

At least by taking herself out of the picture, he can move on and rescue someone else. There's no need for him to worry about her now. She's going to a better place.

She's not a victim.

And she'll never be one. Not ever.

A loud bang disrupts her fogginess, but she doesn't even blink as she slips into darkness.

Everything else bleeds together, no specific memory or dream making any sort of sense. She remembers vomiting a lot and someone lifting her up, lots of shouting, a ride in the back of a van, and then bright lights and sharp stabs of pain as needles are pushed into her skin. Somehow, she's been saved and taken to hospital where her stomach is pumped, and she is hooked up to fluids.

Once she is conscious and able to form words, she's asked over and over if her drinking a whole bottle of vodka and swallowing pills had been an attempt to end her life. She keeps saying no, but they don't appear to believe her because several doctors come in and discuss her mental health and seeing a specialist doctor. Plus, she is asked if she'd like her parents to be contacted, which she immediately declines. She is a legal adult; there is no need to get them involved in something that doesn't concern them.

Lisa refuses to talk about what happened and manages to convince the doctors that her overdose had been an accident, that she was struggling with her studies, and she'd merely been trying to ensure she got a good night's sleep but hadn't realised she'd taken so much.

'Who found me?' she finally asks.

The nurse in her room checks her vital signs. 'Your boyfriend, Simon. He keeps calling and asking about you. He's very worried. Now that you're stable, would you like us to allow him to visit?'

She blinks against the bright lights and winces as the nurse removes the needle in her arm after taking more blood. 'M-my boyfriend?'

'Yes, Simon.'

Then she remembers the man who saved her in the park that night. The kind man with the nice smile and strong arms who'd carried her to the ambulance. She'd said goodbye to him at some point, but she'd never divulged where she lived. How had he known to knock down the door to her university room? How had he known she was in there trying to end her life? And why was he calling himself her boyfriend?

She could tell the nurse that she doesn't have a boyfriend and to send him away, but he's the only person, apart from the people who are paid to look after her, that seems to care about her welfare.

'Yes, please,' she says. 'Let him visit the next time he calls. When can I leave?'

The nurse smiles. 'Not until we're sure you're not a danger to yourself. A mental health professional will visit soon.'

'B-but I'm fine. It was just an accident.'

'Even so, we have a duty of care to ensure you're safe. You were brought into the hospital several nights ago too, weren't you?'

'Y-yes.'

The nurse lays a hand over hers. 'It's nothing to be ashamed of. Sometimes we need a bit of help to get over something horrible that's happened.'

She nods and lies back against her soft pillow, closing her eyes to sleep some more.

* * *

A few hours later, she's jostled awake by the kind nurse. 'Lisa, love, your boyfriend's here to see you.'

She glances past the nurse and sees Simon standing in the doorway, holding a box of chocolates. He nods at the nurse as she walks past him to leave and then comes and stands next to her bed.

'I tried to bring flowers, but they wouldn't allow them in here,' he says, placing the box of chocolates on the table beside the bed.

'That's okay,' she says timidly. 'What are you doing here?'

'I came to make sure you were okay. I had to tell them I was your boyfriend otherwise they would have asked me too many questions.'

'It's fine. Were you the one who broke my door down?'

'Yes. If I'd left it much later, you wouldn't be here.'

'I guess that means you've saved my life twice now.'

He smiles. 'I guess it does.'

There's a long silence while Lisa contemplates what to say, but Simon fills it by asking, 'Do you have anyone you'd like me to call?'

'No.'

'Parents?'

'No.'

'Friends.'

She shakes her head. 'I can't tell my friends. I'll be okay. Maybe I'll get some help from the therapist they offered me.'

She sees Simon's left eye twitch. 'Trust me, therapists are never the answer. All you need is someone to support you, and be there for you. I want to be that person, if you'll let me, Lisa.'

She's touched by his kind words, but she barely knows him.

'How did you know where I lived?' she asks.

Simon stares blankly for several seconds, his eye twitching again. 'When you were taken to hospital the other night after I found you, you asked me to fill out your forms, remember? You told me your details, including your university address and I wrote them down for you.'

She nods, satisfied with his answer, even if she can't quite remember it happening.

'How did you know I was in there anyway?'

'I'd been messaging you, and you weren't answering, and, considering what had happened to you a few nights before, I was worried how you were handling it.'

She sighs softly, exhausted from the conversation. Her head aches and she wants to close her eyes and sleep again.

'I can tell you're tired,' he says. 'I'll leave you be. You have my number in your phone. Call me when you're going to be released and I'll pick you up, okay?'

'Okay, thank you.'

'My pleasure.' He leans forward and plants a gentle kiss on her forehead. 'I'll see you soon, Lisa.'

CHAPTER TWENTY-SIX

Holly

I'm not sure how long we stand in silence and stare at the dead body of Lisa's husband. It could have been ten seconds or ten minutes, but eventually, Penny takes a deep breath and says, 'Well, that escalated quickly.' It's hard to distinguish whether it's a joke or not, but she's not wrong.

The blood from his neck wound is spreading at an alarming rate across the polished floor and there's arterial spray across the walls, worktops and pretty much everywhere. It looks as if someone has just walked around with a paintbrush and flicked red paint everywhere. I take a step back to avoid the oozing puddle soaking into my fluffy socks. Lisa is still leaning over the body. I'm not sure what she's doing, but she's just staring at Simon, her face only inches from his.

'Um . . . I guess we should start cleaning up?' says Penny, turning to a nearby cupboard. She takes out a mop and bucket and another bucket of cleaning products. I catch a glimpse of her Hinch cupboard and silently approve of all the products lined up in order. I wonder if Mrs Hinch has any tips for getting blood off the walls and ceiling . . . probably best not to ask her, though.

'We're not calling the police?' I ask, even though I already know the answer. Penny's just shot a man with an illegal gun and there's a whole wall of notes in the office pod, which plans his murder, albeit not in this way.

'No, we're not,' says Penny. And that's the end of that.

'Lisa, babe . . . you okay?' I ask.

I'm a little worried about her. She's still kneeling in the puddle of blood, staring down at the body, barely moving an inch. Penny and I look at each other and decide to give her a few extra minutes. I sidestep the body and blood and join Penny at her side.

'What's the plan, boss?' I'm proud of how calm I'm staying.

'Get rid of the body and clean up. Delete the CCTV footage. Get rid of the gun. Continue to step two.'

'Got it. Should we be worried about your neighbours hearing a gunshot?'

'No. They're all at work this time of the day and the nearest neighbour is at least five hundred yards away. Plus, the silencer was pretty effective. Be a dear and grab the extra absorbent kitchen roll from the Hinch cupboard, will you?'

I give her a side-eye. 'Are you okay? Why are you speaking like that?'

'Like what?'

'I don't know . . . just . . . never mind.' Penny is probably suffering from shock. She has just shot a guy in self-defence and has his blood all over her. She looks like Carrie from the Stephen King film. I grab the kitchen roll.

'I think we're going to need more than one roll,' I say.

Penny nods, then walks calmly over to the kitchen sink and vomits into it.

Shit.

She's not okay.

I don't know what to do. I should be more panicked. I should be freaking out, but I'm not. For once, I'm the calm one and considering I hadn't wanted to even do this in the first place, I think I'm doing a decent job of holding it together.

Lisa stands up and blinks several times as if she's coming out of a deep trance. 'We can do this. Penny, do you have anything we can roll him up in?'

Penny wipes her mouth. 'The hallway carpet and I have a load of old sheets too.'

'Good. We're going to bury him in the garden. Do you have a wheelbarrow so we can move him?'

'In the shed . . . Where in the garden? I don't want him poisoning my roses.'

Lisa glances out the window. 'What's that right over in the far corner?'

Penny and I glance to where she's pointing. 'It's a sunken trampoline,' replies Penny. 'It's getting filled in next week because the kids don't use it anymore. I'm having about two tonnes of earth and rocks delivered.'

'What's at the bottom? Can we dig a hole easily?'

'Sure, it's just dirt down there.'

'Perfect.'

* * *

Ten minutes later, Simon is rolled up in the hallway carpet and wrapped in numerous sheets. We remove his wallet with his credit cards and ID too. It takes all three of us to lift him into the wheelbarrow, bending our legs and keeping our backs flat. The personal trainer in me wants to ensure we don't pull a muscle while lifting a heavy load. Penny pushes the wheelbarrow into the garage, out of sight. We leave him there and then walk over to the sunken trampoline to check it out. We've all changed our clothes because two out of the three of us were covered in blood and the last thing we want is for some passers-by to see us. However, pushing a wheelbarrow with a large lump in it that looks suspiciously like a body won't help us either, hence hiding it in the garage until the hole is ready.

Penny and I kneel at the edge of the large rectangle. It's going to be tricky to remove the springs and supports, but we get to work. Lisa grabs some shovels from the shed. When the trampoline itself is pulled back, we're left with a hole in the ground about ten feet long, six feet wide and roughly four feet deep. There's a lot of debris and water at the bottom, but otherwise it's the perfect place to bury the body, especially as two tonnes of earth and rock are getting dumped on top next week.

Penny makes us all some cool drinks from the tiki hut and Lisa starts digging. Due to my disability, I realise I can't use a shovel very well, so I head back indoors and start cleaning the kitchen, leaving the other two to dig. We don't say much. At this point, there isn't a lot to say. We know what needs to be done and it needs to be done as quickly as possible, and spending our energy talking isn't going to help us get the job done.

An hour later, Penny calls me over. The hole is finished. They've managed to dig down a further four feet and made the hole roughly three feet wide by five feet long. Penny and Lisa go and retrieve the wheelbarrow, then tip it up and we all watch as Simon tumbles out and into the hole. He remains wrapped up in the rug and sheets, and we have to manoeuvre his body a bit to get him to fit. But once he's in, Penny throws the gun into the hole with him and then makes short work of covering him in dirt.

Now, instead of blood, we're covered in mud, so we change our clothes again before getting to work on finishing the kitchen. I made a decent start, but it still takes almost three hours to clean it. Penny called Aunt Silvia several hours ago and told her we'd be there later than planned. The kids are both fine and enjoying playing with all the animals on the farm and have already been trekking with Aunt Silvia in the fields.

Finally, the white tiles and worktops are gleaming again and there's not a single trace of blood anywhere. It also reeks of bleach and cleaning products, which is making my head a little dizzy. Next, we all take hot showers, then burn the blood-soaked clothes in the fireplace in the lounge. It takes a little while, but by four in the afternoon, we're finished.

We haven't eaten since breakfast, my stomach is gurgling and I'm feeling a little sick, so while I wait for Penny to finish showering, I go outside for some fresh air. I lean against the low wall and stare out across the garden, the sunken trampoline visible, hiding its dark secret.

Thank fuck this day is almost over. Maybe tomorrow will be better. Maybe tomorrow we can figure a way out of this mess we're all in. How exactly do we move forwards from here? Eventually, Simon's absence will be noticed by his friends and family. It's only a matter of time before things start unravelling.

'You okay?'

I turn and see Lisa walking towards me. She has a blanket wrapped around her shoulders, despite the warm afternoon. 'Yes, just getting some air.'

Lisa stands next to me, and we look across the garden in silence for several minutes, listening to the birds chirping and the leaves rustling.

'How do you feel?' I ask her.

'Free,' she replies. 'I still can't believe he was the one who raped me. What kind of monster does that and then pretends to rescue someone, marries them, and then abuses them for years, thinking he's doing her a favour? It's unthinkable. I think he tried to do it before, you know.'

'What do you mean?'

'A few weeks before I was raped, another girl was raped in the same park. She ended up killing herself. She actually killed herself five days before I was raped.'

'Oh my God. You think he was raping girls, trying to find one he could control and abuse?'

'Possibly.'

'Did you see or hear anything else that night?'

'What do you mean?'

'Was it just him or did he have an accomplice or anything?'

Lisa is silent for a moment. 'I don't remember there being anyone else there.'

Approaching footsteps make us both turn around. Penny walks up and joins us. She's freshly washed and has wet hair.

It's like we don't even need words to communicate anymore. We just stare wordlessly into the distance, soaking up the sun's rays, feeling the warmth on our faces.

'Are you okay, Penny?' asks Lisa. I'm pretty sure what she really means to ask is, *Are you okay after just killing a man?*

'I'm surprisingly okay,' she says. 'We're all safe. That's the main thing.' She turns to me. 'Now, we have to focus on Will and whether he's responsible for that woman's death. Drake is still going to be the last one.'

I nod. 'I suppose I should go home and perhaps gather some more information if I can.'

'Do you feel safe going back to him?'

'I . . . I'm not sure.'

'Then we'll all come with you.'

'What about your kids?'

'Aunt Silvia is happy to look after them. I'll just pop back and say goodbye. They're fine. My kids are amazingly resilient.'

Lisa squirms slightly at Penny's remark. If there is something she wants to say, she doesn't say it. It's almost impossible to notice how Lisa won't make eye contact with Penny. She seems perfectly fine with her otherwise, but why won't she look her in the eye?

I nod my agreement. 'Okay, so it's settled. Tomorrow, we go to Edinburgh.'

'What are we going to do with Simon's car?' asks Lisa.

We all turn around on the spot and look at the car in the driveway. 'I'm not digging another hole,' says Penny. 'Not one that big.'

I let out a laugh. 'Let's dump it somewhere and then we'll rent a car using Simon's credit card and drive that to Edinburgh. Plus, I still need to delete the CCTV footage and change the password so Drake can't access it.'

* * *

That's what we do. We head to the farm in Penny's car and spend the night with the kids and Aunt Silvia. The twins are a little confused about why we're all going away and not staying on the farm with them, but Lori leans in close to Lisa as she's hugging her goodbye the next morning and whispers something in her ear. Lisa nods and then Lori beams, turns to her mum and says, 'Good luck, Mummy!'

We drive into the nearest town, rent a car using Simon's credit card, and start the long drive to Edinburgh, but Penny and I share the driving. It's a fun road trip and we stop for several coffees and food along the way.

We decide not to tell Will that Lisa and Penny are with me. They're going to be checking into a hotel nearby so we can meet up. I call into work saying I'm sick and cancel all my clients for the next week.

I say goodbye to the girls and drag my suitcase up the front steps to my house. I'm so tired I can barely keep my eyes open. Plus, I'm sweating, yet I feel cold. Maybe I'm coming down with something. It wouldn't surprise me. My body is running on fumes. I've eaten nothing healthy for the past few days and have not been getting nearly enough sleep. Plus, the stress of cleaning up a murder with my friends is finally catching up with me.

I crack open the front door and am met by a stale waft of body odour and mouldy food. I hold my breath as I step into the house, but then have to let it go when I see the state of the place. How is it possible one person can make this much mess in a few days?

The source of the smell hits me like a smack in the face when I enter the kitchen. Dirty takeaway containers litter the sides. Unwashed plates and cutlery are piled high next to the sink. A mound of soiled washing is dumped next to the washing machine, and the fridge door is ajar.

'What the fuck! Will!' I don't even know if he's home, but I'm met by silence, so I take that to mean he's out. I grab my phone and call him. He picks up almost instantly.

'Hey, babe!'

'Don't "hey babe" me! The house is an absolute state!'

'Oh, you're home already?'

'Yes, I'm fucking home already.'

'Are you not capable of cleaning anything?'

'Don't have a go at me. You know how hard it's been for me lately what with losing my job.'

'Yes, must be so hard for you to sit around and do nothing all day.'

'I've been out.'

'Doing what?'

'Stuff with Oliver.'

I roll my eyes and squeeze the bridge of my nose. 'I can't live like this. How long are you going to be? I need help to clean this up.' I've only just finished cleaning up a murder scene and now I have to clean up my husband's mess too.

'I won't be back till late.'

'What are you doing?'

'I just told you. Stuff with Oliver.'

'What stuff?' I think I'm about to lose it. My voice cracks.

'Stuff! Get off my back!'

I grind my teeth together. 'Are you expecting me to clean all this up by myself?'

'Hey, if you want the place clean, then you clean it. I don't mind it the way it is.'

'You don't . . .' I stop and take a breath. My blood pressure is rising to the point of boiling. No. Calm down. I must remember what Penny said. She told me not to pick fights with him, to keep him on my side and act as normal as possible. But what she didn't say was how I was supposed to react to coming home and finding my husband has turned it into a pigsty and is expecting me to clean it up.

I take a deep breath. 'Fine,' I say. 'Have a nice time with Oliver.'

'Wait . . . what . . .'

I hang up.

I look up at the ceiling and scream. I let it all out. Everything. The past few days come rushing up all at once and it feels good to scream. I kick the bin that's overflowing, and the contents tumble around my feet. I leap back in disgust,

162

picking my way around the rubbish as a load of oil seeps out of the bag.

I send a picture of the mess to the chat group with the caption: *What do I do?*

A few seconds later, Penny replies with: *We'll be ten minutes.*

It's times like this that make me question how we've managed all these years living so far apart from each other. Usually, I'd send a message and they'd reply in the group chat. Penny would send a long voice message that I'd have to put on 2x speed, and they'd give me some advice on how to proceed, but this time it's different. This time they are my physical reinforcements, and they turn up at my door less than ten minutes later, by which time I've managed to locate the black bin bags and made a small dent in clearing the kitchen worktops.

'Fucking hell,' says Penny as she steps inside. She squeezes her nose between her fingers. 'He made all this mess in four days?'

I sigh angrily. 'I swear to God, I don't even care if he killed that woman or not . . . I'm going to kill him myself soon.'

Lisa takes the almost-full bin bag from my clenched hand. 'Don't worry. We'll have this place cleaned up in no time.'

'It's not the point, though, is it?'

'No, it's not,' says Penny. 'But there's no point worrying about it now. We have to stick to the plan and that means cleaning this shithole so you can keep your lazy-ass of a husband on your side and not worry about the fact you suspect him of cheating and/or murdering some woman and getting her knocked up.' Penny exhales loudly. 'Urggh, I need a drink,' she adds. 'I'm getting a serious case of déjà vu.'

'At least there's no body to get rid of this time,' I say.

'Yet,' adds Lisa.

* * *

It takes two hours of solid cleaning before the house resembles a place fit for human living. It smells a lot better too once the

163

rancid food containers are emptied and I've sprayed half a bottle of Febreze and Dettol on every available surface.

Penny and Lisa left ten minutes ago and now I'm making myself some food, wondering when my husband will be home. I had to pop to the local shop to get proper food because it seems Will has been surviving off takeaway and beer. There wasn't a single fresh vegetable in the fridge.

I hate having to do this; to lie and pretend that everything is okay when it's not. I'm not sure how I'm going to get the truth out of him. I don't know what to say or where I need to look to get the information I need.

I take my tuna pasta bake to the sofa, along with my very large glass of wine and adopt the position for the evening. I wish I was with the girls right now.

Food eaten, wine drunk, I wash up and return to the sofa, eventually falling asleep in front of the television and waking up when the door slams. I wipe a slither of drool from my mouth and sit up straight just as my darling husband strolls into the room.

I'm expecting him to be blind drunk, so am pleasantly surprised to see that he's sober.

'Hi,' I say.

'Welcome home.'

'Thanks. Did you have a good evening?'

'Yeah. Looks like you had fun too.' Will glances around at the clean house and I resist the urge to choke him to death right now for being so sexist.

'Yes, loads of fun was had,' I reply dryly.

'Cool. I'm going for a shower.'

'Great!' I say with a grin.

Will narrows his eyes at me, probably thinking I'm acting strange and then turns, strips off his clothes as he walks to the bathroom and dumps them all on the floor in front of the washing bin.

I count to ten before I explode.

Then, I get up, walk to the clothes and bend down to pick them up. The shower turns on and he starts singing so

164

I know I have at least fifteen minutes before he makes an appearance, so I stay crouched on the floor and rummage through the pockets in his jeans and inspect the clothes.

I pull out a receipt. It's dated today, only a few hours ago and is from my favourite restaurant, The Peking Duck, in Edinburgh town centre. Two meals were bought and two glasses of wine. I take a picture of the receipt and send it to the girls before moving on to the other pocket.

He's left his phone in there.

Rookie mistake.

My hands tremble as I type in his password, which has never changed in the past two years. The phone unlocks and now I don't know what to do. Where do I look first?

WhatsApp.

The usual messages are there from me, Oliver, and his mum. A few other random male friends who I vaguely know about, but no other names. No women's names.

Okay . . . Facebook.

I think back to the profile I found of him with a fake name. He's automatically logged in to his normal account, so I click on the swap profile button and there it is. His second profile with the name Malcolm York.

My heart stops.

It's true.

I lick my lips and look up instinctively at the bathroom door, ensuring it's still closed. He's still singing so I'm safe, but this feels too risky. But I don't have time to think now.

I press on the profile and the screen changes. I click on his followers list and scan the names. They are all women. Every. Single. One. They're all around my age, attractive and appear to be single as they don't have anyone in their profile picture with them. I check the messages and there are at least ten chats that are active.

A message pops up as I'm looking through them and it makes me flinch so badly I almost drop the phone. I know I shouldn't, but the tip of my finger presses on the new message before I can think about what I'm doing.

165

It's from a woman called Christina Bell.

Hey, Malcolm. It was great to meet you tonight. I had a wonderful time. Maybe next time you can come back to mine. Thanks for dessert ☺ *xx*

The fact the receipt I found shows no dessert listed makes my stomach clench. I quickly select the button that changes the message back to unread. Then, not knowing where else to look and with merely minutes to spare, I open his photo gallery. There's a folder in the gallery called WHORES.

I open it.

And a garbled cry catches in my throat.

I shake my head and squeeze my eyes shut just in case I'm having some sort of horrible hallucination, but the pictures are still there when I open them again.

The shower switches off and the singing stops.

I lock the phone and put it back in his pocket before leaving his clothes on the floor where he left them. It takes everything I have to walk away and sit back down on the sofa.

My husband is cheating on me with another woman.

But that's not why my mouth is as dry as a desert and my body is shaking.

He has graphic pictures of dozens of other women too. Some tied up, some gagged. It's hard to tell whether it's consensual or not. And a lot of the women look like me . . .

One of them is Leanne Prince, who's now dead.

CHAPTER TWENTY-SEVEN

Lisa

I don't know how to be in the same room as Penny. I know something isn't right between Drake and her daughter and it's killing me to keep it a secret, but if Penny finds out it will destroy her. She should know, but if she did, then she might actually kill her husband with her bare hands and then everything we've done so far will have been for nothing. Penny cannot be the one to kill Drake. The only thing that's keeping me going is knowing I'll be the one to kill him in the end. Either me or Holly, but most likely me. I can't see Holly being able to kill anyone, especially Drake, since she used to be friends with him. I always found their friendship to be an unusual one. For years, I was certain they'd hooked up at university, but Holly was always insistent that they hadn't, that they were just friends. But since he cheated on Penny, she dropped him like a stone, choosing Penny's friendship over his.

Our hotel room is basic but suitable for our needs. We're in one room with a double bed. It's unclear how long we'll be staying here, but it's comfortable enough for now. Penny joked earlier that we haven't shared a bed since we were kids on a sleepover, and she's right. It's been a long time. We used to have lots of sleepovers when we were growing up. I remember one night when we all set up camp in our sleeping bags on the living-room floor and watched scary movies until two o'clock in the morning. First up was *The Blair Witch Project* and we finished it feeling very let down by its lack of horror when we'd been promised by the guy at Blockbuster that it was the scariest movie ever made. However, Holly then proceeded to get exceptionally freaked out when she looked through the glass of the living-room door and saw an eerie reflection staring back at her, which turned out to be her own. Another time, we prank-called the boy Penny was casually dating at the time but had ended up in hysterical laughter because we couldn't keep up the charade for more than thirty seconds.

It had been a simpler time back then, before we grew up and life happened, jobs happened, husbands happened, and kids happened. Sometimes I wish I could rewind back to the start, back before that night in the park or before I'd even left for university. I'd have made so many different decisions. What would my life have been like if that night had never happened, and Simon never raped me in that park? What if he'd found someone else?

After that night, I'd spent several days locked in my halls room, refusing to eat or see my parents or my friends. I even attempted to take my own life, but Simon had somehow saved me again, even though I had no idea how. If I'd known then what I knew now, I would never have spoken to him again. But hindsight is a wonderful thing, or a devastating thing.

After he saved me a second time, he asked to meet me at a local coffee shop. I walked to the coffee shop to meet Simon at the time he suggested. I went inside, pushing open the door, and stepped into the warm, inviting café.

He was already there waiting for me, a large mocha on the table in front of the empty chair. I have no idea how he knew what my favourite drink was, but now, thinking back, it was easy. He'd been following me for a long time. All the clues were there, but I just didn't see them because I hadn't known what I was looking for, or that they were even there. Now, I could easily go back and point out every single red flag.

He stood up as I approached the table and kissed my cheek. 'I'm so happy you decided to meet me. How are you?'

'Fine,' I said, sliding onto the chair, keeping my head down. It was a lie. I wasn't fine.

'I've been thinking about you a lot,' he said.

We locked eyes and I felt myself being sucked into his dreamy gaze. My cheeks heated as he smiled at me, showing off his perfect teeth. I reached for my mocha, but as I did, he grabbed my hand and squeezed tight. I flinched but allowed him to hold it.

'I know what happened to you was awful,' he said, 'but I promise I'll never let anything bad happen to you again. Please don't try and hurt yourself again. You deserve a man who treats you like a queen. You deserve so much more than I can give you, but I want to try. I want to protect you.'

'You don't even know me,' I said. I should have been wary of him being so forward, but I wasn't. I was lapping his attention up and loving every minute. Here was this gorgeous man who wanted to be my protector. Who was I to turn him down and say no?

'But I want to know you. I believe I can make you happy, Lisa.'

And I believed him.

After that, we became a proper couple and there'd never been anyone else. Holly and Penny were shocked that I fell for him so fast, but they never knew about the night we met in the park. I told them I met him at a café.

As far as I knew, he'd never cheated on me during our relationship and marriage. He'd tell me over and over throughout the years that I was *his* and didn't belong to anyone else. The first time he said that it made me feel special and wanted and desired, and that's exactly how I felt, but as the years went by, I realised it wasn't romantic. It wasn't him making me feel special or desired. It was about control and dominance and . . .

'Hey, are you okay?'

I look up as Penny steps out of the small bathroom wrapped in a towel. 'Yes, fine.'

'You look a bit pale.'

'Tired, I guess. And worried about Holly.'

'She'll be okay. Has she messaged back yet?'

I pick up my phone just as it springs to life. 'Holly? You okay?' I put the phone on the bed and press the speaker button so Penny can listen.

'Will met up with another woman tonight. I think she might be in danger. I found photos of women gagged and tied up on his phone. What do we do?'

'What the hell?' says Penny. 'Maybe he just likes a bit of kink.'

'I don't know. I can't tell whether they're consensual pictures or not. The women don't look scared, but how much can you really tell from a picture? I didn't have time to send them to you because Will was going to catch me looking through his phone. But there were pictures of Leanne Prince, the woman who's dead.'

'Was she alive in the photos?'

'Yes, and she was wearing the same underwear she was found dead in.'

'Are you sure?'

'I think so, yeah.' Holly's voice rises an octave or two yet is also a harsh whisper. 'Fuck. I'm living with a murderer. What do we do?'

'Okay,' says Penny, pulling the towel tighter around her chest. 'Let's think about this for a moment. It's not proof he killed her, but it's proof he was with her on the night she died. Holly, you need to decide whether you want to take this up with the police . . . or we sort it out . . . *ourselves*.'

The phone is silent for several moments.

'Well . . . we've come this far,' says Holly. 'I don't trust him.'

I let out a sigh. 'Looks like we're up.'

'Are you sure?' asks Penny, laying a hand on my shoulder.

'Yes. I'm sure. Has Will spoken to you about anything, Holly? Does he seem suspicious?'

'I've no idea. He's just acting normal as far as I can tell. I don't think Will knows anything . . . Wait . . . hang on . . . Oh, shit!'

There's a loud bang, followed by a yelp.

The line goes dead.

'Holly?' asks Penny.

'Holly!' we shout together.

I look at Penny. 'Get dressed . . . quick!'

* * *

It feels like an eternity before we're at Holly's door, banging on it with our fists like two women possessed. I can barely breathe. If anything happens to Holly, then I'll never forgive myself. She knew the risks, but we still let her be alone with her husband, knowing what he could be capable of.

Holly isn't answering her phone. It's been switched off. Fear grips my insides to the point I can't bear it another second. Then, the door opens.

'What the fuck,' says Will as he sees us standing on his doorstep. It's about ten o'clock at night. He's shirtless, barefoot and holding a beer. He stares down at us with a frown on his face. 'What are you two doing here?'

I gasp, wanting to say something, but Penny gets there first. 'Where's Holly?' she demands.

Will chuckles. 'How the hell should I know?'

'She was here less than ten minutes ago.'

'Yeah, but now she's gone. Must have popped to the shops or something.'

Penny takes two steps up to the front door so she's level with Will, squaring up to him. He still towers over her by several inches. 'Look here, you good-for-nothing piece of shit, you'd better start talking right now and tell us where Holly is, or I swear to God I'll pull out every one of your disgusting teeth and make you swallow them.'

I attempt to keep my face deadpan, reiterating the same feelings, but all I can do is dart my eyes side to side and up and down, attempting to catch a glimpse of Holly behind where Will is standing. Perhaps she's hurt? I can't hear any cries for help. Maybe she's unconscious somewhere.

Will lowers the beer bottle from the lips. 'What are you two accusing me of exactly?'

'Well, you're a cheating liar, for a start.'

'Oh yeah? You got any proof?'

'Yes, we do . . . *Malcolm York*.'

That seems to do the trick. What little colour Will has in his face drains away and his eyes dart to the side, as if he's thinking of making a dash for it. If he does run it's not like Penny or I can run after him, not for long anyway. Holly's the fit one out of the three of us.

Will curls his top lip and points a stiff finger directly at Penny's face, but amazingly she doesn't even flinch. My mouth turns dry as I realise the severity of the situation we're now in.

'I don't know what you two think you know or what the hell Holly's been telling you, but you've got it wrong. All wrong. I haven't done anything.'

'Then where is she?' snaps Penny without missing a beat.

Will overemphasises shrugging his shoulders and holds both his palms up towards the ceiling. 'I don't know, and I don't fucking care. She's been acting weird lately.'

Penny narrows her eyes. 'We're watching you.'

Will rolls his eyes. 'You don't scare me. You two are just a couple of housewives who need to get back in their place.'

Penny turns red. 'You sexist pig.'

I reach forward and grab Penny's sleeve, pulling her away from Will. 'Let's just go,' I say quietly.

'Yeah. Listen to your *friend*,' says Will, ensuring the final word is laden with sarcasm.

Penny steps back down to my level. 'This isn't over!' she shouts just before the door slams shut.

CHAPTER TWENTY-EIGHT

Penny
Six and a half years ago

Her husband is away for work overseas, and she's delighted to have their little London house to herself for a few nights, so she treats herself to a face pack, a mini manicure and a bottle of white wine. They've only been married for three months, and she misses him already. His work has got very busy, and he's said he'll be away a lot over the next few months, travelling. She doesn't mind, as she knows he earns a lot and it will help them save money to buy their own place eventually, one they can do up and make their own.

But it doesn't stop her from missing him.

Her phone vibrates against her leg, and she picks it up, already knowing who it is. It's Holly. The poor girl is severely hungover after a wild night out with her work friends, and she and Lisa have been sending her funny memes all day to cheer her up.

Holly: *Finally feeling more human after a greasy cheeseburger.*

Penny: *Jesus, girl, how much did you drink last night?*

Holly: *A lot.*

Lisa: *More than at Penny's hen do?*

Holly: *Yes.*

Penny: *Dear God, I'm surprised you're even alive. What did you get up to?*

Holly: . . .

Penny: *Hols?*

Holly: . . . *Not much. I don't remember a lot of the night.*

The sound of a key sliding into a lock makes her jump. She drops her phone on the sofa and gets to her feet. Who the hell is that? It can't be Drake. He's not due home for another few days.

'Penny, it's just me.'

'Drake? What the hell?'

The front door opens and her husband steps into the hallway, looking slightly dishevelled. His hair is sticking up randomly and he has five o'clock shadow. She greets him with a hug and a kiss, but something's wrong. His whole body is tense, and as soon as he can, he moves away and into the kitchen.

'Are you okay? What's wrong?'

'Nothing, I . . .'

'Why didn't you message me to say you were coming home early?'

Drake drops his suitcase on the floor, heads to the fridge and pulls out a bottle of beer, popping off the cap using the thingamajig on the wall. He takes a long drink, almost downing the whole thing in one go.

'I wanted to surprise you,' he says.

'Well, it's certainly a surprise. Did you have a good flight?'

'Um, yeah. It was fine.'

'Are you hungover?'

'A bit, yeah. Sorry, had a late night.'

She's still convinced something isn't right with her husband. He finishes his beer and drops it into the recycling bin. 'I'm going to take a shower.' And he walks out of the room without another word.

She returns to the sofa, picks up her phone and texts the girls.

Penny: *Drake just walked in from his work thing a few days early.*

Lisa: *Ah, that's a nice surprise.*

Penny: *Yeah, I guess . . .*

Holly: *Drake's there? What did he say?*

Penny: *Nothing much, just that he wanted to surprise me, and he had a late night last night. He looks rough. I can tell something isn't quite right. It's just a feeling.*

Holly: *What do you mean?*

Penny: *Not sure yet.*

Lisa: *Maybe he'll be a little more forthcoming once he feels better.*

Penny: *Yeah, maybe . . .*

She places her phone down and sighs. Maybe she's wrong. Maybe he's just hungover.

But the next morning, her husband can barely look her in the eye as he makes breakfast. She's sitting at the small kitchen table, sipping a coffee while he fries bacon with his back to her. When he speaks it's in a low, slow voice.

'Penny, I need to tell you something.'

'Okay . . .' Her heart starts thumping hard.

'I wasn't on a work trip. I lied to you. I'm sorry.'

'Then where were you?'

'I . . . it doesn't matter where I was, but . . . I slept with someone else.'

The floor seems to swallow her up and her whole world slips away down a black hole. She almost chokes on her coffee. 'What did you just say?'

Drake finally turns around to look at her, tears brimming in his eyes. 'I cheated on you. I'm so sorry. I didn't mean for it to happen.'

She doesn't even have the capacity to utter words. How could he do this to her? They've been married for three months. Three fucking months! They're supposed to still be in the honeymoon phase, for fuck's sake, having sex at every opportunity, but he's fucked someone else and . . .

'Who is she?'

Drake shakes his head. 'A work person. You don't know her. She's married too. It was a mistake.'

'Get out.'

'What?'

She springs to her feet and shouts, 'Get out!' as she throws the coffee mug at the wall next to him. It smashes and spills across the hob, the oil in the pan spitting angrily.

Drake flinches and ducks out of the way. 'Penny, calm down, okay? We can talk about this. I swear it only happened once and it'll never happen again, I promise. Please . . . I love you. I just couldn't carry on with lying to you. I thought you'd appreciate my honesty.'

She laughs, soundly slightly unhinged. 'You thought I'd appreciate your honesty? Really, Drake? Or did you just tell me because you felt too fucking guilty?'

'Well, yes, that too.'

'Get out. Now.'

'Penny . . .'

'Get out!'

Drake holds up his hands and backs away. 'Okay, fine, I'll give you some space, but I'm not giving up on us.' He leaves her standing at the kitchen table, trembling so badly that she has to prop herself up so her legs don't buckle.

She's broken. She never thought he'd cheat. Not ever. She trusted him with her whole heart and now that trust is shattered into a million pieces. There's no way she can ever trust him again.

She needs her girls.

Penny: *Drake just admitted he cheated on me last night.*
Lisa: . . .

Holly: . . .

Lisa: *Oh my God! What!*

Holly: *Did he say with who?*

Penny: *Some skank from work. He didn't tell me her name. He said it was a one-time thing and that it didn't mean anything.*

Lisa: *Babe, I'm so sorry. Do you want me to call you?*

Penny: *Not yet. I may start crying and then never stop.*

Holly: . . . *I'm sorry, Penny.*

The next few days are a blur. Holly calls her several times and just listens as she blames herself, even though she knows it's not her fault. Lisa calls too, and even though her husband tells her in the background to stop spending so much time on the phone, she continues to call, as Penny explains that she wants a divorce.

She can't stay married to a man she doesn't trust, or like. Everything she used to love about him has now gone and been replaced by everything she hates about him. She doesn't want him near her. She spends several hours vomiting one morning. She's barely been able to eat properly, so not much comes up. She sits next to the toilet bowl and cries, then that's when she notices the small plastic container next to the toilet, the one she uses to keep her sanitary pads and tampons in.

She hasn't had to use them for a while.

Oh, shit . . .

CHAPTER TWENTY-NINE

Penny

It takes all the restraint I have left in my body to not punch Will in the face and continue punching him until he resembles a bloody mess of skin and blood on the doorstep. Other than my own husband, I don't think I've hated a man more . . . maybe Simon. Bloody hell, we sure can pick them. What does our choice of husbands say about us? Men like them are the reason women are afraid to walk home alone at night. Lisa is living proof of that, and it makes me sick to think of what happened to her in the park all those years ago. How have all three of us been so blind and not seen how evil our husbands truly are? Or have we always known yet stayed with them out of sheer convenience?

As Lisa and I stand on the pavement outside Holly's house, I take a few moments to compose myself. 'Try calling her again,' I say. I'm not ready to give up on her. Lisa redials, but the phone immediately goes to the answering machine.

'Holly, where are you? Are you okay? Please call us back as soon as you can.' Lisa shakes her head. 'What are we supposed to do? This is all so messed-up. It's all got out of hand.'

She starts trembling and tears leak from her eyes as she puts her phone away.

I wrap my arms around my friend and squeeze gently. 'It'll be okay. We'll find her, I promise.'

'Should we contact the police and report her missing? Or do we have to wait twenty-four hours first?'

'Actually, that's a common myth. Here in the UK at least, you can report someone missing as soon as you suspect it, but I still don't think we should, considering what we've done recently. I don't want to draw attention to ourselves while all this is going on.'

'But what about Holly? This wasn't part of the plan.'

'I think it's safe to say that the plan's gone out the fucking window now.'

Lisa nods against my shoulder as we walk back towards our car. 'Will must be lying about where she is. It took us less than ten minutes to get here from our hotel, and we heard a struggle of some sort over the phone. Something's happened to her. She wouldn't ignore us like this.'

It's true. Yet, in that time frame she's disappeared. Either she's injured and unconscious inside her house or she's escaped and run off and has broken her phone or left it behind. If her phone was working and she had it in her possession, she would have called us by now to tell us she was safe.

We reach the car and lean against it side by side. We can't head back to the hotel to sleep, not with Holly missing.

'I think we need to watch the house,' I say, glancing back down the road towards it. I've always liked the little village where Holly lives. It's so quiet and looks like something out of a romance novel. 'If Will goes anywhere, I want to know about it.'

'Good idea,' whispers Lisa. She takes a deep breath. 'My heart won't stop racing.'

'I know what you mean. It feels as if we're on a roller-coaster, doesn't it?'

'Do you regret starting this whole thing?'

'Not one bit.'

'Me neither. I just hope Holly's okay.'

Our phones remain silent and all messages to our WhatsApp group remain unread by Holly. Things aren't looking good and it's taking a lot of effort for me to remain calm. Exhaustion lingers in the background too, threatening to overwhelm me, but I fight against it, determined to keep going. Because I doubt that fucking dickhead will be going to sleep, so neither will I. For all we know, he's disposing of our friend's body right now.

'Come on. Let's find a place where we can keep an eye on the house,' I say, dragging Lisa back up the road. There's a small lane almost directly opposite Holly's house that works well, so we set up camp there. I wish I'd brought an extra jacket. Even though the evening is warm, there's a strong wind that's setting my teeth chattering.

My phone vibrates in my pocket. I grab it, my fingers trembling, but my heart sinks when I see the name on the screen.

'Don't answer it,' says Lisa, shaking her head.

'I have to keep an eye on what he's doing and make sure he doesn't suspect anything.' I answer the phone to my husband. 'Hi, Drake.'

'Penny, what the fuck? Where are you? Where are the fucking kids? I've just got home, and you're all gone.'

Fuck.

What the hell is he doing at home? He's supposed to be on the other side of the world right now. My heart almost stops as I realise how close he is to my babies.

'I . . . I took them for a spur-of-the-moment trip to Legoland.'

Lisa looks at me in horror as it dawns on her what I'm saying.

'That's bullshit. What's going on? Why wouldn't you tell me you've taken them?'

My mouth opens, but my tongue refuses to work. I have no words, which is very unlike me. What am I supposed to say?

Lisa grabs me and yanks me to the side and ducks down, almost forcing us to collide with a brick wall. 'What the . . .'

Lisa puts a finger over her mouth and then points across the street. 'Penny? What's going on? Why are you not answering me?' shouts Drake.

I cover the phone with my hand and peer out from behind the wall just in time to see Will coming out of his house dressed in a dark jacket with the hood up. Talk about looking suspicious.

I make a decision that I know will come back to bite me in the butt, and hang up on my husband. He immediately calls back, but I ignore it, then block his number. 'I'll follow Will. You let yourself into the house and look around for Holly or any clues as to what's happened to her.'

'Are you sure you don't want me to come with you?' asks Lisa.

'No, I'll keep my phone on. Call me if you find anything.'

'Be careful.'

We quickly hug and then I push myself away from the wall and jog to catch up with Will who's almost at the end of the road. I turn and watch Lisa let herself into the house using the spare key Holly gave us and then follow Will, using everything in my arsenal of knowledge of how to tail someone without being spotted.

CHAPTER THIRTY

Lisa

I don't like the idea of splitting up. In fact, it sends shivers down my spine and a knot forms in my stomach, but it's what we need to do. We must find Holly and make sure she's safe and we need to keep an eye on Will too, so there's no other option but to split up. Holly has to be still inside the house because Will wouldn't have had time to move her before Penny and I had shown up at his door. The thought of her bound and gagged somewhere makes my stomach clench. I can't think about anything right now except finding my friend and getting out of this house as quickly as possible. I just hope Penny will be okay on her own, following Will.

As soon as I close the front door, I turn left and enter the open-plan lounge and dining room. I don't even know where to start looking. I've only been in this house once before (twice if I count a few hours ago when we came to clean) when I came to visit Holly several years ago when she and Will first bought it. They've done a lot of work on it since because the place needed total renovation. I doubt any of it is Will's handiwork. He doesn't seem like the handy type with a paintbrush or saw. Holly loved picking out paint samples and choosing the wallpaper, but she hired people to complete the jobs while she was at work. The lounge is a lovely forest green on one wall and the rest of the walls are cream, but I don't have time to stop and admire the decoration.

'Holly?' I call out, feeling foolish. As if Holly is just going to jump out and yell, 'Surprise, bitches!' and all of this is just some big joke.

The area smells clean and fresh after we scrubbed it earlier. A lingering waft of bleach tickles my nostrils as I breathe in and out as slowly as I can. I'm at risk of hyperventilating if I don't control the pressure building in my chest.

What am I even looking for other than signs of a struggle? Maybe I'll know when I see it. I'd had a good look around when we'd cleaned this place, but back then I'd been focused on cleaning and tidying. Now, I'm searching for clues as to what's happened to Holly.

I give up searching the lounge after five minutes and head upstairs to enter the main bedroom. The house is quiet; too quiet.

'Holly?' I call again, but all I hear in return is the creaking of the boards under my feet.

I close my eyes, steadying my racing heart, and listen.

A tiny scuttle. Like a mouse scurrying across floorboards. Above me.

I open my eyes and look up.

The attic.

Of course! If Will is going to stash Holly anywhere, then he'd use the attic, wouldn't he? Every thriller or police procedural I've ever read tells me that much.

I backtrack to the landing and look up at the small trapdoor in the ceiling. How the hell did he manage to get her up there so fast? I stand on tiptoes and pull on the cord, which dangles tantalisingly in front of me. A ladder automatically unfolds in front of me. I wish Penny were here because she has no fear, except when it comes to the safety of her children.

The idea of going into a dark attic by myself is enough to set the small hairs on the back of my neck tingling.

I creep up the first few rungs of the ladder and poke my head through the dark hole. A waft of warm, stale air greets me.

'Holly?'

Every muscle in my body is telling me to turn around and look somewhere else, but my heart is urging me to continue up the steps. I reach out a hand and feel around for a light switch, but I can't find one. As my eyes adjust to the dark, I see piles of boxes in the far corner and a few strange shapes, which look horribly like body bags.

Stop it. You've read too many thrillers.

Unable to find a light switch, I reach into my pocket, pull out my phone and turn on the torch function. Holding it above my head, I walk up the remaining few steps and crawl into the attic, unwilling to stand up straight for fear of cobwebs dangling from the ceiling tangling in my hair.

Taking a deep breath, I turn the torch onto the body-bag-looking shapes, which turn out to be a few spare rolls of carpet, which reminds me of the rug we used to roll Simon up in. My thoughts briefly turn to him, dead and cold in the ground underneath the sunken trampoline, and then I move on. I refuse to waste any more time thinking about the man who kept me prisoner for so many years and ruined my life. I exhale and turn my attention to the boxes, which are labelled *CHRISTMAS DECORATIONS* and *MISC.*

The attic itself is professionally boarded and isn't damp or leaking. There's even a large chest of drawers up here, although I have no idea how Holly and Will would have been able to squeeze it through the small trapdoor. Now I think about it properly, how the hell *had* they got it up here?

The urge to find out overwhelms the urge to keep searching for Holly. I approach the drawers and shine the light over them. They're at least twice the size of the trapdoor, and it doesn't look as if they can be easily taken apart. It's a solid piece of oak furniture. Quite expensive by the looks of it too, like from one of those high-end stores.

I pull the top drawer open. It sticks so I give it a quick yank, but there's nothing of interest inside bar a few pieces of paper which look like title deeds. I scan my eyes over them. They don't look very old. Apparently, this house used to belong to a man called Timothy Grant. Something about the name sticks in my brain and settles there, but I don't have the luxury of time to think about why it seems familiar, so I keep searching. The second drawer contains more stationery, pens and books, and the bottom drawer is empty. So much for that.

I shake my head, realising I'm being silly for focusing on such an unimportant detail. I'm here to search for Holly and clues. The boards under my feet are pale wood and creak slightly as I crawl over them towards the far corner.

There's plenty of space above my head, but my legs are shaking so badly I don't think I have the strength to stand. Plus, if I did stand, I probably would have missed the small, dark stain on the floor by the stack of boxes. I shuffle over to it and direct the torch down.

The small stain glows dark red.

Is that blood?

My heart leaps. It's an old stain. I reach out a finger and touch it, but my fingertip comes away clean. I hold it to the light to double check just as my phone vibrates.

I shriek and drop the phone, which lands face down on the floor, blocking out the torch beam. The space around me plunges into darkness. I've never been afraid of the dark, but here in the confined attic, I can't stop the fear from creeping over my skin.

The phone vibrates against the wooden floor, intensifying the sound. I reach down and pick it up, fumbling to slide my finger across the screen.

'Penny? Everything okay?'

'Yeah, yeah, all good. Just checking in. You found anything?'

'Not yet. I'm in their attic.'

'Urrggh, creepy. Well, I'm at a pub. He's sitting in a corner with a pint by himself.'

'Weird.'

'Yeah, I think he might be waiting for someone, so I'm settling in for a bit of a wait.'

'Okay, well, let me know if he leaves so I know to get out of here quickly.'

'Will do.'

'Bye.'

I hang up and the torch function lights up the area again, but I scream when a looming humanoid shadow towers next to me. Then laugh when I realise it belongs to me.

I stare at the red stain again. Maybe it's not blood. Maybe it's red paint. I lower my face so it's close to the floor. It's a small spot, about the size of a penny, but further into the darkness, I notice another stain, then another and another. And there's no red paint pot anywhere.

As I follow the spots, I get the same overwhelming urge to turn around, yet my brain is now telling me I need to keep following the trail. I reach the furthest point of the attic from the trapdoor where I entered. There's a wall blocking the way. I assume it's to separate this house from the next, but the wall isn't made of concrete blocks as I'd assume it would be; it's made of wood.

The stains stop at the wall.

I crouch to investigate and gasp as what I see begins to make sense. It's a wooden wall. And there's a door that leads from this house into next door's attic. There's no door handle, keyhole, or any visible means of opening the door, which means it can only be opened from the other side.

I press my ear against the wood.

Listening.

And hear a weak groan.

CHAPTER THIRTY-ONE

Penny

I manage to find a corner of the pub where I have a clear line of sight to Will, but he can't see me unless he gets up and moves. If he does, I can quickly turn my back on him and hide. I look like a typical person trying to avoid looking suspicious but failing miserably, however, I'm hoping no one pays me any attention. I'm good at avoiding eye contact and turning my body away from people so they know not to approach. I have no idea why he is here. Who goes to a pub late at night and drinks by themselves? Losers, that's who. And Will is certainly a loser. And a liar. And a cheater. And possibly a murderer if those pictures Holly says she found are anything to go by.

I have no doubt he is lying about knowing where Holly is. I call Lisa with the hope she's found something, keeping my voice low and head down. I don't like the idea of her snooping around a dark attic by herself. Again, my brain goes into overdrive at these sorts of things. Too many crime dramas, perhaps.

I buy myself a gin and tonic, a double, and am nursing it while shooting glances at Will every few minutes. He is on his third beer already, sinking them like a bloody fish. He keeps looking at his watch, then his phone, then back to his watch. Definitely waiting for someone.

There is only one other person in this dump and that's the barman, who keeps looking at the grimy clock on the wall. I assume it is getting close to last call. I don't want Will to know there is anyone else in the pub, so I purposefully avoid small talk with the barman.

I stifle a yawn with the back of my hand just as the door opens and a young woman walks through it.

Here we go.

She is very well dressed; smart trousers and a white, flowing shirt with a cute pink clutch bag. What the hell is a sophisticated woman like this meeting a low-life piece of shit like Will, who dresses like a homeless person? They kiss each other on the cheek and then she slides into the seat next to him.

The barman sighs loudly.

Damn it, I can't hear what they are saying from way over here, but their body language tells me they are close and friendly. He already has his hand on her leg, and she is sending all the right signals for someone who's enjoying themselves and perfectly happy to have a weirdo run his creepy hand up her leg.

Poor Holly.

I know how it feels to have the person you thought you trusted cheat on you. She was there for me when Drake first revealed he'd slept with someone else, and now I must be there for her, no matter what happens.

The woman laughs. I hear it as clear as day from where I am sitting. Why on earth she'd laugh at anything that man says is beyond me. I feel like I need to do something, but what? It's not like I can just go over there and introduce myself as his wife to scare her off . . .

Wait . . .

That's exactly what I can do . . .

I chug the rest of the gin and tonic and wipe my lips with the back of my hand. This is probably about to get super awkward, so I need the small sliver of courage alcohol some-times brings me. It's an illusion, though, if I really think about it. Kind of like my whole life. A glass of wine or a quick shot of something strong isn't going to solve my problems, but at least it numbs the pain for a little while. Once all this shit is over, I'm going to make a conscious effort to stop drinking so much in the evenings, and sort myself out. I'm not an alcoholic. I can function without it, but I enjoy the soothing sensation it brings me. Like an old friend. But now I have my girls back, I don't need it. Plus, my kids are now my number one priority. That and avoiding going to prison for killing two, potentially three, men.

I stand up and take a deep breath.

Wait . . . I can't do it. I need to be sensible here and not give the game away now, so I only have one other option. I can't let that woman end up like the ones on his phone, whether it's consensual or not; he clearly has a problem. Plus, I feel like ruining his night.

I turn to the barman.

'Excuse me, but I think that woman over there needs help. I just saw that man put something in her drink.'

The barman raises an eyebrow and steps to the side to look at the couple in the corner. 'She doesn't look like she needs help to me.'

'Well, obviously, because she doesn't *know* she needs help, does she? I told you; I just saw him put something in her drink. Can you please just go up to her and tell her she has a call or something and then tell her?'

'Lady, it's 2024. Who calls a pub anymore to ask to speak to someone? I don't even have a landline in this place.'

I grind my teeth together. 'Will you please make some-thing up?'

'Why can't you do it?'

'Because . . .' Okay, I need to tread carefully. 'Because . . . if I go over there, she won't believe me, will she? She'll think I'm his ex-wife or something.'

'Are you his ex-wife?'

'No, I'm a concerned woman looking out for the safety and wellbeing of another woman who clearly doesn't realise she's dating a creep who feels the need to drug her drink.'

The barman sighs as he puts down the glass he's drying. 'Fine.'

'Oh, and don't tell her that I saw it happen. Tell her it was you.'

'Fine, whatever.'

It's at this point I realise if the barman had been a woman, it wouldn't have taken that long to convince her. I don't even feel a little bit bad about lying. For all I know, Will does drug the women.

I watch the barman walk over, while I stay hidden behind the pillar. Will's face turns sour and the woman looks confused as to why she's being asked to come to the bar. Will stands up, glaring as he watches the barman lead his female friend away.

I smirk as he reluctantly sits back down, patiently waiting.

After a couple of minutes, the woman returns to Will and speaks to him. She turns and walks out of the pub, leaving him red-faced. It really looks as if his face is going to explode. I nod my thanks to the barman who tuts at me and returns to drying the glasses.

Will takes out his phone and sends a quick text, then downs the rest of his drink before striding up to the bar. I quickly turn my back.

'What the hell did you say to her?' he asks the barman.

That's my cue to leave. I don't want the barman to get freaked and lay the blame on me, so I sneak around a table and make a swift exit into the cool night air.

I message Lisa and tell her what's happened, and that I'm going to follow Will some more. I warn her that he might be on his way home soon, but the message remains unread. The two ticks stay grey. It makes my stomach gurgle and my heart rate increase a notch. Why isn't she reading my messages?

At this point, Will leaves the pub and begins walking back towards where he lives. I call Lisa, but she doesn't pick up.

Shit. He'll be home in less than ten minutes. She needs to get out of the house.

CHAPTER THIRTY-TWO

Lisa

Am I seriously looking at a secret door in Holly's attic right now? Did I hear a weak groan coming from the other side or is it just my imagination running wild? Maybe it's the wind causing the beams to creak. The lure of the locked door is almost overwhelming. It's like being dehydrated and faced with clean, cool water that's locked in a safe.

I search desperately for some sort of handle or lever, but there's nothing. Why would someone create a door that can't be opened? It's solid and there's nothing suitable around I can use to break through to the other side either. The wall itself is made of wooden boards, so I could break through if I had a crowbar, perhaps. No way in hell am I getting through without one. I need to head downstairs to search. It means leaving this dark attic, which isn't a bad thing because it's creeping me out the longer I'm here. But I can't tear myself away from the wall and the strange noise I heard behind it. It only happened once, and it's been silent since.

'Hello?' I call, keeping my lips close to the boards. 'Is anyone there? Holly? Is that you?'

No sound comes in response. If she did reply, I think I might break through the boards with my bare hands to reach her.

I direct the beam of my phone torch over the door and the wall, searching for any weak spot or sign of entry, but there's nothing at all. I even push against it, hoping it's a push–release type of door.

My phone vibrates, signalling a low battery. The torch function must be draining it quickly because it had at least fifty per cent charge when I turned it on.

'Damn it,' I mutter.

I try calling Holly's phone again to see if I can hear any noise through the wall, but there's no sound at all. Even the moaning I'd heard previously has disappeared, leaving an eerie silence in its place. The phone gives off one last long vibration and then dies completely in my hand.

Now the attic is shrouded in gloomy darkness, bar the glowing hole in the floor at the far end. I have to try and find a torch as well as something to break this wall down. Maybe it's not worth it. Maybe the moan I'd heard was just the floorboards or the wind making the beams creak after all. A sinking dread creeps over me as I realise that now my phone has died, I've got no way of contacting Penny. I really am all alone in this house. Will could be on his way back right now.

Feeling defeated, I crawl across the floor and cautiously descend the steps onto the landing. I quietly close the trapdoor and continue my search of the top floor, stopping to enter the office first.

After five minutes, I have searched the desk and wardrobe. The only thing I've found that's of use to me is a small head torch.

The unmistakable sound of keys in a lock makes the hairs on my arms stand up. I freeze in position. There's nowhere to hide. I can't return downstairs. Unless . . . maybe it's Penny? But then, I've got the set of keys and I'm sure I locked the door when I came in. I creep into the hallway and listen. There's a loud burp followed by a male voice muttering to himself.

Taking a glance at my phone, I realise that even if Penny had called to warn me that Will was on his way home, I would have missed it thanks to the flat battery.

The only place to hide safely is above my head, but if I go back into the attic, I have no idea when I'll be able to leave and no way of contacting Penny to let her know where I am . . . unless I can get through the secret door and escape out through the other house. Since it's semi-detached and the attic space stretches into the neighbour's house, it shouldn't be too hard, unless the trapdoor from the attic is locked, but what does this all mean? Are Will and Holly aware there's a door leading into their attic from their neighbour's house, or is there something I'm missing?

Next door is vacant, and I remember Holly saying she has no idea who owns the house.

I don't have time to think. Time's running out. I have to hide.

I pull the cord and open the trapdoor again. It creaks and groans but I'm able to gently lower it to the floor this time without it crashing down at my feet. The television downstairs blares to life, the volume up louder than is surely necessary. At least it helps to cover my footsteps. I assemble the head torch on my forehead, switch it on and reach down to pull up the steps, sealing myself in the dark attic, which now feels like a tomb.

With the door closed, the muffled sounds of the television sound like static and there's a thin square of light piercing through the floor. I crawl across the floor back towards the hidden door, but as I do, something sharp sticks in my hip. I dig around in my pocket, searching for the reason, eventually pulling out the set of house keys I'd used to gain access to the house. There are three keys on the silver ring, along with a small, plastic nametag that says *HOLLY*.

There's the large silver key I'd used to open the front door and the slightly smaller silver key I assume opens the back door, but there's a third key that I hadn't paid attention to before. It's considerably smaller than the other two and is gold.

'Oh my God,' I whisper. It dawns on me like a lightbulb moment at what I'm seeing. Maybe there is a keyhole in the door and I've missed it.

Ignoring the pain in my knees, I shuffle along the floor, feeling my way in the dim light. The head torch is surprisingly useless at lighting more than a foot in front of me. I bump into the chest of drawers, so circle back to the left to move around it. My eyes begin to adjust so I'm able to find the door again. I scan the beam over the wooden boards, but there definitely isn't any sort of keyhole. The gold key must be for something else.

I place both hands against the door and give it a small shove, hoping I was wrong earlier, but it remains closed. I search the attic once more for something to pry open the door, even searching through the boxes in the corner. The box with MISC written across it has a load of junk, including some old tools. There's a screwdriver, a couple of boxes of nails, a saw and . . . an old claw hammer. That will do.

I manage to wedge the claw in between the gap around the door, and pull. I keep yanking as quietly as I can, and slowly but surely the wood splinters and breaks away. I keep pulling and clawing until I open up a hole big enough to squeeze through.

It feels as if I'm in a living nightmare and sooner or later I'm going to wake up. It's like creeping into a lion's den and not knowing whether the lion is waiting for me. There's a possibility that Holly is being kept in here. I know it's risky, but my curiosity is overpowering my fear. I need to find Holly. And I need to escape this house without being caught by Will, and since this is the only way forward . . . into the dark, creepy attic space behind a secret door I go . . .

The head torch beam picks up on some more flecks of blood or whatever it is. They act like tiny arrows. I follow them and then scan my surroundings when they abruptly stop. All around me are shelves built into the roof, in between the joists and the beams. It's heavily boarded and insulated but still has that damp, musty smell of an unused attic. But there are no boxes of Christmas decorations or old clothes and boots in this part of the attic. But there is a collection of old paint cans, one of which is deep red.

I guess it's red paint after all, but it still doesn't explain what the hell the door is doing between the two houses.

Then my eyes settle on an object that definitely doesn't belong in an attic . . . and my stomach clenches.

CHAPTER THIRTY-THREE

Penny

There's still no answer from Lisa and my messages haven't been received or read. My stomach drops as Will enters his house and closes the door. Now what? I can't very well go and knock on the door and invite myself in for a cup of tea, not after shouting at him and accusing him of possible murder earlier.

I'm out of ideas.

At least I've saved a woman from potential danger tonight. Fuck knows what he had planned for her, and it turns my stomach to even think about it. It can't be a coincidence that he had sex with Leanne Prince the same night she was murdered. No woman is safe around him. That's why I did what I did earlier. I'd rather be safe than sorry. I'd never have forgiven myself if tomorrow morning I'd woken up to the news that she'd been strangled to death.

How long has he been doing this? If he did kill her and others like her, then that makes him a serial killer. My mind can't even take it in. Between the three of us, we've married an abuser, a paedophile and a possible serial killer. Our lives would make an excellent true crime drama and once this is over, I have half a mind to contact Netflix, although if we're apprehended, I expect it won't take long for offers to float in. Everyone loves a fucked-up, true crime drama.

But the more I think about it, the more it doesn't quite add up. Will's not smart enough to be a serial killer. We're talking about a man who can't even keep his own house clean, who has a gambling problem and steals money from his wife. Serial killers are usually stupidly smart and really organised. I can see Will being a cheat and maybe killing a woman in the spur of the moment, but a serial killer?

Something is definitely going on here, but maybe it's not what we think.

There's still Holly to think about, and now Lisa is trapped in the house with Will. I can only assume her phone battery has died. He can't have hurt her yet because I've had eyes on him the whole time, which means she's hiding somewhere in the house, waiting for the opportunity to escape.

There's nothing else I can do but wait and hope that Lisa will be able to find a way out of the house by herself. I haven't felt so helpless since that time the twins both had high temperatures and I sat by the sides of their hospital beds, holding each of their tiny hands, waiting for the medication to kick in and their test results to come back. Thankfully, it hadn't been sepsis as I'd assumed, but a run-of-the-mill infection they'd both managed to pick up at the same time. Usually, a mother's instinct is always right, except at that time I was wrong, but they'd still been very unwell, and I know I'd done the right thing by rushing them to the hospital. I still remember the look on the nurse's face when I shouted at her saying my babies were dying of sepsis. I apologised afterwards, but she had been surprisingly understanding.

Now, I'm here, waiting, assuming the worst but hoping for the best. I assume Holly is dead or unconscious somewhere, tied up in her house by her husband, but hoping she's alive and uninjured. Maybe Lisa has found her, and they are working on an escape plan, or maybe . . .

Wait . . . what is that?

A flicker of light catches my eye. Not in Holly's house, but next door and not at the main windows, but in the small roof window. I move along the road to get a better view and watch the light flickering. It's stronger at some moments than others, but I can't work out where it's coming from. The rest of the house is dark and by the looks of it, no one's lived there for a long time. No car on the driveway, no curtains, and no furniture inside, from what I can see from the road, yet a light is flickering in the attic.

Is that . . .

'Oh, fuck!' I gasp out loud, then clamp my hand over my mouth.

Joy spreads through my body as I realise I'm looking at Morse code. The three of us learned it back when we were kids to send secret messages to each other. For a short time, Lisa and I lived across the road from each other. Holly lived a little further away, so Lisa and I used to swap Morse code messages all the time from our bedroom windows back before we were old enough for mobile phones.

And right now, I'm positive that Lisa is in the attic sending me a message. I watch patiently and say the letters out loud, one by one. Then, once the code begins to repeat itself, I say the whole phrase aloud.

'Holly not here. Trapped. Need distraction. Found something.'

My heart sinks at the fact she hasn't found Holly, but she has found *something*, so that is better than nothing. What that *something* is, I have no idea. A body? A murder weapon? A bottle of vodka? Who knows? But I know I need to get her out of there and quickly.

I pick up a nearby rock. The best and only distraction I can think of is the good old car alarm, so I throw the rock through the back windscreen of the car in the driveway. It blares to life, piercing the darkness like a thorn. Shit, now I need to hide because within seconds Will is going to come barrelling out of the house and look around for the culprit. I leap over the low wall of next door's front garden and squeeze myself down the overgrown side alley, hiding behind some bins, which are in dire need of being emptied and cleaned.

'What the fuck!' Will's voice booms in the darkness. 'My car!'

Technically, it's Holly's car because she pays for it, but I hope she won't be too mad when she finds out what I've done. Loud footsteps echo up and down the pavement as Will shouts into the night. 'You better not try anything else, you sick fuck! I'm going to kill you if I find you!'

Delightful.

Hurry up, Lisa!

There is no way she'll be able to escape through the front door as Will is still patrolling that area, assessing the damage and muttering curse words. I notice he isn't on the phone to the police, which I class as a bit suspicious. Maybe he doesn't want them sniffing around his house. Hopefully, Lisa will be able to slip out of the back door, so I make my way down the alley and wait by the back garden gate.

CHAPTER THIRTY-FOUR

Lisa

The shrieking car alarm makes me jump, but it means Penny has seen my message, which is the best news ever. Thank God, because I had no other ideas. I stop flicking the torch on and off, grab what I've found and race back through the first attic and to the trapdoor. I had searched the second attic as best as I could, but I couldn't open the trapdoor from this side because it was locked from the outside.

I open the first trapdoor and fling it back with a thud, not caring too much about making a noise because the alarm is loud enough to cover it. I close the trapdoor and creep down the stairs, checking the corridor to make sure the coast is clear. Will is shouting and cursing outside, so I head straight to the back door, which is already unlocked, and make a swift exit, only taking a breath when I reach the end of the garden where the gate is, which leads into a small alley.

I open the gate and almost collide with Penny, who throws her arms around my neck. 'Thank fuck!'

'That was horrible,' I say, sucking in precious air. 'Next time, you can search the creepy lair in the attic.'

Penny stares at me. 'What did you just say?'

'Shh! Not here. Come on. Let's find somewhere we can keep an eye on Holly's house. I'll tell you all about it once we're safe.'

'What's that?' Penny points to the locked metal box I'm carrying under my left arm.

'I found it in the attic. I didn't have time to try and open it.'

'What about Holly? We can't just leave her.'

'I couldn't find her. We just have to hope she's okay. The sooner we get to the bottom of all this, the sooner we find her.'

Penny nods in agreement.

* * *

My heart doesn't stop racing until Penny and I find a secluded spot behind a thick hedge. We crouch and poke our heads round the hedge; Holly's house is within sight. Will has turned the car alarm off and stomped back into the house, slamming the front door hard.

It feels as if I've run a marathon. My legs are wobbly and don't feel like they belong to my body. My skin is slick with sweat and I'm in desperate need of a glass of water.

I take a deep breath. 'Okay, so . . . I think something really weird is happening in their attic.'

Penny looks at me as if I have suddenly sprouted horns from the top of my head. 'What the hell are you talking about?'

'I found a secret door in their attic that leads into the next door's attic. The house that's empty. I think maybe they own that house too, or at least maybe Will does and hasn't told Holly. I found an old mattress in there propped up against the side, some discarded clothes and a tripod with a camera. It might be where Will took those photos of the women that Holly told us about, but I can't be sure until I see them myself. That's also where I found this box.'

'That doesn't sound creepy at all,' Penny mutters.

'I know, right? Could Will really be a serial killer? It all fits, doesn't it?'

'I think something else is going on here. I just can't see Will being a serial killer. Maybe he killed Leanne Prince, but . . . Oh, I don't know,' she says with a sigh.

'Okay, so maybe I'm getting carried away, but I have a theory about this box,' I say as I place it in front of us on the ground. I reach into my pocket and pull out Holly's set of keys. Using the faint light from a nearby streetlight, I choose the small gold key and let out a little shriek of delight when it slides effortlessly into the keyhole.

I look up at Penny, who is biting her lip, and then lift the lid.

I'm not sure what I was expecting to find but rolls of cash wasn't one of them.

'Bloody hell, there's thousands of pounds in here.'

'Holly always said she had a rainy-day fund,' I reply. 'So . . . that means Holly's aware of the attic space.'

'You said there was a mattress and a camera on a tripod. Maybe Holly and Will like to get kinky in the attic.'

I screw up my nose. 'Eww! No, I don't think so.'

'What other explanation is there?'

I close the lid to the box and sigh heavily. 'I don't know. What do we do now?'

'What else did you say you found up there?'

I take a few seconds and think about it. 'There was the mattress, the tripod and camera, the box and some discarded clothes, including a pair of male boxer shorts.'

'Gross.'

'The house must belong to Will and Holly. If they didn't own it, then it would be a huge risk to hide all that stuff in an empty house that could be bought at any moment. They wouldn't risk random people moving in and finding the stuff in the attic, would they?'

'Holly would have told us if she owned the house . . . Oh, fuck. I think I've figured it out. I think I've figured out why

Will's stealing money from Holly. It's because he owns that house and hasn't told her, and he needs the money to pay a second mortgage.'

I shake my head. 'But it was Holly's little gold key that opened the box I found, so she must know about it somehow.'

'Maybe she originally hid it somewhere else, and Will found it and hid it up there until he could figure out how to open it.'

'Possibly.'

'Poor Holly,' says Penny, shaking her head. 'You didn't find any sign of her at all?'

'No. Nothing. There were some red stains in the attic that I first thought were blood, but turned out to be spatters of red paint. I found the cans in the attic. But no, there was no sign of her.'

We sit in silence for several minutes. My mind keeps mulling over something else I saw in the attic, but I'm so tired it's a struggle to make sense of it. The tripod and camera. I had checked for film or a memory card, but there wasn't any.

I should have spent longer searching, but I hadn't thought things through up in the attic. I'd just wanted to understand what I was seeing, then to get out of there as fast as possible. All rational thought had left me, and I'd grabbed the box and left.

'I'm certain Holly doesn't know about next door. Remember Holly said a few months ago she was woken up by banging. Do you remember that? She said she was alone at the time, and it really freaked her out. She went round in the morning and found a brick had been thrown through the front window of the house next door.'

Penny frowns. 'I don't remember her telling us that.'

'Maybe she messaged me separately and not in the group chat.'

'Do you chat often without me?'

I mentally kick myself, hoping Penny isn't offended. It's not like Holly and I speak every day outside of the group chat, but sometimes I share things with Holly that I wouldn't share with Penny, and the same goes for Holly. It must have been one of those instances where Holly messaged me personally.

'No, just random stuff usually,' I say.

Penny's lips purse into a thin line. 'Hmm. What happened, then? What did Holly do about the break-in? Did she tell the police or anything?'

'Come to think of it, she never told me what happened. And I forgot about it because . . . well, Simon hurt me the next day and I just . . . forgot.' Tears sting my eyes. They aren't aimed at Simon, but at my own ignorance. I wipe away a single tear and sniff. 'It doesn't tell us much, does it?'

'Not really. We need to get back inside that house and look for more clues.'

I run my hands through my hair and drag them down my face. 'I'm exhausted. I can't even think straight. The house was completely empty. I don't think there's anything else in there.'

'Did you look in all the rooms?'

'No, not properly.'

'Holly can't be far. She must be somewhere in that house or in her house. We have to go back in. Do you have Will's number? Maybe let's call Will and tell him what we know.'

'Yeah, I have it in case of emergencies. Are you sure calling him is a good idea?'

Penny stands up. 'No, but I don't know what the fuck else to do.'

CHAPTER THIRTY-FIVE

Penny

My hands grasp my phone so hard the muscles in my fingers ache. After blocking my husband's calls earlier, I hadn't taken another look at it until now apart from when I tried to get hold of Lisa. The battery's almost dead, but hopefully there's enough to make a call. I press call and wait for Will to pick up. It takes less than three rings for him to answer.

'What can I do for you, Penny?'

'Cut the pleasantries, Will. We know you have Holly locked up somewhere and we know about your creepy attic leading to next door.' There's a long pause on the other end of the line. I switch the phone to speaker mode so Lisa can listen too.

'What the hell are you talking about? Which one of you was in my attic?'

Lisa and I lock eyes. 'That would be me,' says Lisa after clearing her throat. Her voice wobbles. She's never been the most confident of people, but over the past few days, she has finally begun to find her voice, especially since her dickhead of a husband is no longer an issue. I'm counting the hours until I

207

can be free of my own, although before we can get rid of him, we have to get to the bottom of Will's lies.

'Lisa,' says Will. 'Find anything up there besides damp patches and Christmas decorations?'

'I found a beautiful chest of drawers. It's funny, though, how on earth did you manage to fit it through the attic trap-door when it's clearly too big to fit?'

I have no idea what she's on about, but I stay quiet as Will laughs. 'That's the question you have for me? I find myself disappointed.'

While still on the line, I snap a quick picture of the box and send it to Will. Seconds later, he stops talking and sucks in a breath.

'What the hell is that?' he asks.

'Is the picture a bad quality? What the fuck do you think it is? It's a box of money that you stole from your wife,' I reply. 'We need to talk.'

'Look, I don't know what the hell you think you know, but whatever it is, you're wrong. I've never seen that box of money before in my life.'

'I doubt that.'

'If you don't believe me, then I can prove it. Whatever the hell is in that attic has nothing to do with me. I don't even go up there.'

'Who owns the house next door to yours?' asks Lisa. 'Is it you?'

Will laughs. 'You think I can afford two mortgages?'

'You've been stealing money from Holly,' I snap back. 'She showed us the online statements.'

'Yeah, so, what's hers is mine. We're married. That's how marriage works.'

This time it's my turn to chuckle. 'You have a funny idea of how marriage works. What was her name? The woman I saw you with earlier at the pub?'

'What the fuck? You were following me!'

'Checkmate, Will.'

There's a long silence on the line. Lisa and I swap glances, holding our breaths.

'Come to the house in one hour,' says Will bluntly. 'I can prove I'm not lying. I'm not going to be accused of something I didn't do by some wannabe detectives with nothing better to do.' Before I can suggest an alternative, he hangs up.

Lisa sighs. 'I guess that's it, then.'

'Let's use this one hour wisely. Let's search the empty house again. We can also always ask the neighbours if they've ever seen anything going on next door.'

'It's like one o'clock in the morning. I doubt the neighbours will be feeling very talkative,' replies Lisa.

Damn it. I'd lost all track of time. It reminded me of when I'd do the nightly feeds with the twins when they were newborns. Drake was often away, even in the early years, leaving me to do everything myself. Yes, I had Aunt Silvia around to help as a last resort, but there wasn't a lot she could do during the night. The twins would often alternate between breast and bottle feeding. I did a combination of the two because my milk supply had been very low to start with, and I'd eventually given up breastfeeding by week seven because my body felt like a milking machine, and I wanted it back. The hours had melted into each other back then, and so had the days. I remember one time when I was convinced it was a Sunday and Aunt Silvia popped around to take the twins out for a pram walk, which she did on a Thursday afternoon. I'd lost almost a whole week somewhere and I still, to this day, don't know how I managed or what had happened.

'Maybe we can break into next door,' I say, standing up straight and stretching my back. 'It's not like anyone lives there.'

'You don't think he'll be there waiting for us?'

'We won't know until we get there.'

* * *

A few minutes later, we approach the empty house. The street is quiet, and all the lights are off in neighbouring houses,

209

cementing the fact that we most likely won't be talking to the neighbours any time soon. The only light that's on is in Will and Holly's house and it's in their bedroom. Perhaps Will is taking a shower. We sneak into the back garden using the back gate that's barely hanging on by some rusty hinges, and enter the neighbour's garden.

I take off my jacket and wrap it around my right elbow. Lisa grabs it.

'What are you doing?'

'How else are we getting into the house?'

'We're adding breaking and entering onto our list of offences now?'

'Are you really worried about a broken window right now?'

Lisa shakes her head. 'No. Sorry, you're right. Think of the bigger picture.'

'That's my girl.'

I pull back my elbow and smash it against the glass. Nothing happens except my elbow explodes with pain and I bite my lip to stop myself from using every swear word under the sun.

'Guess it's not as easy as it looks in *CSI*, huh?'

I mutter some indecent words at my sarcastic friend and then pick up a nearby rock, feeling stupid. I smash it against the glass and this time it breaks. We hold our breaths, expecting some sort of reaction from someone, somewhere, or maybe an alarm . . . But we're good.

I reach in and twist the lock on the inside of the door, and we step into the dark house.

The air is cold, stale and the place is most definitely empty, bar a random broken table in the living room. The carpets are threadbare, as if a million feet have trodden on them over a long period of time. I keep my phone torch off in case it can be seen from outside. It may be the middle of the night, but if anyone does happen to pass by, I don't want to draw attention to the fact someone is inside this house. My phone is practically dead anyway.

210

I leave Lisa to search the kitchen and head towards the front door where the stairs are situated just off to the right. A pile of mail sits on the floor in front of the door. I bend down and pick up a few of the letters. It looks as if they are bills, and there aren't many. Maybe five or six, no more.

The streetlights combined with the moonlight give me just enough light to read the name on the envelope and when I do, my whole body turns cold.

'Lisa!' I say in a harsh whisper. 'Lisa!'

Fast footsteps approach. 'Did you find something?'

'I know who owns this house,' I say, the letters in my hand shaking.

'Who?'

'Timothy Grant.' It doesn't make any sense, yet there is no mistaking who the bills are addressed to. It's the name my husband uses during some of our sexual roleplaying games. I have no idea why he uses that name, but it can't be a coincidence.

'What are you talking about?' asks Lisa, taking the letters from my hand. 'This says Timothy Grant. Oh wait . . . that's the name . . .'

'Yep.'

Lisa's mouth drops open. Whether it's from the shock of knowing who the house belongs to or because of my sexual deviance, I don't know. I don't ask.

'I've just remembered I found some old deeds in the attic in the chest of drawers. I assumed they were from the previous owner. The name on them was Timothy Grant too.'

'And you didn't think to tell me this earlier?'

'I forgot about the name. I knew it looked familiar, but it didn't click until just now. What does this mean?' she asks. 'Are Drake and Will working together? I thought they barely knew each other.'

I shake my head. 'They don't . . . at least, that's what I thought. Holy fuck.' I need to sit down before my legs give way completely. Not only have I found out my husband is a paedophile, but he's also working with Will somehow and owns a house I know nothing about. I don't want to believe it, but the proof is there as clear as day.

'Are you okay?' asks Lisa. She sets the letter aside and stands next to me, placing a gentle hand on my shoulder as I lean forwards, trying to decide if I'm going to vomit, pass out or collapse. I take a few deep breaths but see nothing but stars.

'I just don't get it,' I whisper. 'Why would he buy the house next to our best friend and not tell me? Does Holly know, do you think?'

'She would have told us if she did.'

I nod, but then a niggle of doubt creeps into my mind. We've all kept things from each other at some point over the years. Holly did know my husband quite well at one point before I met him. Was she keeping secrets for him?

'We need to find Holly,' I finally say. 'I have a horrible feeling she's in danger.'

'We could look around the house again while we wait for Will. Wait . . . someone's coming.' Lisa puts a finger to her lips. We press ourselves against the wall on either side of the front door just as a beam of light pierces the darkness around us. A crunch of gravel tells us a car has just pulled up. A door slams and footsteps echo close by and then fade away.

I bend down and peer through the letterbox and into the street. The car lights are off now, but I see a dark shape standing next to the vehicle. A man.

I'd recognise the silhouette of my husband anywhere.

'He's here, Drake. He's here.'

Lisa's eyes widen. 'What do we do now?'

'How the fuck should I know?' My voice is close to hysterical. Inside, I'm crying buckets and shaking in a corner. A part of me wants to run and hide and forget this whole ridiculous plan, while the other half wants to storm outside and confront my lying, sick husband and have the biggest argument in the history of the world, so loud that all the neighbour's wake up and call the police.

Lisa and I walk into the lounge and sit with our backs against the far wall, our knees bent, our shoulders touching.

Two best friends who have no idea how they've got themselves into such a mess in such a short amount of time.

'Remember when we all played hide and seek when we were kids, and we couldn't find Holly? We were looking for her for over an hour,' says Lisa.

'She was always the best at hiding.'

'I wish she wasn't so good at it now.'

'We'll find her. Or she'll find us,' I say, not believing my own words.

'Do you think we'll get out of this?' asks Lisa, not turning her head to look at me. Her face is blank, not a flicker of an expression anywhere.

'We will. We have to.' I wish I believed it.

The front door bangs open.

We scurry to our feet just as Drake walks into the room and switches on the lights, acting as if nothing is out of the ordinary.

'If you're looking for a shocked response from us, then you're too late,' I say, shooting a dark look at my husband. He should know exactly what it means too because it's the same look I gave him when he told me he'd cheated on me.

'Where are my children?' asks Drake. He doesn't look like the husband I know. Gone is the slick suit and tie, replaced with a pair of old jeans and a checked shirt with the sleeves rolled up. Annoyingly, he looks better than normal.

'My children are safe, far away from you,' I snap.

'Why would you need to keep them safe from me, Pen? I'd do anything to keep them safe.'

'Don't you dare stand there and lie to me! I know what you are.' I don't think I've ever been this afraid and angry at the same time. My body is vibrating with so much emotion, it's a surprise I'm still able to stand.

'Pen, whatever it is you think you know, it's not true.' His voice is so calm, so controlled. The fact he can lie to me so easily is sickening. How long has it been going on under my roof? Since we first met? Since we got married? Has he always been into little kids or is it a new thing?

213

'Then why don't you tell me the truth? Tell me why I found pornographic images of children in your wardrobe. Tell me why you own the house next to my best friend and have never told me. Tell me why you're friends with Will, who's quite possibly murdered a pregnant woman.'

I'm not sure what I expected my husband to do, but it isn't to look as if I've just stabbed him in the heart. 'What the hell? What pornographic images? Are you seriously accusing me of a being a paedo right now? What the hell is wrong with you?'

The sound of the front door opening makes all three of us turn in that direction as Will enters. When he sees Drake standing there, he does a double take.

'What the fuck are you doing here? What's going on?' He looks at Lisa and me for some sort of response, but we're as clueless as he appears to be.

'I think it's time we all had a chat,' says Drake. 'My wife seems to be confused about a lot of things. Wait here, I won't be long.'

Drake turns and walks out of the house. A few beats of silence pass while Will stares at us.

'What is going on?' he asks.

'We could ask you the same thing,' I say.

'Why are you asking me? I didn't know Drake was here. What's he doing here? He's your husband.' This is true, yet it seems I have no idea who my husband truly is.

Seconds later, before I'm able to reply, the front door swings open again and Drake enters, dragging the body of our best friend behind him before dumping her on the floor in front of us.

CHAPTER THIRTY-SIX

Lisa

My first instinct is to rush to my friend to find out if she's alive, but within seconds it's obvious that she is because she's groaning and thrashing around on the floor, desperate to get away. Her hands are tied behind her back and her ankles are also bound together so she's rolling about on the floor like a fish out of water. The skin around her wrists and ankles is bruised and red, possibly the blood supply has been being restricted for a long time. She has a piece of cloth tied around her head, clenched between her teeth. She's drooling and crying and bleeding; her eyes are full of fear.

Penny screams and collapses on the floor next to Holly, who cries even more. Her pupils are dilated so wide it makes her eyes appear black. Penny removes the cloth from her mouth with difficulty. It's tight and has caused a red mark where it's been pulled around her jaw.

Was it Drake who took Holly? Where the hell has he been keeping her? And, more importantly, why? They used to be friends. What the hell is going on?

Both men continue to stand by the door as Penny unties Holly, reassuring her that we've got her and she's okay now.

Once she's free, I crouch down and she throws her arms around both our necks, weeping hysterically.

'I thought I was going to die,' she says in between sobs.

'We've got you now,' says Penny.

My eyes fill with tears as I take in Holly's appearance. Her clothes are torn in several places, her shirt ripped and pulled off one shoulder, revealing her black bra strap. She has a black eye and a cut, swollen bottom lip. Her teeth are stained red. She must have put up one hell of a fight when she was attacked. I can't help but feel proud of her because it's more than I ever did when Simon beat me. I'd never put up a fight because I'd allowed fear to control me. Fear of getting a worse beating. Fear of him taking it too far. Fear of the pain. I'd always just accepted my fate, but not Holly.

And now, no longer me either.

Since Simon has gone, I'm a new woman. If only I'd had the courage to change a long time ago, but that was then, and this is now. I can only move forward from here.

I gently wipe Holly's tears from her cheeks, careful to avoid the cuts and tender areas of her face. Holly smiles and nods, a silent thank you.

'Right, someone had better start talking right now,' shouts Will. 'Why is my wife tied up?' I can't help but notice he hadn't rushed to her side when Drake first dragged her into the room.

Penny ignores him and turns to Holly. 'Tell us everything. What happened?'

'I was on the phone to you, and someone attacked me from behind. I didn't even see them coming. I was out cold and when I woke up, Drake was there. It's them. They hunt and kill people together. They're serial killers. They killed Leanne Prince. It's not just women either. Men too.' She continues to shake and cry.

'Did you know about Drake owning this house?' asks Penny.

Holly shakes her head violently. 'No, not a clue. I never knew who owned the house.'

'What about Drake? The pictures I found . . .' Penny leaves the sentence hanging.

'It's all true,' says Holly with a sob.

My mouth turns dry. It means Penny's children may have suffered at the hands of their father. Lori . . . her pure innocence stolen. I want to do it. Not just for Lori and Luca or Penny, but for myself, and the child I never got to meet.

Drake doesn't deserve to go to jail. He deserves to die.

I know what I need to do, but to do it, I need to get close enough to smell his breath. Close enough to risk my life because at any moment he could kill me, and I know that.

Drake shakes his head. 'I have no idea what you're on about. What pictures? Babe, what's going on?' He directs the question at Holly, not Penny.

Babe?

I catch a glimpse of Penny, who has turned pale. Why is he calling Holly 'babe'?

'What are you talking about?' snaps Holly. She turns to her husband. 'And you! I know you've been cheating on me, you sick bastard. Admit it.'

Will pales and takes a step backwards. 'Okay, fine,' he says with his hands up. 'I've been cheating on you and . . . I'm sorry, okay? I freaked out when Leanne told me she was pregnant. I didn't know what to do. I couldn't risk her fucking everything up, so . . .'

'So, you killed her,' finishes Holly through gritted teeth.

'What? No, of course I didn't kill her. I just left her alone by the river in the middle of the night without making sure she got home okay. The next thing I know, she's been found dead.'

'Seriously? You're saying you were with Leanne the same night she was killed, but you had nothing to do with it.'

Will sighs heavily, as if he can't be bothered to keep up the charade a moment longer. 'Fine. We had sex. We talked. She told me she was pregnant and I just lost it, okay? I didn't realise I strangled her that hard. I just saw red. Look, it's not my finest decision, but I promise I have nothing to do with whatever the hell those two meddling bitches have found in the attic.' He points above him. 'I'm not a fucking serial killer.' He rounds on Drake and points at him. 'You are!'

Drake laughs. 'Okay, I've had just about enough of this shit.'

It all happens so fast.

I barely believe my eyes as the events unfold in front of me.

Drake strides up to Will, pulling a hidden blade from under his jacket and stabs him straight in the side of the neck.

Time stops as all three of us stare at Will standing in the middle of the lounge as he clutches his neck with one hand and starts making gargling sounds as blood drips from his mouth. It's as if his body hasn't registered it's dead yet. Blood spurts out of his neck wound like a fountain is being turned on and off, coating his hands in red and running in rivers to the floor.

The blood doesn't stop. I can't even look away. It doesn't disgust me at all. It's completely fascinating to watch as his life drains from his body in thick, oozy spurts. The knife is still embedded in his neck. His eyes are wide.

Drake yanks the knife from Will's neck and it's enough to finish him off. Will crumples to the floor, lying in an expanding pool of his blood, and takes his final breath, all while the blood still flows from the hole in his neck.

It's at that moment Holly begins to shake while crouched on the floor. She covers her face with her hands. She's making a horrible sound. I can't bear it, but then I realise something.

Holly isn't crying.

She's trying not to laugh.

CHAPTER THIRTY-SEVEN

Holly
Six and a half years ago

As she tosses another shot back, having no idea what it is, her head spins and she almost topples off the stool she's perched on. She erupts into childish giggles and accidentally knocks the line of shot glasses over, their purple contents spilling across the bar. She yanks her clutch bag out of the liquid before it ruins the beading while her work friend, Jane, starts to mop it up with a load of napkins. She's also giggling loudly, her movements exaggerated and clumsy.

Holly hasn't been this drunk in a long time. Not since Penny's hen do last year. But she's out tonight on a work night out, and all of them are getting on it big time. Just a bunch of rowdy personal trainers having a good time, dancing to some cheesy rock music in a bar where there's also a sticky dance floor. She doesn't even know what bar she's in, nor what the time is. Will has messaged her a few times, checking in, but she's switched her phone off because he's doing her head in. She doesn't message him when he's out with his mates, so why should she reply?

Jane leans over to her. 'Where is everyone?'

'I dunno . . . dance floor, I think,' Holly mumbles.

'Come on, then.' Jane grabs her arm and tugs her off the stool, but Holly pulls her arm free and shuffles her bum back onto it.

'Na, too drunk. You go. I'll be here . . .'

Jane stumbles away towards the group and leaves her at the bar. She holds her hand up, signalling a bartender, but he's busy over on the other side, so doesn't notice her.

'Well, well, look who it is,' says a familiar voice.

She turns and attempts to focus her eyes on the tall, dark and handsome man who's appeared next to her, standing a little too close for her liking. It takes a further few seconds for her drunk brain to recognise him.

'Oh my God . . . Drake?'

'Yeah!'

She flings herself at him, wrapping her arms around his neck, but her body is too slow to react and instead she falls into him, and he catches her.

'Whoops,' she giggles.

'Whoa, I haven't seen you this drunk since our university days,' says Drake with a laugh. He props her back up on the stool and stands closer, ensuring she doesn't topple off again.

'You know what I'm like with shots.'

'I do, I remember very well.' Drake holds her gaze for several seconds. 'How are you, Hols? I haven't seen you since my *wedding*.'

'Oh, I'm good. You know, wedded bliss and all that crap,' she responds with a roll of the eyes.

Drake smiles. 'Yeah, I know. How's Will?'

'Will is a lazy bastard who couldn't find my g-spot if I gave him a fucking map and compass.'

Drake bursts into laughter. 'Okay, no more shots for you. Who are you out with?'

'Friends.' She glances over her shoulder, waving her hand vaguely in the direction of the dance floor. Drake looks over, but then straight back at her. He slides his strong hand against the small of her back and brings his mouth so close to her ear that she feels his warm breath.

'I've missed you.'

Without turning to look at him, she whispers, 'Fuck off.'

'I mean our friendship,' he adds quickly.

'I'm sure you did,' she replies coolly.

'Who am I kidding? Hols, you look incredible right now.' Then he shifts her whole body so she's facing him and his body fits nicely between her thighs. He leans closer, but she leans back ever so slightly. 'Do you remember the night we first kissed back at university?'

'You mean the night you forced your tongue down my throat and then we had ugly sex on the floor of your tiny bedroom.'

Drake's eyes don't leave hers. His gaze is burning a hole straight through her and it's suddenly got really hot in this bar. 'I've got a lot better,' he says.

'Lucky Penny.'

'Holly . . .'

'Drake . . . I may be drunk, but you're my best friend's husband.'

'Right . . .' She moves away slightly, but as she does, he grabs her hips and pulls her closer.

'Not so fast,' he whispers.

'Drake . . . I'm drunk. I can't . . . I . . .' Oh God, this isn't happening. Not again. She never told Penny that she and Drake had drunken sex at university. It only happened once, but it felt wrong because they'd been friends for so long. But now . . . he's here and she's wasted, and he smells so good, and . . .

Drake's fingers gently brush against her naked thigh and then travel upwards, as her breath catches in her throat and her internal temperature climbs. Her body automatically leans into him.

'What are you doing here, Drake?' she manages to ask.

221

'Work,' he whispers back. 'But I was hoping to run into you.'

'Did you know I was here? Does Penny know you're here?'

'Yes, and no.'

She nods and takes a deep breath as the room spins around her. 'Okay.'

'Okay.' Drake takes her hand and leads her out of the bar and into a waiting taxi. Oh God, what is she doing? Why is she doing this? Why . . .

They're sitting next to each other, their thighs touching as he takes his hand and runs it up in between her legs. That's all she needs to lose her mind completely. She climbs on top of him and rides his fingers until she almost climaxes. He leans in close to her ear while he pumps his fingers into her.

'I want to cum on your face later,' he whispers.

And she falls off the edge completely.

* * *

The next morning, she feels like someone has lit a fire inside her head. Last night is just a haze of sweat, cum and orgasms and warm, running water. They took a shower together at some point and she remembers him pressing her hard against the tiles and . . .

Oh God . . .

She scurries out of bed and barely makes it to the toilet bowl in time. She's a horrible, terrible, disgusting person. She can't believe she slept with her best friend's husband.

'You okay?'

She turns and sees Drake standing in the doorway of the bathroom wearing nothing but his boxers. 'Do I look okay to you?'

Drake smiles. 'Sorry. Can I do anything to help?'

'Tell me last night didn't happen.'

'It wasn't that bad, Hols.'

222

'No, I . . . I'm not saying it was bad. It was good. It was more than good, but . . .'

'Holly, look, I know it was wrong. I'm sorry, but . . . I've wanted this for so long. I can't stop thinking about you.'

She flushes the toilet and stands up on wobbly legs. 'What are you saying?'

'I'm saying . . . I . . . I love you, Hols.'

'No, you love Penny. *Penny*. Remember, your wife.'

Drake rolls his eyes. 'Fuck my wife.'

'Hey, that's my best friend you're talking about.'

'Some friend you are.'

She points a stiff finger at him. 'Fuck you!'

Drake runs a hand through his hair. 'Fuck,' he says. 'I'm sorry. This is all my fault.'

She stomps past him and into the hotel bedroom where there's a mess of scattered clothes. She begins to pick up her items and steps into her underwear. 'Look, as far as I'm concerned, this never happened, okay? It. Never. Happened. You're going to go back to your wife. I'm going to go back to my husband, and we're going to get on with our married lives, and then everything will be okay.'

Drake sighs. 'Can you really do that, Hols?'

'Yes, I have to. I will not be responsible for breaking up my best friend's marriage.'

'What about yours?'

'And mine. Whatever. Please just . . . can we forget about last night, please?'

Drake nods. 'If that's what you want.'

'It's what I want.'

Drake's eyes scan her body, and she gets the familiar tingle between her thighs. She's in trouble. She's in big fucking trouble.

* * *

Penny has just revealed to the group that Drake has come home and admitted to cheating on her with a woman from work, but only she knows the truth. Now, she has to console her best friend, all the while knowing it's she who's destroyed her marriage because her husband can't keep his guilty conscience in check and his dick in his pants. A part of her wants to tell Penny the truth, but she can't let her lose her husband and best friend in one go. She'd never survive. Drake doesn't tell Penny the truth either, which must mean he thinks the same thing.

Penny has kicked him out of their house. Holly's not sure where Drake's staying. Penny's putting plans in place for a divorce, but then she calls the group WhatsApp, something the others rarely do, preferring to message instead.

'Penny? Are you okay?' asks Holly without saying hello.

Lisa comes on the line and asks the same thing.

'No, I'm not. Girls . . . I'm pregnant.' And then Penny starts wailing like a banshee. Holly doesn't even hear her as the blood rushes to her head. She feels as if the whole world is spinning. Lisa attempts to calm Penny down, but all that's going through Holly's mind is *shit, shit, shit, shit!*

'Were you trying?' she manages to get out.

'No, not really. I mean, we talked about kids, but not yet. We've only just got married and we wanted to spend more time together as a couple, but . . . oh God, now what am I supposed to do? He's admitted he's cheated on me, but I can't raise this baby by myself.'

'Of course you can,' says Holly. 'You're the strongest woman I know. We'll help you. You won't be alone.' She doesn't know why she's saying this. The fact is that nothing she says seems genuine. She's a fucking liar and hypocrite and she hates it.

'Have you told Drake yet?' asks Lisa, taking the words out of her mouth.

'No, not yet,' says Penny, sniffing loudly. 'Urrggh, what a fucking mess my marriage is.'

'I'm so sorry,' says Holly as a gut-wrenching pain almost makes her double over.

'I need to think about this. I need to talk to Drake. Like he said, maybe his affair was a one-off and it didn't mean anything.'

'Wait . . . you're not thinking of going back to him, are you?' asks Lisa.

'I don't know . . . But I think we need to have a long talk. I'll call you girls later.'

'We love you,' says Lisa.

'Love you,' says Holly.

'Love you back.' Penny hangs up.

Holly hangs up, then screams as she hurls her phone across the room.

* * *

Six hours later, she's barely managed to move off the sofa because she's been staring at her phone, hoping it will ring, but what result is she wanting to hear? That Penny's marriage is ruined and she's leaving him and now has no husband and is pregnant with his child. It's not what Holly wants, but it's not up to her, is it? She's the bitch who's started all this. She's the idiot who slept with Drake.

Her phone vibrates and she practically jumps on it without looking at the screen.

'Hey.' It's not Penny.

'Drake, why are you calling me?'

'Penny's just told me that she's pregnant.'

She holds her breath and then sighs. 'Yes, I know.'

'We had a long talk.'

'And?'

'And she's willing to give me another chance.'

She closes her eyes and takes a deep breath, determined not to allow the tears to flow. 'Okay,' she says quietly. 'Is that what you want?'

'Not really.'

'Then what is it you want, Drake?'

225

'You.'

'You can't have me.'

There's a long silence and then he says, 'I have an idea.'

'If the idea is to continue sleeping together behind my pregnant best friend's back, then you can forget it.'

'I know about you, Holly.'

It takes a few seconds for her to understand what he means, but even then, she's not sure. 'What are you talking about?'

'I can help you. I love you and I want to protect you, even if we aren't together the way I want to be.'

'Drake . . . you're making no sense right now.'

'I've bought the house next to yours.'

'What!' The word comes out much louder than she expects. She flinches and lowers her voice. 'What the fuck are you talking about? Why would you buy the house next door?'

'Leverage. Holly, listen to me, okay? We can make this work, you and me. Together. I promise you. I have money. Penny will never have to know a thing.'

She stands up and paces up and down the lounge. 'Drake, I don't know what it is you think you know about me, but you're wrong. Us sleeping together was a mistake. I won't cheat on my own marriage even though I despise my husband.'

CHAPTER THIRTY-EIGHT

Holly
Now

I can't help it. I want to keep up the charade for longer, much longer, but it's impossible now Drake has murdered my husband in cold blood. It's more than I ever thought possible. I've been hiding out for the past few hours with Drake while the girls have been trying to contact me, but it was all part of the plan. The look in Penny's and Lisa's eyes as Drake plunged the knife into Will's neck was a work of pure art, a thing of beauty. I kneel on the floor, attempting to stop myself from giggling, but I'm not laughing at my friends. I manage to control myself as I look up at the girls.

It's then that I see it blossom behind their eyes.

Betrayal.

No. They don't know the whole story yet. When they do, that look will leave their eyes, and they'll love me again.

I look at Lisa who is shaking her head, her eyes so wide it looks as if she's taken some sort of potent drug and is revelling in its effects.

I never expected them to figure it out, but now I'm about to bring us closer than ever before. Because we've always been close, but after this, there'll be nothing that can come between us. Nothing can stop us. I've known for as long as I can remember we were meant to be together for ever. They will understand soon enough that everything I've done, I've done for them. I love my girls. My bitches. It's never been about anyone else, not even Drake. Not that the poor bastard knows that. He'll find out soon enough. It has always been about my friends; my best friends.

Because yes, good friends will die for you, but only best friends will kill for you.

'N-no,' says Penny.

'It can't be true,' adds Lisa. 'What's so funny? Your husband is dead!'

Penny steps backwards away from me, like being near me is repulsing her. I want to reach out and pull her close again, but I sit back on my heels and allow her the space she needs to come to terms with the fact her best friend is a liar and worse . . .

'I think we had better explain ourselves, babe,' says Drake. He stands next to me, reaches out his hand and pulls me to my feet. I brush myself down and take a stance next to him.

Penny crawls across the floor towards Lisa, who kneels next to her. They clutch each other as if their lives depend on it. I don't like it. I want them to hold me like that. It's fine. They'll see sense soon.

'Please tell me this is all a joke and that's why you were laughing,' says Penny.

I stay where I am and tilt my head to one side. 'It's not. Why would I joke about something like this?'

'Y-you? But . . . I don't understand. Are you and Drake . . . together in this?'

Drake and I look at each other and smile. His is real; mine is fake.

Then Penny's mouth drops open. 'Oh my God . . . it was *you*. You're the woman Drake cheated on me with, aren't you?'

'Yes.'

'What the fuck!' She leaps to her feet. 'You slept with my husband and then had the audacity to pretend to comfort me while I was in pieces. What the fuck is wrong with you? How can you be so heartless? I thought you were my best friend!' It's interesting that she's angrier with me than she is with Drake, meaning she doesn't care that he cheated on her, but she does care that it was with me.

Drake stupidly puts his hand up, attempting to get between us, but Penny shoots him a warning look. 'Don't you even start!'

'Look, I never meant for it to happen,' I say. 'It was merely a means to an end. I promise you it hasn't happened since. I've just been using him for other means.'

'What's that supposed to mean?'

I sigh. We're getting off-topic here because this isn't about Drake. 'Penny, the truth is that Drake and I have been in contact and working together for a long time to rid the world of those who deserve to die. I can't stand by and see innocent people hurt, locked up or killed for something they didn't do. It started at university. I can explain later, but Drake has been helping me because he's been in love with me from when we first met, and he'll do anything I ask of him.'

Penny frowns at me. 'You expect me to believe that? Why would he have married me if he was in love with you?'

'Because I didn't love him the way he loved me, and so he married you in order to stay close to me. Ask him yourself.'

Penny glances at Drake, who is holding his tongue until it's his time to talk, like the good lapdog he is. 'It's true, Penny. I did love you in my own way. You're the mother of my children, but I've always loved Holly, and even though she doesn't love me back, I wanted to be with her in another way.'

'By helping her kill people!'

Drake shrugs. 'It's brought us closer together.'

He's wrong about that but I allow him his moment in the sun.

Penny almost gags. 'Are you saying that you're a team of serial killers?'

I tilt my head. 'I prefer the term vigilante killers.'

'Whatever. A killer is a killer. Why would you want to kill people? I don't understand.'

'Why wouldn't I want to kill people?' I respond. It's clearly not enough of an answer for either Penny or Lisa because they both start crying, and I find myself disappointed in them.

'Girls, I'd never hurt either of you,' I say. 'Everything I've done is to protect you and others like you. Lisa, you of all people should be thanking me. You should understand.'

'What do you mean?'

'I only kill people who deserve it. Like Simon. Rapists. Murderers. Paedophiles. They all deserve it. And sometimes they get away with it and slip through the net. It's not right.'

There's a brief silence.

'How many people have you killed?' asks Lisa.

I take a deep breath. 'Six.'

Lisa half-laughs and half-gasps. 'Six! Who?'

'Does it matter? They don't deserve to be remembered by their names. One of them liked to put out cigarettes on her nine-month-old baby.'

Penny's face turns pale and Lisa gulps loudly.

'Do you know what she did? She blamed it on her husband, and he was the one who went to prison. Can you believe that? Don't worry, the baby is fine. She's gone to social services.'

Lisa opens her mouth, wanting to speak, but she doesn't get any words out.

'And where does Drake fit into all this?' asks Penny. She doesn't even look at her husband, but keeps her eyes locked onto me. 'When did all this start? Explain it in full. I want all the details.'

'Drake has been in love with me since our university days. I never realised it until much later after we slept together, but he always kept a close eye on me. While at university, a friend of mine on my course got attacked and molested by a man in a nightclub, practically in front of everyone, but no one did anything about it. She was so drunk she couldn't even stand, so I stepped in. The man ran off and I followed him, but I lost sight of him so I went back to my friend. She refused to press charges or take it any further and it made me angry.

'After that, I saw more and more of the same. I couldn't stop seeing injustice going on in the world, yet no one was doing anything to stop it. So . . . I put a stop to it. I saw that man again trying to do the same thing to another poor drunk girl. This time, I didn't lose him, and he ended up dead. Drake must have put two and two together. He found out but continued to keep an eye on me.

'After that, I guess I got a thirst for it, for punishing people who deserved it. Drake noticed a few things and told me that he knew what I was doing. He wanted to help. Even though I turned him down and said I wouldn't sleep with him, he wanted to stand by my side. Even after he met you, Penny, and you guys got together.

'Ever since then, he's been my accomplice of sorts. He helps me get rid of the bodies and sometimes helps me drug my victims or clean up the mess. Whenever he goes away on some of his long work trips, he's usually with me.' I don't add that he's also my scapegoat. If it ever looks like I'm going to be caught, then it's him who will go down for the murders, not me.

Drake slides an arm around my waist and pulls me against his body. It's all I can do to stop myself from ramming an elbow in his ribs and watching him flail on the floor in agony. He makes me sick. He's a useless pawn now that I've used him how I see fit. He thinks there's a chance I'll change my mind about him, that I'll figure out he's the one for me after all these years, but he's wrong. This has never been about Drake.

'We make a great team, don't we?'

Penny looks as if she's sucking a lemon. 'I don't believe this. All this time my best friend and my husband have been going on secret murder sprees together. Wait . . . what about the pictures I found in Drake's wardrobe? How do you explain them? Holly, if you kill bad people who deserve it, then why haven't you killed Drake before this if he's a paedophile?' She's angry and that's okay. I was expecting anger, fear, loathing and tears. I'm ready for it all because I know the love we have for each other will override any of that eventually. I just have to give it time to sink in because I know it'll be a shock to my friends.

To be honest, I'd been secretly hoping I wouldn't have to explain myself in detail and that they'd accept me for who I am, no matter what, but murdering people is perhaps a step too far when it comes to our friendship, but it won't be for much longer. They'll come around. They have to, or things will get very unpleasant.

At this point, Drake steps up and faces me. 'Hols, what's she talking about? What pictures?'

'They're fake,' I reply smoothly without looking at him. 'Drake's not a paedo. I planted them on the laptop. There was no guarantee you'd find the pictures, of course, but on the off-chance you did, then you'd start to mistrust him, perhaps want to get rid of him. And if Drake happened to stumble on the pictures on his laptop before you found them, then it wouldn't really matter by that point. It's not like he'd question his wife as to why there was child pornography on his own laptop. But, as it happened, you did see them because he was stupid enough to leave his wardrobe door open and it was the start of everything. Well, that and the life insurance.'

Penny gulps. 'That was fake too?'

'Yep.'

'This whole thing was a set-up?'

I nod. 'In a manner of speaking.' I then turn to Drake. 'Would you go and grab something for me from the back of your car? You know what I mean.'

Drake smiles. 'Be back in a sec.'

Yes, good riddance for now.

All three of us watch him leave the room. Once he's closed the door, it's just me and the girls. Exactly how it's supposed to be.

'Finally, he's gone!' I say with a laugh as I let out a long breath.

Penny and Lisa look at each other and then back at me. 'Any other surprises you want to throw our way?' asks Penny.

'Girls, I did all this for you. Lisa, I knew you weren't happy with Simon. He was abusing you, I could tell, but you refused to tell us, so I took the matter into my own hands. Let's face it, since we all got married, our lives have been torn apart and we barely have time for each other anymore. I love you girls.'

Penny laughs, but it's not a joyous laugh. It sounds fake. I'd recognise her fake laugh anywhere.

'Are you saying that you set us up to murder our husbands?'

'No, not at first. I was going to suggest the idea, but everything started happening on its own, so I moved things along as I saw fit. Nothing was random. Not even Simon turning up. I looked him up on Facebook and messaged him the address.'

Penny looks at Lisa for some backup, but Lisa is staring blankly at the wall.

'Why couldn't you have just killed them all yourself? You seem to know what you're doing. Why did you have to involve us?'

'Because I wanted to empower you and save you from your husbands. You're my girls. We've grown up together, done everything together. I didn't want to do this on my own anymore, not with Drake. I was sure that once your horrible husbands were out of the way, then you'd understand why I do what I do.'

'You are fucking unbelievable!' snaps Penny. 'You honestly don't see what's wrong with what you're doing? You've been killing people, Holly! And you've set us up for murder!'

'Can I remind you about something, Penny? It was actually *your* idea to kill our husbands in the first place, remember? I didn't even have to suggest it. You came up with the idea all on your own and Lisa agreed, so I played devil's advocate for a while to see just how serious you were about the idea. Turns out you were very serious, so I messaged Simon where Lisa was once the kids were safely out of the way and . . . Well, you know what happened next.'

Penny's face falls. And that's the moment the truth hits her like a tonne of bricks.

CHAPTER THIRTY-NINE

Penny

My brain can't seem to comprehend what's happening. I can see and hear everything that's going on, but none of it is registering as reality in my brain. This cannot be real. I cannot be standing in front of my best friend after she's revealed she's a murderer and that she was the one who slept with my husband. Nothing makes sense. Someone is going to jump out from behind a door and yell 'Just kidding!' any second now. They have to, because the truth is incomprehensible.

As the words Holly has just spoken sink in, the urge to vomit makes its way up my throat. I can't stop it and I lunge to the side of the room and retch. Nothing comes up. I retch again and take a deep breath. My body wants to purge the past few days, but there's just nothing there.

Oh fuck, it's true.

It *was* my idea all along. Holly didn't even want to go through with it, but I see now that it was all an act. She's played us from the start and she's a fucking good actress too. The conniving bitch.

Am I the true monster in all this? I convinced both Holly and Lisa to go through with this plan. I'm the one who came up with the idea, all because of Drake changing his life insurance . . .

And it turns out that was all a set-up too. If that hadn't happened, if I hadn't found those fake pictures in his wardrobe, would I have even suggested the crazy idea of killing our husbands? But then Lisa told us about Simon, and after that everything seemed to spiral.

It's like Holly's a stranger to me now. Looking at her sends a jolt of fury through my veins which makes me want to lash out and scratch her eyes out. Once, back when we were about ten, Holly and I had a vicious fight. She pulled my hair. I bit her arm. We scratched each other's faces and arms to shreds like we were squabbling cats. Holly's mum had to pull us apart. The funny thing is, I don't even remember what our fight was about.

'All this time,' I say quietly. 'All this time you've been working with my husband behind my back. And it was you who slept with him. Your betrayal hurts worse than anything else.'

'Oh please, as if you really care about Drake. Since he cheated on you, you couldn't care less about him. I did you a favour. He never loved you, Penny. As hard as it is to hear that, it's the truth.'

A primal scream erupts as I throw myself towards her, bending down in a crouch as I rugby tackle her to the floor. A loud thud follows as I land on top of her. My arms flail about as I punch her over and over in the face, but she must have seen it coming because she has her arms up, blocking her face so all I'm hitting is her forearms.

'You fucking bitch! I'll fucking kill you for this!'

Lisa shouts from across the room, 'Penny, stop! Don't!'

The next thing I realise, Lisa is dragging me off Holly and telling me to calm down. Why the hell is she protecting her? Just because she didn't sleep with her husband.

'Get off me!' I snap, shrugging her off. I don't attack Holly again, but I do let out another scream and kick the nearby wall, which hurts more than I expected, but I'm so revved up, that I barely notice as my big toe starts to throb.

I glare at Holly while she composes herself and wipes blood from her nose.

Good. I hope it fucking hurts.

'Are you finished so I can explain further?' asks Holly. Her tone is sharper than before. She's no longer acting like it's a big joke. Her eyes have darkened. Maybe they were always dark, but I just never noticed. How could I not? How could I not see the monster behind them?

'What else is there to explain?'

'The truth is, Drake isn't completely innocent in all of this. He might not be a paedo, but . . .' She gulps and her eyes flick to the side.

'What? Spit it out.'

'I think he did hurt one of your children. I don't know which one, and I don't know the details, but he did tell me a few weeks ago when he was drunk that something happened and he . . . lost control. It's another reason why I knew he had to go.'

I freeze, barely able to breathe. 'W-what? When?' Tears stream down my face so thick and fast I can barely wipe them away quick enough before more arrive. Snot pours from my nose, and I feel the urge to vomit again. I hold onto the wall to stop myself from collapsing. 'Y-you're lying.'

Lisa lays a hand on my shoulder. 'No, she's not. I think it was about a year ago.'

My head snaps around to look at her. 'Did you know? You knew! Please tell me you haven't been lying to me as well.'

'I don't know the details, but I do know something happened. Lori and Luca told me as much while I was tucking them in. I'm sorry. I should have told you, but . . . I just didn't know how.'

A gargling noise escapes my throat. 'What did he do?' I scream at Holly. 'Tell me now or I swear to God, I'll kill you.'

Holly holds her hands up, palms facing me. 'I don't know. I swear!'

I choke and gag as emotion overwhelms me. I've prided myself on always being the one in control of my emotions, never showing them, not to anyone. But it's impossible to hold them back any longer. I'm a bad mother. I'm the worst mother in the world. I never saw this happening. I hate myself.

A silence falls over the room. I'm exhausted. I don't have any fight left in me. What else is there left to say? All I want to do is get home to my children, wrap my arms around them and then never let them go. I want to lock all the doors and never allow Drake anywhere near them again.

All three of us turn to look at the body of Will who is still slowly bleeding out like a stuck pig on the floor. The puddle of blood has increased substantially in the past few minutes, but the carpet now seems to be absorbing a lot of it. It's going to be a bitch to clean. Then again, it's probably better to just rip the whole carpet up and burn it. At least when we'd cleaned up at my house, we'd been able to wipe the mess off the tiles and Lino.

That's the next job, I assume, once the three of us have sorted out this fucking mess that used to be our solid friendship circle. Now, our friendship feels as if it's been blown apart.

'I am so fucking relieved that twat is dead,' says Holly.

I don't say it, but I agree with her.

But I still can't seem to move past the fact my friend lied to us. I don't care what she says or how she says it, she still tricked us into committing murder.

'You've taken this too far,' I say, shaking my head.

'I haven't taken it far enough. There's still Drake to get rid of. Two down, only one to go.'

Lisa looks down at the floor. I just stare at Holly without blinking for ten seconds.

'Holly . . . you have to see that what you're doing is crazy. You could have gone to the police and—'

'It was your idea!' she shrieks.

I jump in alarm because I hadn't been expecting her to react so violently. I hold my hands up. 'Yes, I know, and I was wrong, okay? I was wrong to come up with the plan to kill our husbands. I should have suggested we deal with it in a better way. We should have gone to the police.'

'You're such a hypocrite, you know that?' she snaps.

'Look, I'm sorry for everything, okay? I'm sorry if you thought that Lisa and I agree with what you're doing, but this has to end.'

'And how do you expect this to end?' asks Holly. Her eyes flick to the door. 'Because if you think I'm going to let you walk out of here and into the nearest police station then think again.'

Shit.

'Is that a threat?' I snap. 'You won't kill us, Holly. I know that for a fact.'

This situation just got complicated because I have no idea how to proceed. There's a dead man on the floor bleeding out. Plus, Holly's lapdog could arrive back at any second. No doubt she has some sort of escape plan in place, but it's difficult to judge her thought process. She's unreadable and has no intention of being caught. Would she really kill us to escape?

It's at that moment the front door opens, and Drake walks into the room holding a gun.

CHAPTER FORTY

Lisa

My mind is blank. After seeing Drake slice Will's throat open, all I can see is blood clouding my vision. Despite that, I'm not upset. Not even a little bit. Will meant nothing to me, other than the fact he was my best friend's husband, but now it appears she didn't even care about him in the first place. Like Penny, I'm more distraught that Holly has lied to us. I can't guarantee that we would have agreed with her, but had she told us the truth from the start, we might have been somewhat more understanding.

But now Drake is here holding a gun, pointing it towards Penny, and I have no idea what to do. Is this part of Holly's plan or is Drake taking matters into his own hands now? It's clear that Holly has been using him, but just how far will she go to get what she wants? She wants Penny and me to join her side, but surely, she can't expect us to do it at gunpoint.

Holly steps forward. 'It's okay, give me the gun. I can handle this.'

'We can't trust them, especially my dear wife,' he says. 'I know her better than she thinks I do. She'll turn us in to the

240

police.' His outstretched arm is shaking and there's a darkness in his eyes that tells me Holly doesn't have control over him anymore. He's doing this off his own bat to protect himself.

'They won't,' says Holly. Her voice is calm, but she's slowly stepping closer towards him with her hand out as if she's attempting to tame a wild animal.

My eyes widen as Drake gestures with the gun, switching from aiming at me and Penny every couple of seconds. He isn't sure who to aim at. Any swift movement could set him off. His finger hovers over the trigger, merely millimetres from being fully depressed.

'Drake . . . give me the gun,' says Holly. Now she's firmer, telling off a naughty child, but it causes him to laugh.

'Hols, I know they're your best friends, but do you really trust them more than me? We've been planning this for years. You and me, remember?'

Holly stares at Drake and then lowers her arm. She stands still for a moment and then laughs. 'You're right. It was you and me, but I'm afraid to say that if you expect me to choose between you or my girls, then there's no competition. I'll always choose them.'

I gulp back the lump in my throat as tears spring to my eyes. Despite her faults, her murderous mind, Holly loves and cares about us. It makes me glad she's on our side, especially since she can easily lead men on for so long, using them and getting them to play to her rules of the game. And she wasn't even sleeping with him.

Drake lets out a weird sort of growl. 'You can't choose them, Hols. I know you. You won't risk your best friends turning you in.'

Oh shit. He's just signed his death warrant.

Holly pulls out another gun that's tucked into the waistband of her jeans and points it at Drake. I recognise it as the gun Penny used to kill Simon. How the hell had she managed to get that? I thought we buried it along with his body.

'What the hell are you doing?' he asks.

'Taking out the trash, once and for all. You've outlasted your usefulness.'

Drake frowns. 'What the . . .' He points his own gun at Holly. 'Don't you dare choose them over me. Not after everything we've been through.'

'Sorry, Drake . . . chicks before dicks.'

Drake lets out a guttural scream and pulls the trigger.

The empty click of the barrel makes all of us freeze.

Holly laughs as she raises the gun.

But she's too slow.

Drake has already lunged forward at her.

The gun with the silencer goes off like a jet of pressured air as he tackles her to the ground.

Penny ducks and throws herself to the side. I move fast and throw myself at Drake, who's too distracted by attacking Holly to see me lunging at him. I knock the empty gun out of his hand, and it skids across the floor, landing next to Will's body.

Before I can think of my next move, Drake turns and punches me in the face and stars spin around me as my head snaps back and hits the floor. I'm on my back, unsure which way up I'm facing. Drake grabs my hair and gets hold of my arms, which I fling about, hoping I'll smack him somewhere it hurts, but my brain is struggling to focus.

Penny screams.

Holly is desperately scrambling to her feet.

Drake grabs my throat and squeezes. There's no air. The more I breathe in, the tighter his hands become. This is it.

Another high-pressure shot erupts and Drake freezes. His grip loosens, his eyes glaze over, and he slumps down on top of me. The warm liquid coats my chest as he bleeds out.

CHAPTER FORTY-ONE

Holly

I don't know what I ever saw in Will, to be honest. He's always been weak and unable to make up his mind or form an opinion of his own, so it did shock me when he decided to cheat on me with a woman who looked almost exactly like me – Leanne Prince. Plus, God knows how many other women he's shagged along the way. But as I said, I didn't care and had no qualms about Drake stabbing him in the neck and ending his miserable life. No one steals or cheats on me and gets away with it.

But Will had finally served his purpose as my husband. I did think about letting him in on my dark little secret, but I couldn't trust him as far as I could throw him.

Drake, on the other hand, is different. He's always been my friend and yes, we slept together, and I felt bad about it, but he has had his uses.

When I'd sent him out to get the gun earlier, he probably thought he was the one in control and he could trick me. But he was wrong. I had loaded the gun in front of him earlier and then secretly slipped the bullets back out again when he turned his back. Penny isn't the only one who can handle a gun. Then he'd come in and pointed it at the girls, like I expected him to. It was all too easy, really. Because he might think he knows me, but I know him too.

The truth is, if he really did know me, then he should have realised I'd always choose the girls over him. They are what this whole thing has been about from the start. Drake has only ever been my puppet to use as I see fit. Now, with all three of our *husbands* out of the way, nothing can stop The Bitches.

I saw my chance to dispose of my puppet once and for all, so when Lisa threw herself at him, I grabbed the gun and shot him in the back while he tried to choke her to death.

It's such a shame he died so quickly, but never mind. All that matters is Lisa is safe. As are we all.

I fall back on the floor when I see him slump forward.

'Lisa, are you okay?' I hear Penny ask.

I don't watch them, but I hear them shuffle around. Penny swears loudly as she pulls the dead weight off Lisa. A few seconds later, a shadow passes over my closed eyes, so I open them and see both Penny and Lisa kneeling over me.

'Thank you,' says Lisa. 'You saved my life.'

I smile. 'Well, I wasn't going to let him kill you, was I?'

'Don't think this changes anything,' says Penny. She's still pissed, but at least it doesn't look as if she's going to finish the job and kill me anymore. 'Are you hurt?'

I do a quick mental check of my extremities. 'No, I'm fine.'

'Good.'

Then, as quick as a flash, Penny grabs the gun off me and points it at my head. Touché.

'Penny, what are you doing?' shouts Lisa.

'What does it look like I'm doing?' she shouts back. 'Holly, I can't let you get away with this. You can't honestly believe that what you're doing is okay. You've killed people. You manipulated us into planning to kill our husbands. And I actually *have* killed someone because of you.'

'I can get us all out of this if you just trust me,' I say, keeping my voice calm, my eyes never leaving Penny's.

Penny narrows her eyes at me. 'I don't believe you.'

'Do you honestly think I would have done all this and not had a contingency plan in place?'

Lisa steps forward and stands next to Penny. She places her hand on Penny's outstretched arm and gently pushes down, lowering the gun to the floor.

'Let's hear her out.'

Penny shakes her head. 'Even if you do get us out of this, I don't think I can ever forgive you.'

'That's okay. You're an amazing mum and friend, so I wouldn't expect you to. But just know that everything I've done has always been for you two, and also for your kids.'

'That's even worse because you've killed people for us! We never asked you to do that.'

'No, but who else is going to keep us safe. They were bad people, Penny. How do you not see that? You were more than happy to kill your own husband when you thought he was a paedophile, and you killed Simon with hardly any remorse whatsoever. You're more like me than you realise.'

I see Penny's angry exterior start to waver. She's thinking about it and that's all I need her to do right now. Because I can get us out of this, but I need her to trust me, and she and Lisa need to do and say exactly what I tell them.

'I don't get it,' Penny says. 'Are you saying that we either have to hand ourselves in or join your twisted game? I have children, Holly. I can't just abandon them and go around the country killing people even if they do deserve it.' I don't tell her that that's exactly what she's done this week.

'So, you admit that the people I've killed deserved to die?'

'I think they deserved to be jailed.'

'And me?'

Penny sighs. 'I don't know!' Then she screams and punches the nearest wall. 'Motherfucker!' She jumps around, clutching her right fist against her chest. 'Just tell me what your plan is to get us out of this and then I'll decide whether or not I think it'll work.'

'That's not how this works,' I say. I look at Lisa. She hasn't said a lot, so I'm not too sure what's going through her mind, but I'm taking the silence to mean she's open to the idea. 'You either trust me or you don't. If you do, then I'll get us out of this, but if you don't, then you're condemning me to life in prison. Lisa, as soon as I realised Simon was hurting you, I began to put a plan in place to help you. The same goes for Drake when I thought he might have hurt one of your kids, Penny. Do you trust me?'

Lisa's eyes shift towards Penny who is still tending to her injured hand. Then she looks at me and nods once. 'Yes, I trust you.'

Lisa steps away from Penny and stands beside me. We both look at Penny. Her eyes dart from the two bodies on the floor to the two of us, and then she closes her eyes.

'Fuck it. We've come this far, and if we all land up in prison together then at least I'll get to spend the rest of my life with you bitches.'

CHAPTER FORTY-TWO

Penny

The next few hours are a whirlwind. Halfway through, while we're cleaning up after not one but two dead bodies, I begin to wonder if maybe Lisa and I are making a huge mistake in trusting Holly, who has, after all, lied to us for a long time. But she's got just as much to lose as we do. If her plan fails, then she'll end up in jail too, and since she's the secret mastermind behind everything, she'll probably get a worse sentence.

We follow her directions to the letter. We drag both bodies into the back garden of the empty house and dispose of them down an old air raid shelter shaft that apparently no one knows about except Holly. She says she stumbled on the secret bunker years ago. I dread to think how many other bodies are down there, but the waft of decay and death soon tells me my answer. It's where she keeps all the bodies.

It's the reason why Drake bought her the house and why she chose it. He was watching her. I'm not sure whether he meant to use his knowledge as leverage eventually, or whether he was just obsessed with Holly from the start, but whatever the reason, he sure went out of his way to spend as much time with her as possible, marrying me so he could remain close to her. The bunker isn't on any plans of the house and grounds and unless you know it's there, it's almost impossible to find. The house will remain in Drake's name (or Timothy Grant's name) and will never be sold. It will just sit there and continue to fall into disrepair, and nothing can ever be done about it because it belongs to a fake dead man.

That's it.

It's all over.

Our husbands are dead, and I can finally return to my children and begin to piece together the remains of our lives. Everything will change now. I don't even know how to explain to my children that their father is dead. Maybe I'll just say that he left us. I haven't fully decided, but I have a feeling they won't be too shaken up about it, especially after what Lisa and Holly have told me. The fact Lisa knew something had happened and didn't tell me is still playing on my mind.

But Holly has thought of everything.

The house is cleaned to within an inch of its life, made easier by the fact there's no furniture.

The bodies are disposed of in the bunker.

The attic is cleared of the camera and gross mattress. Apparently, Will would take his women up there and take raunchy photos of them. And he had stolen the box of money from Holly, but she knew about it and was aware of what he was doing in the attic. It didn't look like he ever hurt the women, but he was a creep through and through. But he did kill Leanne and her unborn child, so that's more than enough reason to be glad he's dead.

I'd love to know the whole truth about why Holly turned into a serial killer. I know she said that she started at university, but why did she feel the need to keep going? People aren't just born a serial killer. They're made. At least, that's what I understand from the true crime documentaries I watch. I have a feeling I won't be watching them as religiously anymore. After having lived through my own crime spree, I've seen enough blood and death to last a lifetime. It's not as fascinating in real life.

Another part of me is somewhat proud of her and mildly impressed that she has been able to get away with it for so long, but the scale of this whole thing is mind-blowing. It brings into context just how much planning has gone into this.

Holly provides Lisa and me with notes on exactly what to say to the police for when we return home and report our husbands missing. I know I'm going to struggle to play the distraught wife of a missing husband because I'm not upset that he's gone. All I want to do right now is curl up with my children on the sofa, one arm around each of them, and watch a Disney film. I don't even care if it's one I've seen a hundred times. I just want to feel them next to me and never let them go.

But I trust the process. I trust Holly. And, despite the dread of being questioned by the police, I'm almost certain that we'll get away with this.

Once everything is clean and we're ready to go our separate ways, Lisa and I stand by the rental car and look up at Holly's house.

'Some girls' weekend, huh?' I say.

Lisa chuckles. 'Quite possibly our most chaotic one yet. It beats Ibiza.'

The sun is just peeking over the horizon, so we watch the sunrise together, our shoulders lightly touching.

'Are we bad people now?' asks Lisa after a few minutes of silence.

'I don't really know,' I answer slowly. The lines between good and bad, right and wrong have blurred so much in the past week that I can't distinguish them anymore.

I will eventually inherit Drake's money from his disappearance, although due to UK law, I have to wait seven years before I can declare him officially dead. I questioned Holly about this and asked why we couldn't just dump his body somewhere to be found, but she said it was too risky. If there's a body, then there's a crime. However, thanks to my prenup, I do get a large amount of compensation because technically he has left me alone with the children to raise and that was one of the stipulations in the prenup.

Lisa will probably eventually get compensation for Simon's disappearance, although that's less likely due to the fact the flat she lived in was owned by him, and according to his will, he didn't leave anything to her, but she doesn't care about that. She doesn't want anything to do with him anymore. She doesn't want or need his money. His family will eventually report him missing, but the plan is to say she left him because of his abuse, which is true, and she's going to move in with me.

A few minutes later, Holly walks out of the house. She smiles at us standing side by side. 'Can I join you?'

'Sure,' I say. 'What's the plan now?'

'I'm sure you'll be wanting to get back to your kids.'

'Yes, and Lisa's coming with me. She's going to live with me for a while.'

'Good. That's good.'

'What about you?' asks Lisa.

'I'm going to stay here,' says Holly. 'I still own the house. There's still a mortgage to pay. Plus, it means I can keep an eye on the empty house. If I sold my own house, the new owners might not be so understanding about having a derelict house next door.'

'Especially one with a secret door in the attic,' adds Lisa.

'Right.'

I stand up and stretch my arms above my head. 'What are you going to say about Will?'

Holly sighs. 'Well, I have all the evidence I need to show the police he was stealing from me, plus evidence he knew Leanne Prince. They'll probably put a warrant out for his arrest in connection with her murder, and since he'll never be found, they'll assume he's on the run. Since we were married, everything, including our house, belongs to me.'

I'll give it to her; she sure has thought of everything. 'I guess this is goodbye, then.'

We all turn to each other, standing in a circle.

'I guess so,' says Holly. 'Just remember what I've told you. Stick to the plan.'

Lisa sniffs and then throws her arms around Holly's neck, erupting into quiet sobs. 'I'm not sure how I can ever thank you enough for saving me from Simon.'

'Your continued friendship is thanks enough. You know I love you both so, so much, right?'

Lisa pulls away from Holly, finally letting her go. I don't know how to do this. I'm not even sure what I want to do.

'Maybe I'll organise another girls' weekend soon,' I say. It's a lame joke, but at least it breaks the tension.

Holly laughs. 'Sounds good. I look forward to it.'

'Take care of yourself, Hols.'

'You too.'

I give her a smile and turn to walk away, but then I stop and run up to her, wrapping my arms tight around her shoulders. She hugs me back, but neither of us sheds a tear. I'm not sure our friendship will ever be the same again, but I know I don't want to spend the rest of my life hating this woman.

'I love you, Penny,' she whispers in my ear.

I'm not sure I feel the same way anymore.

* * *

Her words stay with me as we drive back to Aunt Silvia's. We take the rental car to a drop-off location, then rent another, again using Simon's credit card. It's a long drive and I somehow survive it by drinking copious amounts of coffee. I drive the whole way because sitting and doing nothing in the passenger seat will just cause my brain to overthink everything, so I stay focused on the road instead. Lisa spends a lot of the time asleep, so I put the radio on, listening out for any news stories of relevance, but they never arrive.

I cry hysterically when I'm reunited with Lori and Luca. As soon as they see me, they shout, 'Mummy!' and run into my outstretched arms, wrapping theirs around me so tight. I breathe in their scent and sob into their hair.

'We missed you, Mummy,' says Luca.

'I missed you too, my babies. I missed you so, so much.'

I look up as Aunt Silvia walks up to us. 'You've had an eventful time, I take it?' she asks.

I hold her gaze but don't respond. I'm not sure what she thinks she knows, but I'm grateful she's not saying anything in front of the twins.

'Mummy,' says Lori when I finally let her go.

'Yes, baby.' I tuck a stray strand of blonde hair behind her ear.

'When is Daddy coming back?'

Straight to the point, I suppose. There's no point beating about the bush.

'He's not, baby. Daddy is never coming back.' I watch her reaction, but she barely bats an eyelid. Luca doesn't either. Lori leans forward and hugs me again.

'Thank you, Mummy.'

And I start crying all over again.

CHAPTER FORTY-THREE

Lisa
Six months later

A lot has happened in six months, or maybe I should say that not a lot has happened because despite having to go through a few police interviews and do lots of annoying paperwork, the three of us are living our lives quietly and happily minus our husbands.

Holly is still living in Edinburgh. Neither Penny nor I have seen her since we said goodbye six months ago, and our three-way group chats have dropped off the face of the earth. Penny doesn't talk to Holly, so Holly and I chat separately. I think Penny's just trying to forget everything that happened, and I don't think she'll ever forgive Holly for what she did. I do miss our group chats. I miss The Bitches. But I'm glad I'm still in contact with Holly. She's doing well. She is still working as a personal trainer. I'm not sure if she's keeping up with her extra-curricular activities. I haven't asked her because I'm not sure I want to know the truth. I do keep an eye on the news in Edinburgh, though, but so far there haven't been any suspicious murders that sound like they were committed by Holly.

I hum quietly to myself while I wait for my next walk-in patient. I've managed to get a job as a pharmacist and now I see patients to provide advice about prescriptions and look over small injuries. I feel stronger every day since I've been able to eat more and put on weight. Penny even persuaded me to join the local gym with her and we exercise three times a week together. My hair is shiny, my skin clearer, and Penny constantly tells me how bright my eyes are.

And all it took was killing my husband.

I don't think about Simon at all, only in passing. A few days after Penny and I returned to her house, the sunken trampoline was filled with rubble and earth, burying him even deeper. He was reported missing by his parents and his colleagues at work, and I was interviewed regarding his disappearance. There was CCTV footage of him driving to Wales to track me down, but since we deleted the CCTV at Penny's house there was no evidence to suggest he ever arrived. His own car was found abandoned, and after investigation, the cops found out about the two cars being rented with his credit card, but that's as far as it went. He's still missing, but I told the police about his beatings and was honest when I said that I didn't care where he was. His parents never liked me, and they blame me for pushing him away. Whatever.

Penny and I rarely bring Holly up in conversation either, only when we need to.

I'm still living with Penny and the kids. I'm saving up to move out, but Penny keeps saying that there's no rush and if I want to stay for ever then I'm welcome. But I can't do that. Penny has her own life and I need to start living mine too. We're happy, though, and spend many an hour after the children have gone to bed, laughing and drinking wine in front of a cosy fire.

Penny has met a new man, but so far hasn't mentioned to him that she has children. I don't blame her for keeping him at bay. It's hard for either of us to trust men again. I certainly won't be venturing into another relationship any time soon even though I'm desperate for a baby of my own. But there are other ways to have a child, so I may explore my options soon.

I look up at a knock on the door.

'You have a walk-in, Lisa. Seems to have a nasty cut above her eye.'

'Okay, thanks.'

A few seconds later, a timid-looking woman walks into the small consultancy room. She has a cut over her left eye, which is also slightly bruised. I look down at her wrists, they are also bruised.

'Hi, what can I help you with today?'

'Um . . . some ointment perhaps, for my eye? I didn't think it was worth going to the doctor for,' she adds with a smile.

'Let me take a look.' I stand as I slip on my plastic gloves and turn her head up to the light. She winces as I gently touch the area. 'I'm afraid there's not a lot any ointment will do. It's not bleeding. Can I ask how this happened?'

The woman blushes and coughs. 'Um . . . I walked into the side of a kitchen cupboard door.'

I sigh, shaking my head slightly. 'Is that the answer you're sticking with?'

'Excuse me?' She rushes to her feet, backing away towards the door. 'I came here for help, not to be accused of lying.'

I hold up my hands in surrender. 'You're right. You did come here for help. I know you didn't get that cut and black eye from a cupboard door.'

The woman shakes her head. 'You don't know what you're talking about.'

'And those bruises and scratches on your arms. You either have a very big cat or . . .'

'I have to go.'

'No, wait. Please.' I reach out. 'What's your name?'

'Heather Morrison.'

'Heather, who's doing this to you?'

She squeezes her lips together, tears streaming down her cheeks.

255

'Heather, you don't have to defend him anymore. Trust me.'

'H-her.'

'I'm sorry?'

'Her . . . my wife. But I can't . . . I've reported her, but nothing ever gets done. She's in the police and can easily make sure my claims never get filed. She has friends in high places. I've tried everything.' Heather begins to weep, bringing out a tissue and dabbing her eyes.

I place a hand on her shoulder. 'I have friends in high places too . . . and they can help. I promise you.'

THE END

ACKNOWLEDGEMENTS

A huge thank you to my twin sister, Alice, and our best friend, Katie, who, while we ourselves were on a girls' weekend, somehow managed to come up with the idea for this book while talking about what would happen if our own husbands died or if we killed them. A morbid topic of conversation, yes, but it inspired this book, so . . . thanks, girls!

Thank you to my husband, Scott, who never takes anything I write personally.

Thank you to Joanna, for suggesting the location of the burial site for one of the husbands. I told you I'd get it into one of my books one day!

Big thanks go to both Jasper Joffe and Kate Lyall Grant, who picked my book out from their enormous open submissions pile, saw the potential in my story, and asked me to sign with them. It's been an absolute pleasure, and I hope to write many more books with you!

Thanks must also go to Jamie Taylor, who beta-read *Horrible Husbands* for me before it went out on submission and helped me iron out a few issues. I'm so glad you loved the girls as much as I do.

Thank you to the whole team at Joffe Books who have handled the editing, design, formatting, marketing and all the jobs it takes to get a book from a submission piece to a fully-developed and polished book.

Lastly, thanks go to my loyal readers who continue to read my books, no matter how dark and twisted I make them. Thank you for sticking with me during my transition to being a traditionally published author and for your support throughout my career.

THE JOFFE BOOKS STORY

We began in 2014 when Jasper agreed to publish his mum's much-rejected romance novel and it became a bestseller.

Since then we've grown into the largest independent publisher in the UK. We're extremely proud to publish some of the very best writers in the world, including Joy Ellis, Faith Martin, Caro Ramsay, Helen Forrester, Simon Brett and Robert Goddard. Everyone at Joffe Books loves reading and we never forget that it all begins with the magic of an author telling a story.

We are proud to publish talented first-time authors, as well as established writers whose books we love introducing to a new generation of readers.

We won Trade Publisher of the Year at the Independent Publishing Awards in 2023 and Best Publisher Award in 2024 at the People's Book Prize. We have been shortlisted for Independent Publisher of the Year at the British Book Awards for the last five years, and were shortlisted for the Diversity and Inclusivity Award at the 2022 Independent Publishing Awards. In 2023 we were shortlisted for Publisher of the Year at the RNA Industry Awards, and in 2024 we were shortlisted at the CWA Daggers for the Best Crime and Mystery Publisher.

We built this company with your help, and we love to hear from you, so please email us about absolutely anything bookish at feedback@joffebooks.com.

If you want to receive free books every Friday and hear about all our new releases, join our mailing list here: www.joffebooks.com/freebooks.

And when you tell your friends about us, just remember: it's pronounced Joffe as in coffee or toffee!